Ben Richards was born in 1964 and lives in East London. He has worked as a Housing Officer for Newham and Islington councils and currently lectures at the University of Birmingham. *Throwing the House out of the Window* is his first novel and won the Texaco/Eastside award for first-time novelists in 1994.

'Ben Richards' accomplished first novel convincingly evokes the energy and angst of contemporary urban life' *The Times*

'Brutally funny' *Independent on Sunday*

'The novel's strength . . . lies in its wry humour and a refreshing sense of compassion as Richards details the grey deprivation, casual violence and small delights of a London he clearly loves' *Observer*

'Written with pacy irony, this attractive first novel takes us vividly through the pangs of disappointed love, troublesome colleagues, even more troublesome tenants, sink-estate racism, violence, crime and insanity, all with a light-hearted nonchalance which makes the pain so much easier to bear. More, please' *Oxford Times*

'Where Richards excels is in chronicling the uncertainties, from creeping half-light insomniac fears to bursts of frustration and anger that seem to erupt from nowhere and everywhere. He has got the rhythm of a young adult's urban life off to a tee in its utter contradictions, its terse humour and its occasional sheer bewildering pointlessness . . . There is so much in this book, and it's all so deftly handled, with a freshness and integrity easily lost by others' *What's On – Birmingham*

'A startling debut . . . a colourful and highly enjoyable piece of fiction' *Maxim*

'A likeable and engaging novel' *Time Out*

'The housing officer: a hero for the nineties! The former officer who wrote this novel has made the most of his experience. His twentysomething narrator, Jamie, is a housing professional working in east London's front-line . . . Ben Richards is particularly strong on describing office life with its mixture of support and conflict, rivalry and friendship. And he firmly points up the overlap between Jamie's work and the same urban problems – loneliness, violence and racism – that he faces in his free time.

This novel is a perceptive, sometimes hilarious, account of the stresses and rewards of life as a housing worker. While it is careful to offer no solutions, its contemporary authenticity makes it fascinating reading.' *Housing Magazine*

Throwing the House
out of the Window

Ben Richards

First published in 1996
by HEADLINE BOOK PUBLISHING

First published in paperback in 1996
by HEADLINE BOOK PUBLISHING

A HEADLINE REVIEW paperback

10 9 8 7 6 5 4

ISBN 0 7472 5279 3

Printed and bound in Great Britain by
Clays Ltd, St Ives plc

HEADLINE BOOK PUBLISHING
A division of Hodder Headline PLC
338 Euston Road
London NW1 3BH

This book is dedicated to Rossana

Acknowledgements

For their early and invaluable encouragement I should like to thank Harry Lansdown and Emi Bulman. I should also like to thank Julia Cream, Geraldine Cooke, Darley Anderson, Tara Lawrence, Elizabeth Waite, all at Eastside Books, and GNASH! Finally, thank you to both my families.

Contents

Part One   3
Part Two   117
Part Three   209

PART ONE

The Beginning of History

In the courtyard beneath my window, two children are kicking a football against a wall which bears a new sign reading NO BALL GAMES. They play in a sustained, absorbed kind of way without speaking to each other until a window opens in one of the flats opposite and their mum calls them inside. They continue the game until she calls out again, slightly more impatiently, their names filling the courtyard, and then one of them picks up the ball and they trot back to their stairway.

I stand watching them, clenching and unclenching my fist to get rid of the weals from the plastic handles of the carrier bags that I have just hauled back from the supermarket.

'You should put that stuff in the fridge,' says Helen, glancing up from her laptop computer at the bags that I have dumped by the side of the sofa. 'There's frozen stuff in there as well.'

'In a minute.'

She returns to her work, fingers clicking furiously on the keyboard – a fast typist. She pauses from time to time and twists her head to look out of the window. There is something silently irritable and impatient in the gesture, the tendons in her neck taut like a wishbone, a wisp of blonde hair falling from behind her ear. Sometimes she pushes it back but it falls forward again almost at once. She is preparing a paper for a seminar.

'Helen,' I say suddenly, 'if we had a child what would it know?'

'What are you talking about? We're not going to have a child.'

'I don't mean that. I mean, it would be strange, that's all. Any child. It would know such different things from us. From what we knew. Even quite recent things that have just disappeared . . . that seem long ago now . . .'

Her hands remain above the keyboard like a concert pianist waiting for the twitch of the conductor's baton. She is frowning, thinking about her work. I can't explain it to her. Entire countries are disappearing, collapsing in on themselves, tearing themselves apart. There are things I took for granted, that I knew before, that were part of things, that don't exist any more.

'Why does that worry you so much?' asks Helen, narrowing her eyes at the screen and tapping a key. 'It's not all bad, there are ways that it's positive. Everything changes. It always has. There's no such thing as a Golden Age.'

'. . . Not even necessarily good or bad though. I'm not saying that. What a kid will know though, a kid that's born now, will be so different.'

'Well, take it easy, Jamie. We're not going to have a child.' And her fingers return click-clicking to their task again.

'It's called a hypothesis, Helen. An interesting launch pad for a general conversation. I'm not talking Mothercare.'

But all Helen's attention is on the computer screen in front of her, the neat blue square like a window into a sea aquarium gradually filling with white letters.

I turn my head to the window. The flag on the post office roof is cracking in the wind against an eye-aching grey sky. From where the men are fixing the road, the wind has stolen a long streamer of pink tape which has been preventing pedestrians from passing through their work site. Now it is entwined in a plane tree, snaking around the upper branches like the sad tail of a kite lost on its first launching. It flaps in the wind as if trying to liberate itself from the sharp branches which hook and twist it. A pigeon gurgles obscenely on the window-sill, its oily chest puffed out like a little *Duce*. I rap with my knuckles on the window-sill to make it go away. Then I pick up the bags and take them to the kitchen, putting tins in cupboards, toilet paper in the bathroom, salad, vegetables and three bottles of wine in the fridge, and a large bag of frozen oven chips in the freezer compartment.

Later that night when we are drinking one of the bottles of wine and watching TV Helen tells me that she has been thinking that we should maybe split up, or at least try living apart for a while. All day, the air has been becoming slowly contaminated – truncated conversations, pointless questions met with silence or negatives. Helen's announcement is not unexpected but I still feel the shock of the words, articulated clearly for the first time. We have been living together for over two years.

'We hardly talk properly any more, we rarely have sex, and you don't like my friends,' she says, lighting a cigarette.

All of these statements are true, especially the last one. Helen left her job as an education officer to do a Ph.D. on Feminism and Post-Modernism. This has brought with it a group of dull polite friends who swap e-mail addresses and give papers at conferences on the horrors of meta-narratives and masculinist binary structures. I have become suspicious recently as to the nature of her relationship with one of these gestating academics; a thin-lipped, gold-rimmed-spectacled, post-everything called Neil who is writing his thesis on Discourse and Docklands and talks about Bourdieu and Baudrillard as if they were close personal friends.

'Where are you going, Jamie?' Helen returns to the offensive. 'You just seem to be treading water. You get ideas but you do nothing about them. And you've become . . . cynical.' She drops a cigarette butt into an empty packet and shakes it vigorously. She looks at me as if expecting me to defend myself but I've got nothing to say, although I would certainly dispute the cynical accusation. Where am I supposed to be going anyway? My days are filled with broken-down central heating systems, noise nuisance complaints, tenants who turn their flats into shrines to serial killers and mass murderers.

I pour myself a glass of wine which has gone slightly warm and gulp it down, pouring another one almost immediately. Helen gets up and goes into the bathroom. I hear the taps being turned on and the bath filling up. Angry clouds of steam start to billow out until Helen shuts the door and clicks the lock.

An' I'll Tell You Another Thing . . .

The rest of the weekend is so bad that going to work on
Monday morning is almost a relief. I slump down at my desk,
which is a mess of unsorted paperwork: insurance claims,
notes from reception requesting repairs and rent cheques,
letters waiting to be signed. Tiny islands of mould float on the
cold dregs of coffee in the mugs left during the weekend. I lean
back in my chair and nod to Trevor, who is on the phone to a
tenant.

'No, I'm sorry, Mr Williams, trimming the hedge is not an
emergency.'

He rolls his eyes at me, phone wedged between head and
shoulder.

'I'm sorry you feel like that, Mr Williams.'

He puts the phone down and straightens the blotter on his
immaculately tidy desk. 'Jamie, how are you man?' biting into
an egg and bacon sandwich. Trevor never appears to get
depressed or grow weary with the job. He always dresses
smartly, drives a bright red Sierra with a white child's seat in
the back and appears to be completely at ease with himself. I
tell him about splitting up with Helen and he listens sympathetically while alternating between his sandwich and a cup of
coffee. 'So she lodged you,' he says, and I have to admit that
this is more or less the state of things even though I have been
carefully saying 'we thought' and 'we decided' in an attempt
to make it sound like a mutual agreement.

7

When the office opens to the public my telephone rings straight away. 'Jamie, Mr O'Leary is in reception for you.' I shut my eyes for a second, imagining him waiting below, every passing second increasing his impatience. Peering over the balcony – one of the advantages of being on the upper floor of an open-plan office – I shudder as I see him, standing with his hands in the pockets of his long leather jacket, a swallow tattooed on his neck, staring around aggressively at the office potted plants, welfare rights posters and scattered children's toys. His body appears to be straining forward, and his lips are moving slowly as if he is already rehearsing the threats he will make if I do not immediately agree to whatever it is that he wants. Trevor grins at me.

'Nice one, Jamie, just what you want on a Monday morning. Careful of those mad eyes.'

O'Leary has a habit of staring straight into your eyes without blinking as he speaks to you. Trevor knows this because O'Leary used to be his tenant. Then he got sent down for driving the getaway car in an armed robbery and, when he came out, Trevor cunningly got him a transfer on to my patch on the grounds of marital breakdown. I cross myself as I gather my pad and make towards the staircase.

'An' I'll tell you annuver fing. If I don't get a new flat in one week, I'm gonna be down this office Monday mornin' and there's gonna be trouble.'

He is staring at me, the swallow throbbing slightly above its vein. I want to say how ecstatic I would be to give him a transfer. The Shetland Isles? Burkina Fasso? At the very least, back on to Trevor's patch. I look at his clenched fist with its thick stubby fingers, the nails bitten right down to the flesh.

'I'm sorry, Mr O'Leary, but I really think there's not much chance of you getting a transfer. It's council policy you see . . .' He stands up.

'Just get it sorted. All right? I gotta get out of this area. I can't live 'ere any more.'

Then he puts his face close to mine and hisses, 'I want a transfer.'

I gather my papers together.

'Right, well, it's out of my hands now, Mr O'Leary. I'll be giving your details to our allocations officer and you must direct all your inquiries to him from now on.'

''Ow many times do I 'ave to tell yer. I ain't bothered about that. JUST GET IT FUCKIN' SORTED.'

And the door of the interview room bangs shut behind him. When I return to my desk, there is a note from Trevor.

'Your ex rang. Phone her at home.'

'Helen?'

'Jamie, listen. I've found a place with a friend. I'm going today, well, right now actually.'

'Who's the friend?'

'Oh, erm, someone from college who's got a spare room. I think it's better if I just go, Jamie. I couldn't stand another weekend like this one. I'll ring you later to sort out coming to get some stuff and everything.'

'OK.'

'I'll leave the phone number.'

'OK.'

'Speak to you later, Jamie.'

'See you.'

A car alarm begins its nagging, pointless alert in the street outside. I look at the phone, momentarily quiet and misleadingly benign. When I get home tonight she will be gone. The telephone rings again mercilessly. 'Jamie, I've got Mrs Begum, Mr Kitchener and also Mrs Connolly from the Tenants Association in reception.'

'Tell them they can all fuck off.'

'I beg your pardon?'

'Oh, nothing. Tell them I'm on my way down.'

The helicopter from the London Hospital is churning up the

air as I get off the tube at Whitechapel. People on the platforms peer up at the sky, trying to catch a glimpse of it as it hovers above its landing pad. I emerge on to the wide pavements of the Whitechapel Road, where the market traders' hands move swiftly, dipping into the money pouches for change, whipping fruit from stall to scales to bag, while at the same time watching for other unauthorized hands squeezing the fruit, and performing rapid mental arithmetic, their eyes already on the next customer. 'That's four fifty love . . . yes please?' In front of them the red-faced dossers circle drunkenly, hands outstretched to the passers-by. I dodge past a continuous flow of fob-watched nurses with blue coats over their uniforms and flat black shoes, elderly stern Bangladeshi men with walking sticks, thin-faced Somalis, kids eating greasy fried chicken, beer-drinkers sprawled on white chairs outside the pub. The morning fish stall has gone, leaving just a fishy smell and empty white polystyrene ice-boxes, the cheap nylon dresses are being taken down leaving bare their hanging frames, the fruit traders are beginning to shift boxes of oranges into the vans parked behind the stalls. The wind whips up sheets of newspaper and empty plastic bags and they gather height like released balloons. From the edges of the City, the Nat West tower grimly surveys the East End like an impassive sentry.

I buy a pint of milk and a loaf of bread from the Seven–Eleven and walk away from the crowds, towards the statue of a Victorian philanthropist who, facing away from the multitude and holding high a moralizing stone finger, is almost eclipsed by the heavy trees which line the pavement. A group of Bengali kids are sitting on the wall by the entrance to my flats. One of the smaller boys nods at me shyly as I pass. I have seen them grow up, watched them playing rounders or cricket in the courtyard below, dressing up at Eid to sally out with the family, hanging from their balconies to talk to their friends in the flats underneath. Sometimes their mothers and little sisters also appear, calling to the children from the window, while the older boys come and go quickly, car keys always in their hands.

I turn the key in the lock, open the door and walk into the flat. Empty. Helen is not sitting on the sofa awaiting my return anxiously so that she can spring into my arms and recognize how terribly mistaken she has been. Instead there is a note on the table. 'I took some things which are mine. I'll phone you. H.' I look at the records and try and find something of mine she's taken but she hasn't. She's even left the records I bought for her on her birthday and which she always claimed, perhaps with some justification, I had bought for myself.

I fall on to the sofa with the remote control and turn on the TV. In ex-Yugoslavia the Bosnian Serbs have taken a mountain over Sarajevo from the Bosnian Muslims, but the Croatian Croats have pushed the Croatian Serbs out of a UN-protected enclave in a disputed area, and meanwhile the Serbian Serbs are saying that it's nothing to do with them any more and a flak-jacketed reporter is discussing the possibility of another cease fire in front of burned-out apartment buildings. There is a report on the moral dilemmas of creating designer babies out of the eggs of an aborted foetus, and a right-wing Tory MP claims that the latest sex scandal will not make him resign.

I remember Helen and her friends discussing the changes in the world at one of Helen's academic dinner parties. According to their analysis, it was all to be greatly welcomed and would lead to a different kind of politics free from the tyranny of totalizing ideologies, based on movements from the margins and communities of resistance. Normally I would try and avoid arguing with Helen's friends, but there was a provocative arrogance in their tone which suggested that anyone who disagreed with them was either stupid or an ex-Stasi member. 'Where are these communities?' I asked aggressively. Because in the community I was working in, people were still pushing glass and shit through letter-boxes and Mr Rogers was threatening to beat the fuck out of his neighbours for complaining

11

about his all-night music. I was aware of my voice rising self-righteous and opinionated, saw eyes dropping to the table, heard the murmuring of the subject being tactfully changed. In the end only Neil and I were left arguing and I began to start shouting, accusing him of being the type of bandwagon-jumper who would have been a Maoist in the sixties – same face, different jargon. I really hated Neil. Not just because I thought something was going on with Helen, but because if they were giving out Ph.D.s in smugness, he wouldn't have had to bother with all his fieldwork. And because he had little glasses that made him look like Himmler, and a nose that had two indentations as if someone had pinched it together. And because he had never worked, never even poked his nose outside the placenta of academia, and yet felt entitled to make all kinds of claims about the way the world was changing. And because he said 'exactly' in a way that managed to be patronizing even though he was agreeing with you. Anyway, people began making their excuses to leave and Helen and I ended up screaming at each other drunkenly in the kitchen, our joint anger blazing incoherently among the wine dregs and ashtrays. This concluded with her hurling a cup of coffee at me. For some time afterwards I kept finding the stains in unexpected places as if we had a secret ghost in the house weeping coffee tears.

I wander into the kitchen and begin to butter slices of bread, folding them double and cramming them into my mouth one after the other. From the window, I watch other people in their kitchens in the flats opposite. A man and woman are laughing, a bottle of wine on the pine table in front of them. The light is changing unbearably outside, the dropping sun lighting the sky from behind a bank of clouds. The couple turn and look at me and the woman says something laughing to the man. Skunk hour.

Later, I phone the number Helen left. A girl answers. 'Let me speak to Neil,' I say. 'There's no Neil living here,' she

answers. 'Well, tell him he's a cunt,' I say and giggle inanely.
After I replace the receiver, the telephone rings again almost
immediately. I switch on the answerphone in case it is Helen
calling to remonstrate with me but it is Eduardo, my Spanish
teacher, who asks me to call him back as he has something he
wishes to discuss. I contemplate picking up the phone but I
am in no mood for conversation. The phone clicks down, the
tape rewinds, and a bright red number 1 appears on the
message counter. I stare at it for a second before going to the
kitchen to find something to drink.

Coriander Leaves

I met Eduardo – a Chilean exile – through an advert pinned to the notice-board in Helen's university department. I had always been interested in Latin America and was even talking about saving up to go there. Helen arrived home one evening, dropped the card in front of me and announced, 'You can start by learning Spanish. I'll even dial the number for you if you want.' I was Eduardo's only pupil and we spent less time on grammar than on his experiences following the coup in Chile. For translation practice we would work on documents with names like 'Ultra-leftism: the Trojan Horse of Imperialism'. This meant that my vocabulary was heavily biased. While I could talk about the inequalities generated by dependent capitalism, I had far greater problems with more straightforward situations such as buying a train ticket or booking a hotel room. Helen found this out when we went on holiday to Madrid and told me I was wasting my time and to get a new teacher. But I had got used to evenings in Eduardo's kitchen listening to him railing against the stupidities of the world, and he had long stopped charging me anyway.

Eduardo's wife went back to Chile – after he had an affair with an English woman from the solidarity campaign – leaving Eduardo to bring up his daughter Soledad, who hangs around with the youth from the estate and refuses to have anything whatsoever to do with her country of birth. Her mother paid for her to visit Chile last year and she hated it. Her cousins laughed at her accent and mocked her clothes. 'All they listen to is Sting,' she protested when I asked her about it. She shouted at men who made comments to her in the street and they would humiliate her with insults she did not understand. Eduardo used to insist that she accompany him to solidarity events, which she did sulkily and under the utmost duress. These events are few and far between now, and Soledad is one person who does not feel nostalgia for the days when Chile was high on the agenda of international concern.

The purpose of Eduardo's phone call turns out to be to invite me to dinner the following evening. 'I have someone I want you to meet,' he says when I call him back the next day. 'A visitor from Chile. Come with Helen, of course.'

'No, it'll just be me, I'm afraid. We've split up actually.'

'Oh, really? Helen is very intelligent girl. Very nice girl.'

He almost says it as if our separation is proof of Helen's intelligence and good nature but I decide he did not mean it that way. I put the phone down feeling glad that I have something to do that evening. It will be like that now, planning things more carefully, not being able to rely on company. And suddenly I look around my flat and feel a sense almost of exhilaration. 'It's not that bad,' I say out loud, stretching my legs on the sofa and reaching for the remote control.

In his kitchen Eduardo is expertly chopping fresh coriander and sprinkling it on a tomato and onion salad. There are few more relaxing places than this kitchen. The walls are covered with old campaign posters and photos of a bizarre array of public figures that Eduardo finds amusing: Saddam Hussein, Julio Iglesias, Lady Diana and the Pope. Cassettes are carelessly scattered around the tape machine – a mixture of techno, cumbia, jungle and tango – reflecting Soledad and Eduardo's diverse tastes. There is a pile of computer magazines, since

Eduardo is a great enthusiast of technology and the Internet in particular. He conducts a series of intense debates about the political situation in Chile with a group of people he has never met, and always blames the large phone bills on Soledad gossiping to her friends. Bottles of red and white Concha y Toro wine are stacked on an old sideboard which opens to reveal a large collection of Ballantyne's whisky and Spanish brandy that Eduardo gets cheap from some shady source. Sometimes I have ended evenings at Eduardo's surrounded by empty wine bottles, clutching a large tumbler full to the brim with brandy in my hand.

The smell of the wet fresh coriander mingles with that of the lamb which is roasting in the oven.

'It's a good thing Helen didn't come,' I remark.

'Why?' The coriander-green knife pauses briefly.

'She's a vegetarian.'

Eduardo sniffs. 'Why?'

'I never really knew actually. Not out of any great love of animals. She ate fish.'

Then I feel guilty because I do know really why Helen was a vegetarian. She didn't like meat. It was no big deal for her. She wouldn't care whether there was animal fat in biscuits, but I know that I am trying to present it as a pretension: faddy bourgeois Helen. And it works.

'The British are strange about these things. In Chile the only reason for not eating meat is because you can't afford it,' Eduardo answers, the knife chop-chopping again rapidly, leaving tiny fishbone scars on the wooden board.

We are drinking white wine while Soledad and her boy-friend Patrick are sprawled in the living-room giggling and semi-watching *EastEnders*. There is no sign yet of Eduardo's visitor, who apparently went out in the morning to visit the British Museum and has not returned.

It turns out that she is the daughter of the man with whom Eduardo's wife began living after returning to Chile. 'My stepdaughter,' Eduardo says frowning. 'No, my stepdaughter-in-law.'

'Your half-stepdaughter?' I offer. 'Your ex-wife's step-daughter?'

Eduardo tells me that her father was a well-known journalist in Chile who had to leave after the coup. He took his family into exile, first to Canada, then Mexico, and finally back to Chile when his exile was finally lifted. In contrast to Eduardo, however, it was he who stayed in Chile while his wife returned to Mexico. He then started an affair with Eduardo's wife, whom he had known before the coup. Meanwhile, his daughter found life in the new country far from easy. She was expelled from the university where she was doing teacher training, and finally her exasperated father paid for her to come to Britain and stay with Eduardo. The fact that he is looking after the wayward daughter of the man who is living with his ex-wife does not seem to strike Eduardo as even remotely strange.

Soledad and Patrick wander into the kitchen.

'When's dinner, Dad? I'm starving.'

'When your *prima* gets here.' He checks his watch slightly anxiously.

'She's been gone hours. Typical Chilean, always bloody late. I'm starvin', man.'

'Well, eat some bread or something and stop moaning.'

At this point there is the sound of a key in the door. 'Thank God for that,' says Soledad loudly. 'Can we eat now please?'

'Jamie,' says Eduardo, frowning slightly at his daughter, 'this is Ana María.'

The first thing I notice about her are her black almond eyes. They stare at me curiously, almost aggressively. She has long black straight hair tied back with a red ribbon, a round lightly freckled face, and a sloping chiselled upper lip. On her finger she is wearing a ring with a lapis lazuli star. She shakes my hand formally. 'I am very pleased to meet you.' Her English is good and clear, with a faint Canadian accent.

'How did you like the British Museum?'

She flops down at the table, takes an orange from the bowl and begins to roll it around with the palm of her hand. For a minute I think she is not going to answer me at all. Then she fixes me with an unswerving gaze and says, 'Very interesting. Especially all the things the British steal from other countries.'

'Steal? Don't you mean rescue?'

'Sure, like you rescued our nitrates, like the Americans rescued our copper.'

She takes the ribbon out of her hair and slouches in her seat, letting her hair fall forward over her face so that only her nose pokes out, making her look like a cavewoman.

'Our friend is joking,' Eduardo butts in. 'Apart from stealing, the English are extremely fond of irony.'

Ana María shakes her hair back, pours herself a glass of wine and drinks it greedily.

'Very funny,' she says.

I feel slightly uneasy, as I have an infallible ability to get on badly with some people from the moment of first opening my mouth. I have never been sure what strange chemical is responsible for this, I just see the person looking as if they have a high-pitched whistle blasting their eardrum.

Soledad, with whom I have always got on well, glares ferociously at her half-stepsister.

'Well, Chileans can't talk. I mean, look at 'em. They've got a two-thousand-mile coastline and they go and steal the little bit Bolivia had. And apart from that, Chileans are the biggest thieves I know. When I was in Santiago I was always having to stop people nicking my stuff. Didn't stop the bastards getting my Walkman. Thieves, man. The other thing about 'em is that they never arrive when they're meant to.'

Patrick giggles. 'Maybe I should say that in my restart interview. I'll only accept a job in the Bolivian Navy.'

'Actually,' says Ana María, looking at me, 'if you knew

19

anything about history you would also know that the people responsible for the War of the Pacific were the English. And there is a Bolivian Navy. They practise on lakes.'

' "The horrendous English whom I hate'," adds Eduardo unhelpfully. 'Neruda said that. But tonight we make an exception for Jamie. Maybe he is not really English. You have a little Irish ancestry, Jamie?'

'Sorry, no. Anyway, that's just stupid, all that stuff. I don't mind being English. And I've known plenty of Irish who were a long way from being poets.' I glare at Ana María but she doesn't even acknowledge it and continues to roll her orange around the table. Patrick raises his eyebrows at me sympathetically.

'Jamie,' he says. 'A mate of mine, their Staff's just had pups. Do you want one?'

'Er . . . no thanks, Patrick. Nowhere to keep it really.'

He nods. 'Same for me. 'S a shame 'cause they're beautiful little dogs. Tyson – that's the mum – wicked dog, mate. Stupid name for a bitch though, innit? Tyson! Stupid name all round for a dog really. Too predictable. If I 'ad a dog I'd call it Sputnik. Sounds good, dunnit. Oi Sputnik, c'mere boy.' He laughs.

'So,' says Eduardo, putting on a large blue fish-shaped glove and opening the oven door, 'what do you have planned for tomorrow, Ana María?'

'I thought I would go to the cemetery and see the tomb of Marx.'

Soledad rolls her eyes. 'That'll be thrilling. How you gonna be able to sleep tonight?'

But Ana María just glances sideways at her as if at something very small and insignificant, and then up at the picture of Salvador Allende staring nobly from the kitchen wall, as if asking him to give her strength in the face of such stupidity.

Later, while I am helping Eduardo to wash up, he says to me, 'You know Jamie I want to ask you favour. If you have time to look after Ana María a little. Invite her out. I have asked Soledad but . . .' he shrugs comically, 'they don't really see eye to eye about much. And really she is quite unhappy you know, quite homesick. She can't spend all her time in museums and cemeteries.'

'Well, I'm not sure if *we're* going to see eye to eye actually. What if she says no?'

'Ah no, she likes you Jamie, she likes arguing. It is traditional in her family. I knew her father you know. Very intelligent, very arrogant man. I was partly responsible for expelling him from the Party and now he is living with my wife.' He laughs and passes me another plate, warm and slippery from the hot soapy water. 'But Ana, she is really very sociable and she is lonely at the moment. I am worried about her.'

'Well, OK, I'll give it a try.'

'Thanks, Jamie.'

Soledad and Patrick poke their heads round the door. 'Later, Dad. We're off out.'

'Yes, well, not too much later please.'

When they have gone, Ana María wanders in and sits at the kitchen table twirling a strand of hair around her finger. She certainly does have the look of someone who is thoroughly bored. Maybe she is about to try another argument. She didn't say much at the meal but snorted contemptuously when Soledad and I started talking about soap operas.

'You should see Chilean soaps, Jamie,' said Soledad, cutting her eyes at Ana María. 'Third World, man. Seriously underdeveloped.'

Patrick giggled and Ana María scowled. 'They're not all Chilean anyway,' she retorted. 'Most are Venezuelan . . . or Mexican.'

'There you are then,' crowed Soledad triumphantly. 'They can't even make their own soaps. They have to get them from other countries. Anyway . . .' she added spitefully, '. . . if it's such a brilliant place what are you doing here?'

21

'So what else have you been doing since you got here?' I ask Ana María quickly. She is rolling an orange around the table again. I am beginning to suspect that this might be her normal prelude to a fight, like a shark's rapid wiggling movements before moving in for the strike.

'Oh, you know, I have been to some museums, some art galleries . . . London is a horrible city,' she adds suddenly.

'You can't say that until you know it better. It's an acquired taste. Have you been on a pub crawl yet?'

'What is that?'

'You go from bar to bar having a pint of beer in each one and end up very drunk.'

She laughs. Ana María might be a bit of a Stalinist but I noticed that she was stacking the wine away tonight.

'I haven't been in a pub yet.'

'Well, you can't not go to the pub. Marx and Lenin, when they were in London, all the time not spent in the library they were down the boozer.'

'The what?'

'Oh, it's another word for pub.'

'You are joking again, I think.'

'No, seriously. We could go to the pub where Lenin used to drink. They used to have to throw him out at closing time. Call Mrs Lenin and get her to take him home. Well all right, that bit is a joke, but it's true. Lenin went to loads of pubs. Why don't you come some time? One weekend. We could finish up in one of Lenin's regulars.'

She looks down shyly a moment. 'Yes, all right,' she says, and then smiles at me, her face dimpling unexpectedly. Eduardo pours me some brandy and pats me on the shoulder.

As I walk to the bus stop later that night it begins to spit with rain and rubbish swirls around the streets. It is hard to think of a place that I would rather not be than waiting for a bus in Clapton on a rainy evening. The bus does not arrive and I

22

stand waiting in the cold beneath the strange orange glow of the street lights. Little diamonds of broken glass are scattered around the bus stop where somebody has punched the casing for the timetable. There is still a maroon smear of blood where the knuckles made contact. A couple of drunks – man and woman – lurch down the streets arguing. They stop on the corner against a front wall shouting at each other and the man swings his arm and hits her on the side of the head. Then he walks off. The woman leans against the wall, the can of beer still in her hand. A dark-windowed car speeds past exuding aggression, ignoring the red lights in its path. The bass from the stereo is thumping like a giant's heartbeat, as if the music is fuelling the car's movement. I think what a miserable spectacle London must present to somebody seeing it for the first time, and wonder what it must be like to see this city with the eyes of a newcomer. It would be strange to have to think about your movements, to have no inner map of its directions, no fluency with its patterns. My hopes rise as a 253 turns the corner, but as I get on the driver, who is wearing a Walkman and smoking a fag – both I am sure against London Transport regulations – says wearily, 'Only going as far as Hackney Central, mate.'

When I finally get home there is a fat red 0 on the message counter of the answerphone. I try to decide whether I mind the flat being empty and decide that I don't. Then I look for the bottle of brandy which is supposed to ensure that there is always alcohol in the house and which is having to be replenished more and more frequently in order to achieve this. There is a late-night programme on TV where a member of the public takes phone calls, eventually choosing one of the callers as a date. I dial the number but it is engaged. Later they debate whether there is too much sex and violence on TV. There are two numbers you can dial to register yes or no. I dial the no number – annoyed that there is no opportunity to register a not enough vote – and have better luck this time as a voice tells me my vote has been registered. Sure enough the graph monitoring the calls rises slightly in favour of the no and I decide that this is a good omen. I dial Helen's number but put the phone down before anybody answers. Outside, the sound of drunken singing crescendoes down the street. I set the alarm, determined to go to work the next day, and turn the light off thinking of all the people who might come and see me in the office. Unable to go to sleep, I drift into a strange trancelike state which is neither sleep nor waking, where I become obsessed with finding a missing tenancy file. Sleep comes at last with its stupid flickering anxious dreams.

Frau Hilda

The estate where I work is not really a single estate but rather several which have merged together. The housing office is on Jarvis Road, which slopes down to the start of Meadowdown North, the basis of which is formed by six identical tower blocks – Shakespeare, Tennyson, Byron, Milton, Wordsworth and Shelley. Satellite dishes creep down the walls of the blocks like inverted octopus suckers. In the early days of satellite TV we used to insist that people take them down, but were forced into a humiliating retreat when most people simply laughed and told us to try to come and take them down ourselves and see what happened. A series of bench-lined paths leads down to a large grassy space, an old abandoned laundry building, and an area for playing football enclosed by high wire fencing. The laundry building once belonged to four older walk-up blocks – Blake, Herbert, Donne and Keats. Standing slightly apart is the crescent-shaped Pope House which is commonly known as the granny block. Behind these smaller buildings is Folkestone Road with its line of scruffy grille-windowed shops – newsagent, launderette, off-licence, bookie's – and behind that some older blocks of flats and maisonettes which form part of Meadowdown South.

Most people who live on the estate are trying to leave it. Twenty-five minutes on the tube from Whitechapel, a fifteen-minute walk from the tube station, it is part of a depressing sprawl of estates, hemmed in by canals and gasworks, roads without shops which appear to go nowhere in particular, and isolated pubs which are either called the British Lion or the British Bulldog. It is not a place which is ever likely to be gentrified, since the raw material for such a process – street property – is almost completely absent. There are only a few pockets of small terraced housing, some of which also belong to the council. The most frequent complaint from the tenants is that they cannot move to wherever they want to go because the council has given all the decent housing to Asian families. 'If I was a Paki you'd move me quick enough,' they say sullenly when I tell them that they are unlikely to qualify for a transfer. 'You've gotta be a Paki to get anything from this council.'

Walking through the estate one morning after a series of noise-nuisance and rent-arrears visits, I meet Mrs Khan, wearing a bright pink and green sari and pushing a pram, the rest of her kids dancing and tripping around her feet.

'How is my transfer going?' she asks, shielding her eyes from the sun with her hand. 'You know they come again last night.'

'What did they do?'

'Oh, nothing much, just shouting, you know, and hitting letter-box.'

'Make sure you write it on the diary sheet. And the time and everything.'

She rocks the pram gently to and fro on the pathway.

'Yes, but please, Mr Collins, please hurry up.'

'I'm doing my best.'

One of the children twists round her legs, peering up at me with long-lashed olive eyes and giggling. The paving stone I am standing on is broken, cracked in the middle. The council have painted pink fluorescent crosses on dangerous paving stones as if they were plague victims. I step aside and it rocks slightly, freed from the pressure of my weight.

'Remember to write it on the diary sheet, yeah?'

Throwing the House Out of the Window

Mrs Khan sighs in answer and pushes the pram off, the children trotting along behind her. As I continue walking back towards the office, I am distracted by the sight of the Chair of the Tenants' Association, Hilda Connolly, bearing down on me. It is too late to dive for cover into one of the blocks.

'Hello, Jamie.'

Hilda hates me. She thinks that I am a young whipper-snapper who dresses unsuitably for work. I know that Hilda does absolutely nothing in her capacity as tenant representative to dispel the idea that the council is prejudiced against white families. Hilda's list of undesirables, however, goes much further than other ethnic groups. She is also obsessed with homosexuals, single mothers, ex-offenders, teenagers, children, pigeons, most classes of domestic animal apart from cats, and drug-dealers. The latter is a fairly elastic category which includes anyone that Hilda does not like the look of. She hates council workers unless they hold a rank of some importance, in which case she becomes disturbingly ingratiating. But her real venom is reserved for caretakers, whom she hates with a frenzy which at times approaches dementia. On Tuesday mornings she carries out a single-handed inspection of the estate, after which she presents me with a list of caretaking omissions ranging from the reasonable to the absurdly petty. If she had her way the estate would be transformed into a secure childless Hildaville of locked gates and parking spaces, cleaned by slaves and administered by a junta of righteous, like-minded, silver-haired citizens.

'Hello, Hilda.' I look at the large brown buttons on her coat instead of her face.

'I'm glad I've caught you, Jamie. There's a couple of things I wanted to bring up. Do you know there are squatters in Wordsworth House?'

'Yes. I've just been to see them. They'll be leaving soon.'

'Well, I hope so, Jamie. We don't want that sort around here.

27

Also, Mrs Davis has been to see me. The man on her stair –
coloured chap – has been playing his music until all hours and
she wants you to go and see him.'

'Tell her she must put a complaint in writing.'

'Yes, but surely you could go and see him in the meantime.
She's got dreadful lumbago and its hard enough to sleep at the
best of times. And she says he has all sorts going in there at
every hour of the night . . . you don't know what he's up to,
she's worried he's selling heroin . . .'

'Tell her not to worry, it's more likely to be crack.'

Her face puffs up like the fish that can turn themselves into
iridescent footballs. 'It's no laughing matter, Jamie. I keep
saying, and I've said it at Neighbourhood Policy Group
meetings, it should be us the tenants who decide who lives
here. If we were in control of allocations policy . . .'

If Hilda were in charge of allocations policy, Bosnia would
seem like a multi-ethnic paradise. I let her moan on, staring at
the boarded-up window of an empty flat where somebody has
written 'Paula Roberts is a dirty slag.' The flat has been empty
for months and it was only supposed to have minor repairs. I'll
have to get on to Building Works when I get back to the office.
Who had the keys last?

'Are you listening to me, Jamie? It's not good enough, her
nerves are shattered by the noise.'

'OK, I'll look into it. Is that everything?'

'No, Jamie, it isn't. Now, I put a crisp packet outside my flat
the other day to see how well the caretaker was doing the
sweeping. Two days later – two days, Jamie – it was still there.'

I look at her disbelievingly. 'Surely, it would have
blown . . .'

'No, Jamie, it would not. It would not have blown away.
Because . . .' she looks at me with malicious triumph '. . . I
weighed it down. With a large stone inside.'

'Very cunning,' I murmur, coughing slightly, and grateful
that nobody is around to witness this exchange.

Throwing the House Out of the Window

When I finally get back to the office, I approach Bob Townsend, the allocations officer. He grunts at me. 'I hope you're not here to pester me with transfers.'

'I want to know what's happening with Mrs Khan. Racial harassment case.'

Sighing, he taps into the computer. 'Yeah, she's nearly there.'

'Well, that's what you said a fortnight ago. How long?'

He swivels round on his chair to face me, fingering his bushy moustache. Bob has been here longer than anybody else. Management would love to get rid of him but know they are just going to have to stick it out until he retires. Bob reads the *Daily Express*, supports Spurs and always claims that he votes Tory. I'm not sure which makes him a more pathetic individual but I suspect that the last bit may just be a wind-up. 'You don't need to convince *us* that you're a loser, Bob,' Trevor always says when the subject comes up.

'How long's a piece of string?' Bob growls in response to my question. 'I don't know. She's not Category One. Could be weeks, could be years. It all depends. If you bastards would stop finding these bloody cases we could clear some of the backlog. And another thing, Collins, I've had mad dog O'Leary on the phone saying that you told him I'd get him a flat in a week.'

'Would I say that? I just mentioned that from now on he should direct his inquiries to you.'

'Well, good news, sonny Jim. He's coming to see you on Monday.'

'He'd better not wind me up. I'm dangerous when I'm provoked.'

'You're about as dangerous as my son's gerbil, you sad fucker.'

'Just get on with doing what you're meant to do and get Mrs Khan a transfer, you miserable fascist Tottenham git.'

'Did you just call me a yid? I distinctly heard you call me a yid. You can't get away with that in this authority, mate. I'll have you for racial abuse. Did you hear that, Trevor? Collins just called me a yid.'

'Shut up, Bob, you wanker, I'm trying to do some work.'

'I'll be getting my mate O'Leary on to you lot.'

'Even O'Leary wouldn't be your mate, Bob.'

This bickering is interrupted by my telephone ringing. I stare at it for a second and then sigh and pick it up.

'Mr Collins, Mr Collins . . . oh please Mr Collins it's my roof, there's water pouring in, I think I'm going to drown Mr Collins, I'm a pensioner, I've always paid my rent Mr Collins, it's an emergency . . .'

'Hi Karen.'

'Saw through it again, you clever devil. Listen Jamie, buy me lunch, it's your turn you know. I'm going out of my mind here, if I don't talk to somebody normal I'm going to turn into a raging psychopath and massacre the entire office.'

'OK.'

'Meet me at Mauricio's in twenty minutes.'

'See you later.'

Karen works in the neighbouring housing office. We sometimes meet for lunch in the one reasonable café which lies almost halfway between our offices. Karen and I started working in the borough at around the same time and met up on an equal opportunities training day. We ended up going to the pub for lunch and failed to return for the afternoon session. Karen is sharp-tongued and self-composed, always seeming to know what she is doing and why. Helen – who claimed that Karen was bitchy and aggressive – would sometimes accuse me of having a thing for Karen when we argued. She was right but not in the sense that she meant it. The thing I have for Karen is that I wish I could be more like her.

I walk towards Karen's office along the main road which cuts across the borough, the route from London to Essex leading out to the sort of places that people on the estate would like to move to: Ingatestone, Billericay, Chelmsford. The dreary stretch which runs by our office has no distractions for the drivers of cars and lorries entering or leaving the city. There is just one strange depressing shop by the bus stop which sells cheap plants and stale cheese rolls wrapped in cellophane, as well as renting out a small unchanging selection of soft-porn videos. Nearer to Karen's office however, where streets from other parts of the borough converge in a snarling roundabout, there are a few pubs, some shops and Mauricio's café.

I see Karen immediately, sitting in a window seat, her long straight blonde hair curving over the shoulders of a light suede jacket. She waves at me from her seat by the window and points to the cup of tea she has ordered for me.

'I also ordered,' she remarks as I sit down, 'beans on toast with a fried egg.'

'Fine.'

'So Helen's left you,' Karen muses after I have once again failed to present our separation as a mutual parting of the ways. She sprinkles pepper on to the dome of her egg and then splits it neatly open with her knife like a surgeon making the first delicate incision. She watches intently as the yolk slowly trickles down and then looks up and smiles as if she has just performed some ingenious trick.

'Well, you know, we thought that all round it would be better if we stopped it now so we could still be friends and everything . . .'

I stare at the little oily patch on the surface of my tea and consider taking up smoking again.

'. . . And I'm making a list of all the people I know who might be prepared to have sex with me.'

'Ugh, what an unpleasant thought. Well, at least it won't take you very long to write it.'

'You're right. So far, yours is the only name I can think to put on it.'

31

She laughs and stirs her tea.

'The plane, the plane . . . Fantasy Island, Jamie.'

'That's what's great about friends, the way they rally round when you're in trouble.'

'I'll rally round to the pub with you but that's my limit.'

'It's all right. Just buy me another cup of tea.'

A man pushes through the door of the café wearing a trilby hat and a shabby grey suit with a matching beard. He lurches up against the tables.

'You've got no brains,' he cries, 'none of you, you're all so stupid, you fucking stupid useless cunts.'

'Oh for God's sake,' mutters Karen, tensing visibly and putting down her knife and fork.

'He's harmless.'

'I know that, you fool, he's one of my tenants.' She gets up and takes him by the elbow. 'Come on, Mr Moody, why don't you calm down or they'll throw you out.' Mauricio, the owner, is staring belligerently at Mr Moody in a way that makes this prediction seem fairly accurate.

'You're all stupid fuckers,' says Mr Moody, but more quietly and fumbling in his pocket for some change. He doesn't have enough for a cup of tea, and Karen signals to the owner that she'll make up the difference. Mr Moody sits down at the table next to ours, muttering to himself. His trousers stop some way before his shoes and his skinny white legs end in day-glo green socks. Perhaps when they kick the patients out of their institutions into the warm embrace of the waiting community, they insist on this sock code as a form of tagging, in case policy changes and they decide to round them all up again.

'Listen, Jamie, I've got a new job.'

'What as?' My stomach clenches with disappointment and envy.

'In research. I'm going to be working for a housing research centre.'

'What's the pay like?'

'Oh, it's a bit better, but the main thing is to get away from all of this, you know, I can't handle much more, I'm burning out. I'm tired, Jamie. I've started to hate people.'

She looks at me suddenly over her cup of tea. 'Are you OK, Jamie? Really, are you all right?'

'I don't know. It's just everything at the moment . . . it would be better if the weather was nicer,' I say pathetically.

Mr Moody suddenly howls with laughter. 'Dogger, Fisher, Cromarty, German Bight,' he yells. 'Rising to gale force imminent. Blow winds and crack your cheeks . . . nice weather if you can get it.'

Karen and I look at each other, fighting to swallow mouthfuls of tea without laughing. She puts her hand to her mouth, her cheeks swollen with tea.

'Stupid fuckers,' mutters Mr Moody, glaring at Karen over the cup of tea she has just provided for him. I suddenly feel quite light-headed and cheerful.

'I'm all right I think. I think therefore I'm all right. I think I'm all right. I'm a bit of all right . . .'

'Get a grip, Jamie. Or you'll end up like . . .' and she jerks her head over to Mr Moody, who is muttering and fashioning a boat out of his paper napkin.

'No, really. I'm OK. You're a bastard though, leaving me like this without even talking it through. You've ruined my day. Who am I going to have lunch with now?'

Back in the office, an irate tenant tells me that her neighbour has poured weedkiller over her carefully nurtured geraniums because he claimed the leaves were brushing against his part of the wall. When she confronted him about it he told her that next time it would be more than just the geraniums. She has thick glasses and plays with the zip of her blue fleecy jacket. 'What are you going to do about it?' she asks. The question floats irrelevantly away, soap-bubble words drifting up and bobbing gently against the ceiling.

Red Red Eyes

Insomnia lifts you out of the ranks of the normal and dangles you among the lunatics and serial killers. It leaves you with red eyes and a sore stomach. Wriggling and twisting among the covers, putting on and casting off night attire, crazed thought patterns, images incessantly repeating themselves: he dives to the right and saves the penalty, he dives to the right . . . The first ghastly sound of the birds, light slowly stealing in through the gap in the curtains, falling asleep half an hour before you have to get up for work. Insomnia is cunning. Whispering that if you get up and do something, you might miss the moment when it lets go of the scruff of your neck and drops you into sleep. Threatening you with never sleeping again so that you are trapped in a vicious circle of anxiety and sleeplessness. Worst of all it is part of you, something inside and intrinsic to your mind, the frantic, angry buzzing of a wasp banging against the sides of a jar.

I lie star-shaped on the bed holding my eyes shut. I don't care, I don't care, don't care was made to care . . . They were brushing against my window, it's not going to bring my flowers back is it, breach of tenancy condition number two, not to cause a nuisance or disturbance . . . and now the shipping forecast . . . a canoeing holiday, suddenly rolled over, trapped in by my spray deck, inhaling water, kicking and kicking, my knees red and raw, crying afterwards for my mum who wasn't there . . . he dives to the right and saves the penalty . . . I dropped the brick on my sister Catherine's toe and it burst open . . . he won't make you laugh, Helen . . . the dog chewed out its stitches after being spayed, its insides fell out on the living-room carpet, I couldn't see it was blood, just a spreading dark stain, why did it try to bite Dad, it's in a lot of pain love . . . are they awake as well now, are they laughing, talking, FUCKING . . . are they . . . is she . . . he dives to the right . . . don't care, don't care . . . we stole the girl's glasses and buried them in the garden while they led the child to the railway line, a question of degree . . . though three men dwell on Flannan Isle, how does it go? Something about cormorants, an unfinished meal and an overtoppled chair, where did they go the three lighthouse keepers . . . he dives to the right . . . his name is Jamie he is a housing officer Jamie couldn't sleep they didn't live in Islington or Camden Town and he didn't get a clothes allowance like some of his friends his mum took him shopping no those shoes won't last six weeks I said no and I mean no I'm not asking you I'm telling you Jamie like when he dropped the brick on his sister's toe and saw her eyes widen in surprise and pain and he was frightened a dark spreading stain on the living-room carpet snarling pain it tried to bite Dad was his Dad frightened when he sleeps he dreams but he can't sleep now because she's not laughing now what *is* she doing now then Jamie he was frightened of the grey light seeping through the gap in the torn curtain.

'God, you look terrible,' says Trevor, leaning back in his chair with his hands folded behind his head.

'Thanks.'

'No man, you really do. You're a state.' He adjusts his tie as if my dishevelled state somehow threatens to contaminate him.

'Look, fuck off all right, Mr Clothes Show.'

Trevor looks hurt. 'I was concerned, that's all.'

Throwing the House Out of the Window

I gaze down at my rent arrears printout and plan harsh letters to pensioners, single mothers, and other vulnerable members of the community. If I feel like a bastard there's no reason why I shouldn't behave like one. Helen phoning snaps me out of my bleary-eyed state.

'Hi, Jamie.'

'Oh, how're you doing?'

'Yes. Fine, thanks . . . erm . . . I was wondering whether it would be OK to come round tonight and get some stuff.'

'Sure, of course, what time?'

'About eight. Does that suit you?'

'About eight. Sure yeah, see you then.'

'See you.'

A crazed *Luftwaffe* of starlings passes overhead as I stare out of the window waiting for Helen, and the evening smell of spices wafts up from the flats below. A drunk sprawls on the wall with a can of Special Brew in his hand, haranguing the passers-by without meeting their eyes. He has a foaming white beard stained ochre by nicotine around the mouth like a clown. A trail of piss runs from where he is standing, across the pavement and into the gutter. My neighbours Harold and Phyllis, left behind when the Jewish community abandoned the East End for more salubrious areas, shuffle past him along the street with their shopping trolley. Sometimes they ask me to change a light bulb, fill in their housing benefit form or arrange their Dial-a-Ride. Their flat always smells of over-boiled cauliflower. 'You're a good boy,' says Phyllis, the soft sagging whiteness of her ageing face coloured by brightly rouged cheeks and brown-painted eyebrows. 'Drives you mad, Jamie,' says Harold, a lugubrious ex-tailor, as he pains-takingly signs his name at the bottom of the forms, drops of sweat beading on his nearly bald head. 'All their bleedin' forms, drives you mad it does. Make the most of being young, boy' – as if housing benefit forms were invented as a special device to torment the elderly. Sometimes when I have filled in a form for them, I find a bar of chocolate or ten Rothmans cigarettes dropped through the letter-box. I wonder what they will make of Helen's absence. Phyllis has never liked her much because she thinks she is slovenly and has never seen her once clean the walkway.

A car turns into the street and makes its ungainly approach over the speed humps before pulling in under the flats. Helen gets out. I crane my neck to see who is driving but can only see a hand on the steering wheel. Helen leans through the window and says something to the driver. I pull back from the window because I know she'll look up.

'Hi, Jamie.' She kisses me on the cheek as she comes in and then says, 'Wipe your face, you've got lipstick on it.'

'Do you want a drink?'

'Have you got a beer?'

'No. Wine.'

'White?'

'Yeah.'

'OK then.'

She is looking nice, her hair tied back with a blue ribbon, wearing a new jacket.

'That's a new jacket.'

'Yes, my mum took me out shopping.'

'Is she all right?'

'Yes, she's fine. She sends you her regards. She was upset, you know, she always liked you.'

'Mmm,' I say noncommittally, since Helen's mum never supplied me with any evidence of this affection.

Helen looks around the flat, her hands resting on her knees, the heels of her loafers together so that her feet form a V. I give her a glass of wine.

'How did you get here?'

'I got a lift with a friend. I'll have to get a move on actually, because they're coming back for me in an hour.'

'How's your house?'

'Oh, you know, it's fine. I was dead lucky that Claire had a room going in her house.'

'Claire?'

'You've met Claire. You were quite rude to her I think.'

I remember Claire. She was part of the post-modern praetorian guard, a cultural anthropologist doing her research on the social construction of sexuality. Her command of the jargon was second only to Neil's, and she had two favourite words – 'gaze' and 'other' – which she used with monotonous regularity. 'Other' could also become a verb in her lexicon with 'othering' a major offence, second in gravity only to the masculine gaze. She had had a serious run-in with my friend Colin at a party, their dislike for each other increasing exponentially as they talked. Hostilities had commenced as soon as Colin had established that she was from Morningside in Edinburgh, and escalated dramatically when they began discussing whether young children had a sexuality or not. It was probably the first time in his life that Colin had been accused of 'othering' children through denying them the freedom to explore their sexuality.

'Claire? Isn't she that mad Scottish woman who kept insisting that it was OK to molest children?'

Helen rolls her eyes. 'Well, I don't think that was exactly what she was saying but you weren't in much of a state to listen that night. And calling her a 'fucking pervert who should be sent to Broadmoor' wasn't exactly the most tactful way of expressing your reservations about it.'

I can't help giggling slightly as a sudden image of her outraged face flashes across my mind.

'I don't think I said that, you know. I think it was Colin.'

'Well, that would make sense. Whatever, she was really hurt. That's sometimes your problem, Jamie. You think that because you think something you're entitled to say it. You never care that it might be insensitive or even wrong.'

I am about to remind Helen that I didn't actually say it, when her words suddenly remind me of an incident when I was very young. A kid who lived near us had a wooden sword. It was large, curved like a sabre and painted with blue and white stripes, and we all laughed at it and said how babyish it was. I remember taking it and holding it away from him, saying, 'Where did you get this then?' And he looked at me desperately, his eyes filling with tears, and said, 'My dad made it for me.'

'You don't care if you hurt people, Jamie.'

'Yes I do. It's just I don't always realize.'

'Yes, you're pretty stupid for someone who's always right.'

'*I'm* always right! That's pretty funny coming from you. I haven't exactly seen you or your friends plagued by self-doubt.'

'I might have known you would drag my friends into it, Jamie. I wonder what it is about them that makes you so angry.'

'Well, I'd tell you, but you said you only had an hour.'

Helen's eyes flash dangerously at me. 'Oh, I don't think you'd need an hour to tell me that you find it threatening that there are people around you who aren't just floundering about, but are actually doing something with their lives. They may have their faults but at least they're not . . .' She pauses.

'Not what? Come on Helen, don't hold back, at least they're not what?'

She looks straight at me, her eyes glittering. 'At least they're not failures.'

'I can't think,' I say coldly, 'how I could ever have thought that I loved you.'

Helen flushes and turns her head away.

Suddenly she shakes her head and laughs harshly. 'What am I doing? I didn't come round here for this. I'm going to get some stuff together.'

Watching Helen go through the videos and glasses and

books is interesting rather than depressing. It makes me remember where things came from and who the moral owner really is. She picks up books, hesitating from time to time, sometimes throwing them back like a discerning angler unwilling to bother with minnows.

'If it's yours take it,' I say. 'Don't just leave it because it's crap. And that copy of *One Hundred Years of Solitude* is mine but you can have it if you want.'

She removes it from the box disdainfully and throws it back, but the next book she picks up is a guide to Madrid, where we went on holiday two years ago. It was September and we stayed in a cheap hotel opposite the Prado listening at night to the perpetual whine of cars and motorbikes in the busy street below. We would wander for miles around the city, stopping in tiny bars to drink beer and eat *tapas*. The bed in the hotel creaked loudly and sometimes we would throw the crisp white sheets on to the floor to make love, falling asleep there in each other's arms. Helen turns the book round in her hand several times. There is a postcard tucked into the pages – Goya's picture of a drowning dog staring at an oncoming wave. 'Do you want to keep this?' Helen asks.

'No, you have it. Let me have the card, though.'

She looks at me for a moment, sadly, almost tenderly, and I want to say that I didn't mean what I said, that I can remember that other time when we lay in a noisy hotel room in the late September heat of a strange city. We remain almost transfixed in silence, the nostalgia of fading light filling the small living-room.

A car hoots downstairs. 'Oh, there's my lift.' She goes to the window. 'Yes. Right then, Jamie. I don't think we should see each other for a little while. And please don't ring my house again.'

'What are you talking about?'

'You know perfectly well. Phoning and asking for Neil and swearing.'

'Are you seeing him?'

'For God's sake, Jamie. Right, I'll see you.'

'I'll give you a hand.'

'OK.'

We carry the stuff downstairs. Claire is sitting in the car. 'Hello,' she says briskly in a Miss Jean Brodie accent as we put the boxes in the boot. She is wearing a checked skirt and the pixie boots that were fashionable at the beginning of the 1980s. Something about her just irritates me intensely.

'Hi, how's your research going?' I ask and Helen shoots me a warning look. I can't help it but I snort with laughter. Claire flushes and slams her door shut. As Helen gets into the car I see a look on her face that I know very well. She is trying not to laugh.

Later, in the bathroom mirror, I notice that I still have a lipstick kiss on my cheek like some sleazy adulterer in a cheap farce.

But is it Art?

Colin phones, wanting me to come to a private view at an art gallery in Mayfair.

'Loads of free beer,' he says.

Colin is a painter. He comes from a housing scheme in Edinburgh where his slightly wayward talent was encouraged by a community art project on his estate. Strangely enough, I met him through my sister Catherine. She was a punk at the time and had taken advantage of our parents' absence to have a party. Predictably, the assortment of punks and skins who had turned up proceeded to trash the house while Catherine sat forlornly crying in our parents' bedroom, rivulets of mascara running down her face. I was also pretty worried, since my parents apportioned blame on a strictly fifty-fifty basis, and there would be little chance of convincing them that it had had nothing to do with me. Colin had been one of the uninvited guests with his friend Blackie, a pale skinny character who turned out to be a martial arts expert who had done time. Blackie wandered into the bedroom, saw Catherine's distress and decided that things had gone too far. Within about ten minutes, they had cleared the house and Catherine and Blackie were snogging on my parents' bed while Colin and I took a couple of blues and sang along to Clash and Bowie albums. Colin explained to me that Blackie was 'soft like that really, can't stand to see a lassie greetin' '. After that, Colin had just attached himself to my family. He had a special knack for twisting my mum around his little finger, knowing just the right moment to turn on the charm, when to give gruelling accounts of shared needles and shattered lives, and when to be the responsible brother figure who would make sure nothing happened to me. I can see them now, Colin at the kitchen table, devouring another plate of food 'that was magic, Mrs Collins' before we retired to the bedroom to skin up. My mum said that Colin was an original, in which she was right. She forgave him almost anything because she said that he knew how to love unconditionally. He outlasted Blackie, who did not love Catherine, even conditionally, and their relationship was exhausted after about a week. She cried again when he packed her in, but this time Blackie was unmoved.

An evening out with Colin frequently ends in a brawl as he decides, usually correctly, that someone is patronizing him and repays them with a head-butt. He hangs around with a group of poseurs and social climbers for whom he has the utmost contempt but with whose world he also remains endlessly fascinated. They are a strange mixture of actors who have had minor parts in films, artists who exhibit in tiny galleries to their friends, and musicians who are always in the studio and on the verge of a major breakthrough. They meet most frequently in clubs and at parties, always appearing to treat Colin like an amusing toy, extremely deferential to his face and sniggering when his back is turned.

'No, I don't think so,' I reply to the art gallery invitation.

'Come on, Jamie, you radge, loads of free booze. We'll have a laugh at all the wankers.'

'All right, I'll meet you at the tube station.'

'Marble Arch at seven-thirty. See you later, Don't be late 'cause we've got to get to the free bar before it all runs out.'

I arrive at the tube station first and wait by the barrier. There are a few other people waiting and we glance at each other from time to time. Nobody wants to be last to be picked up. A girl steps forward to her boyfriend who wraps his arm around her murmuring apologies and excuses about security alerts at King's Cross. In the next stream of people ascending the escalator I see Colin, taking the steps two at a time, his ever-present Crombie coat flapping around him. He is stocky, with a large powerful head, cropped dark hair, mocking eyes and a small scar over one eyebrow.

'Sorry I'm late. Some idiot must have left their bag on the train again. How you doin', Jamie?'

'Not bad.'

The place in which the exhibition is held is packed with the usual crowd drinking bottles of Becks. There are lots of crop-haired or naturally balding men – it's hard to tell – with thick-rimmed glasses and black leather jackets talking earnestly to each other. There are goatee beards and Björk lookalikes. There are also a few executives in suits, and women with suntans and long legs. I can't see much art but there is a kind of shark feeding-frenzy going on around the free bar, over which hangs a canopy of cigarette smoke. It is far too hot because of an enormous fire roaring in one corner of the room. Colin keeps meeting people. He introduces me to Henry, who has Tintin hair, little oval-shaped glasses, a brightly coloured waistcoat and has just got back from China where he was 'with' Gilbert and George. 'Big fuckin' deal,' says Colin. 'Gilbert and George are wankers.' Henry ignores him. 'I'm sure I know you,' he says to me. 'Haven't I met you in Shoreditch?'

'That's right,' says Colin. 'This is Wolfgang, he's always in Shoreditch.'

'Well, I'm very pleased to make your acquaintance, Wolfgang. You must be of German origin?'

'No, no,' says Colin. 'He's a Bosnian refugee. He's had a very traumatic time. The Serbs murdered his whole family. They had to airlift him out. The shock turned him mute.'

'Oh, look,' says Henry, 'there's Dan. Excuse me a minute, I must go and say hello to Dan. Back in a sec.' He disappears.

'Hang on,' says Colin. 'I'll go and get some more beers.'

While Colin is battering his way efficiently through the crowd to the bar a girl sidles up to me. 'Don't you think Malcolm is just frighteningly talented?' She is pretty, with long chestnut hair, wearing a black dress with red roses printed on it, and a cocaine smile.

'What? Oh yeah, right, frighteningly so.'

'I love him to death.'

'Erm, that's nice. Who's Malcolm by the way?'

She turns reproachful eyes on me. 'Oh right, another one who's only here to get pissed. Malcolm's the artist.'

'Yeah, of course. I was only kidding. It's not a very big exhibition, is it? I mean there only seem to be about three paintings. Well, I suppose they're not really paintings . . .' I stare at a triangle of blue neon tubes with a swastika in the middle.

She looks around her, sways slightly and puts her hands to her face theatrically.

'Yes, you are right. You are so very very right. But there's not room for Malcolm's bigger . . . installations. Do I appear to you to be glowing?'

'You appear to be off your fuckin' face, Iona.' Colin has returned with the drinks and passes me two bottles of Becks, sticking another couple into his coat pocket.

'Ah, Colin. How very delightful to see you. It is always so nice to hear your reasoned and temperate voice.'

'Aye, right. Now beat it, we're trying to have a conversation about art here. Not that there's any about in this room, mind you. Go and do another line with the rest of your pals. And tell Malcolm that Nazi chic is so awfully *passé*.'

Iona seems both used to and unperturbed by this vitriol. She smiles serenely at Colin.

'Ah, yes. I would be offended by your superior moral tone were it not for the fact that I know there's not an ounce of hypocrisy in clean-living Colin Ferguson.' She smiles at me,

'Nice to have met you,' and drifts away.

'Listen, Colin. I'm going to make a move.'

'Don't worry, Jamie, we're out of here in a minute. These were the last free bottles. From now on it's three quid. Er . . . Jamie, could you lend me a tenner for the pub?'

In the pub it seems that the change to a charging policy for beer in the art gallery has provoked a similar response among the beautiful people. It is a relief to be in the familiar surroundings of beer pumps, purple velour-covered seats and tables with half-filled pint glasses, little puddles of split beer, and ashtrays. It is also good to escape from the log fire which has been roasting the backs of my legs. Iona comes in and waves at me. 'I think she's after you, Jimmy,' says Colin.

'No, she's in love with Malcolm. He's frighteningly talented.'

'He's frighteningly shite actually. And she's just a coke-head although she's not as bad as him. Wouldn't kick her out of . . .'

'Why do you hang around with all these people?'

'The thing is, Jamie, all the people I've ever met have been either boring or pretentious. And, at the end of the day, give me the pretentious ones. Like Dostoevsky said, man reaches truth through talking shite. And at least you can have a laugh, get a shag, take a few drugs and not get so fuckin' bored. What's the option?'

I go to the toilets. I am getting pissed. There is something reassuringly familiar about a pub toilet when you are drunk; the swing door, the leaking cistern, the water that periodically hisses down over the white porcelain, standing on wet tiles and aiming your piss at the fag butts floating alongside the yellow lozenges, making them disintegrate and release their last saffron filaments of tobacco, the felt pen graffiti: BNP, ANL, LUFC, IRA, Pompey, Milwall – pride of London, NO SURRENDER, I suck men's cocks – write time and place below . . .

When I come back up the stairs I notice that Colin is talking to someone I don't know and that his head is lowering in a way that I have seen before and which starts alarm bells ringing. The stranger has a finely sculpted public school face and is carrying a silver-topped cane. He is saying in a deliberately exaggerated upper-class accent, 'Oh, I get it, you're one of those who thinks we should all be out painting murals on council estates and being in touch with the real world. You've got no time for the nasty capitalist art world because it's got no time for you.'

'No, I don't think that actually, you patronizing English cunt. I've got no time for the capitalist art world 'cause it's full of mingin' bastards like you. And carry on talkin' to me like that and I'll stoat you in the head.'

From the slight smirk with which Silver Cane greets this statement I can tell that he does not realize how little time is left between threat and action. Previously Colin has only been taxiing down the runway, but now it is obvious that he is about to switch the engines to full throttle. I quickly hurry to the table.

'Listen, Jasper or Rupert or whatever your name is, I think you'd better go.'

'Yeah, beat it, you prick,' says Colin, who continues to stare at him threateningly as he rejoins his group of friends.

'Can't you ever go an evening without starting a fight, you crazy bastard?'

'People just talk to me the wrong way.'

'Well, talk to them the wrong way back. You don't have to inflict GBH to give them a lesson in etiquette.'

'Aye, well, sometimes it's the best thing for them. Get a drink in, Jamie.' And he gulps back the rest of his pint and gives me a disarming grin.

'Just don't batter anyone while I'm at the bar.'

We lurch out of the pub pissed at closing time, with me still sober enough to keep an eye out for Colin's adversary.

'D'ya wanna come back to mines, Jamie?'

'No, you're all right, I can get the bus from here.'

'All right, Jamie, you're magic you are. No really, ye're ma best pal. I fuckin' love you Jamie, you know that. Don't you worry about wassername. She'll come back.'

'Yeah, right, well, see you later Col.'

'D'ya wanna get some chips?'

'No, no, I'm not hungry.'

'OK Jamie, could you lend me a pound so I can get some? I'll pay you back, you know that Jamie. Thursday, right? When the giro comes.'

I give him a pound and he grabs me by the ears and starts affectionately pummelling my head against his shoulders. 'Ye're fuckin' brilliant, Jamie. No really . . .'

'Let go of me, you mad bastard.'

He lurches off down the street waving behind him and crashes into a lamppost. He steps back and pretends he is about to head-butt it, and then disappears laughing around the corner.

At the bus stop I meet Iona, who is standing with a group of people.

'Ah, you have got rid of your rude friend. We are going to a party. Would you like to come?'

One of the girls in the group looks at her friend and smiles knowingly.

'Er, no thanks.'

'Oh, why not?' She takes my hand. 'I would like you to come.'

'No, really, I have to work tomorrow.'

She does not let go of my hand. 'I think it could be nice if you came.'

'Iona, this is our bus coming.'

'Will you come?'

'No, really.'

The bus pulls up and the doors open. The driver stares in a

bored way at the people waiting to get on.

'This is your last chance.'

Stupidly and against my better judgement I get on the bus. She is still holding my hand.

Hello Cruel World

The receptionist raises her eyebrows as I come into the office at 10.30. 'Tubes were terrible this morning,' I mumble. Roy, my section head, looks over the balcony, looks at his watch and then returns to work.

'I've been turning lots of tenants away,' says Mary, 'but there's a couple still waiting.' I turn and see Mrs Khan and smile at her. 'Let me just get myself sorted out.' Upstairs, the sight of Trevor hard at work in his crisp suit and tie is almost too much to bear. I lurch into the kitchen and put the kettle on, trying to find a mug that does not have a small tropical rain forest growing in it.

Not surprisingly, we did not stay too long at the party, which was full of intense people, strange furniture and weird lights. We ended up sitting under a lampshade made out of the helmet of a German soldier from World War Two. I began kissing Iona in the taxi back to her flat. When it came to paying for the cab, it seemed that we had no money until Iona found a rolled-up tenner in her purse, sucking the end quickly before unrolling it and passing it to the driver. She had a rose tattooed on her shoulder. When I woke in the morning I panicked. 'Where am I?' And then saw Iona's hair spread across the pillow and remembered. I found my clothes and went to the desk to write a note saying that I had gone to work and leaving my phone number. There were lots of invitations to clubs and one-nighters on the notice board above the desk;

51

Strawberry Sundae's, Madame JoJo's, Pushka. I recognized some of the names because Colin has sometimes tried unsuccessfully to make me go to them. On the desk there were strings of beads, a half-smoked joint in the ashtray, a bank statement which showed that she was £745.69 overdrawn, a letter which began 'Darling Iona, Goa was heavenly . . .' I shut the door quietly behind me. On the bus I thought about Helen, her mum taking her shopping, her face trying not to laugh as she got into Claire's car.

The kettle begins to scream. My boss comes into the kitchen.

'Hello, Jamie.'

'Hi, Roy.'

'Listen, Jamie, try not to come in like that, you know. It looks very bad to the tenants.'

'I know. Sorry.'

'Got a hangover?'

'How did you guess?'

He picks up a coffee cup, peers inside and recoils, wrinkling his nose.

'I'm going to start a washing-up rota soon . . . You can't go out partying in the week. Well, some people can, but you can't pull it off. You look like the living dead.'

'Thanks. It seems to be a habit in this office to tell me what a sorry case I am.'

'Well, take the hint, Jamie. There's a one-day strike coming up, I hear.'

'That's right.'

He takes the mug handle between his finger and thumb as if he is holding a dead rat by the tail and puts it in the sink, blasting it with water from the tap.

'Mmmm. I don't think many are going to go out.'

'Maybe, maybe not. I can't discuss strategy with the enemy of course.'

'Well, I'll be opening the office.'

'Of course. You're a management lackey. A sell-out to the

bosses. The unacceptable face of . . .'

'Yeah, well, less of that, otherwise I might start becoming a real bastard and crack down on latecomers and huge flexi-debits.'

'OK, OK, as management lackeys go you're part of the progressive wing.'

'Well, don't ride your luck, Jamie.'

'Yes *baas*.'

'And eat some chewing-gum or toothpaste or something before you talk to any tenants.'

'Aye aye, skipper.'

'And I want to know what's going on with Mrs Khan. I've had a Councillors Inquiry and a phone call from the Anti-racist Monitoring Group.'

'I'm just about to see her. It's Bob. He's moving at the speed of a tortoise with no legs. Lean on him for me.'

'Right. Keep me informed, Jamie.'

Downstairs I hold the door open for Mrs Khan so that she can push the pram into the interview room. She sits down and takes one of the kids on her lap. The child reaches up to her face murmuring and chortling. She takes its chubby arm absent-mindedly in her hand and waves it about as she talks.

'Please Mr Collins, do you live every night with people screaming at you, throwing things through letter-box? Do you lie awake worrying that maybe your house is going to burn down?'

'No.'

'You don't know what it's like. For you I am just problem. Problem at work. Then you go home and it's all forgotten.'

'Actually that's not true.'

Is it true? I don't know any more. Everything gets mixed up: the small complaints with the big ones, the genuine problems and the petty moaning. I certainly worry about work at home. But this usually involves tenants who might get violent if their hot water is not restored half an hour after it has broken down.

Or it is just a general sense of worry which diminishes somewhat on Fridays and then crescendoes throughout Sunday evening.

'You are a nice boy, I know, I don't want to be rude to you. But you don't understand.'

'You see, my problem is that you're telling me this and I'm telling someone else and he's probably telling someone else. I gather you've been in touch with the Monitoring Group?'

'Yes.'

'I'll give them a ring and see what we can do.'

At this point one of the children pushes the red panic button which has been thoughtfully sited at exactly the right height for a five-year-old child. People come running as the alarm begins to shriek, except for Rosemary McKee who is used to this occurrence and already has the key out ready to switch it off.

After Mrs Khan has gone I phone the Monitoring Group, hoping that I don't get Khaled, who treats all council officers as if they were representatives of the British National Party – ignoring the fact that his organization only survives with a hefty council grant – and with whom I have had several bust-ups in the past. My hand is sweating slightly on the white plastic receiver and I can feel my pulse beating. A tiny muscle in my nose starts to twitch irritatingly. I will have to go home this afternoon and go to bed. Fortunately, it is Paula who answers.

'Who's been dealing with Mrs Khan?'

'Khaled.'

'Oh.'

'Only joking. I know how much you adore each other. It's me actually.'

'Good. Erm . . . can we meet up to have a chat about it? This afternoon?'

'Oh, let me just consult my Filofax. Yes, I think I can squeeze you in. About three?'

'Fine. Do you want to come to the office?'

'Yes, OK.'

I rest my head on my arms and contemplate falling asleep at my desk. I think about Mrs Khan. Have I stopped caring any more? Have I become routinized into indifference? Do I just see all tenants now as people to be feared, laughed at or ignored? Part of what Helen said was true. You have to take responsibility for things and stop feeling sorry for yourself. I need to put my house in order and I could start by doing some serious work on this case.

I remember what I can of the party last night but it makes me feel too uncomfortable – somebody blabbering on to me about beauty being everything, somebody telling me about feeling betrayed because their partner had turned out to be gay but hadn't told her, Iona smiling beatifically and leading me downstairs, waiting silently in the cab office, a red rose, her hair fanned out on the pillow in the morning . . .

On the way home that night, I stop off at the supermarket. A fat woman with white leggings pushing a trolley in front of me turns to see her son picking up a Cadbury's Creme Egg from the chocolate aisle. She puts her hand on her hip. 'Liam! Put that down now.' The freckle-faced kid puts it back but doesn't release his grip on it. 'Put that down Liam or I'm gonna break your fuckin' jaw.' I stare at the woman. *I'm gonna break your fuckin' jaw?* The kid is five years old. The woman notices me looking at her and stares at me challengingly as if Liam's is not the only jaw that might get broken. I open a carton of eggs and spin each one round in its cardboard nest to ensure that none are yolk-glued to the sides.

When I get home that night there are two messages on the answerphone. One is from my sister asking if there is any chance of me doing some babysitting. I don't recognize the voice on the second message at first and then I realize that it is Ana María. She doesn't really say anything in her message apart from the fact that she called to speak to me but I wasn't in and could I call her back.

I start slicing onions to make a sauce for some pasta. The kitchen is full of grey light and I can't find the tin opener. I think about my conversation with Paula that day. 'This could be a really difficult case,' she said. 'It's more organized than it looks at first. It's not just kids behind it.' I drop the spaghetti in the boiling water and wait for the brittleness to give before pushing it down until it curves and submerges. When the food is ready, I take it into the living-room, and sit in front of the TV eating. Each mouthful is an effort, however, and finally I pick up the half-eaten food and stand over the bin scraping the mess of pasta and tomato sauce into it. The pungent smell of raw onion has lingered depressingly on my fingers. *I'll break your fucking jaw*.

I know that if I spend the evening watching everything on TV this noose of depression will tighten even more, so I pick up a book. Gradually, as I read, it begins to release its grip on me and time loses its stickiness. I curl my legs on the sofa, pausing sometimes to look up at the window, before returning to the page. 'Nastasya Fillipovna' I whisper to the empty room, savouring the sound of the name. 'Nastasya Fillipovna.' It has a soothing effect on me.

The telephone ringing interrupts me. It is Iona and she sounds slightly subdued.

'You didn't stay for breakfast,' she says.

'No, well, I was really late for work. I thought I'd just leave you sleeping.'

'What are you up to?'

'Reading.'

'Oh, right.'

There is a pause and I struggle desperately to think of something to say.

'Do you want to go out for a drink some time?' she says suddenly. 'What about Friday?'

'OK, yeah, Friday's fine.'

'Do you know the French Protestant church in Soho Square?'

'No.'

'It's on the north side of the square, a red brick building. Meet me there at nine.'

'OK,' I agree, wondering what would be wrong with meeting at a tube station.

After putting down the phone, I turn on the TV. The *Late Show* is doing an appreciation of Michel Foucault. I flip channels. There is a programme about atrocities in Bosnia on one side while on the other there is a *Carry On* film. I continue to flip the channels quickly to and fro: Sid James, Slobodan Milosevic, Hattie Jacques, Kate Adie, Sarah Dunant, Kenneth Williams, David Owen, Michel Foucault. 'Carry on Ethnic Cleansing,' I say, but there is nobody around to hear me.

Black and Gold

I don't quite keep my promise to take Ana María to a pub Lenin used to drink in. Instead, I meet her after work one night at Whitechapel tube station, arriving early so that she doesn't have to stand waiting for me. A man in a dirty pea-green anorak is selling a paper called *Worker's Shield*, the headline of which reads 'Yugoslavia – Return to the Road of Lenin and Trotsky!' Or rather he is standing trying to sell it because they are not exactly going like hot cakes. 'Expose the imperialist carve-up of Yugoslavia,' he mutters hoarsely. 'For a revolutionary class-war against racism.' On the wall behind him, veiled women brandishing assault rifles decorate a line of flyposters advertising a meeting on the future of Islam. A man pulls back the curtain of the photo booth to find one of the woman dossers sprawled on the swivelling chair. Her mottled face breaks into a grin and she raises her can to him. 'Fuck sake,' he mutters and draws the curtain again.

Through the crowd coming up the steps, Ana María emerges, carrying a book in her hands.

'What's the book?' I ask.

She turns it round to show me the cover. 'Roque Dalton,' she says. 'Poetry.'

'I've never heard of him.'

'He was from El Salvador. He was a guerrilla. They executed him.'

'The death squads?'

Ana María smiles ironically and shakes her head.

'Unfortunately,' she replies, 'he was executed by other guerrillas.'

'Why?'

'It was a very confused situation. Nobody really knows. There was a big split.'

We walk down the Whitechapel Road, past the old brewery with its gold-lettered arch that is being converted into luxury flats. SHOWFLATS – AVAILABLE FOR VIEWING is written in red letters on a long white banner hanging from the top of the building.

'This pub,' I say as we pass the Blind Beggar, 'is famous because of two local gangsters who shot a man in here. They were twins. Now it's a bit strange because it's like they've become heroes all of a sudden.'

Ana María peers inside the conservatory which has been added to the pub. 'It doesn't look like a place where somebody gets shot.'

'No, well, it's probably changed quite a bit.'

'Who are those people?' She points to a large group standing on the other side of the road looking at the Blind Beggar and listening to a tubby man in a deerstalker hat.

'Tourists. They come round here on walks. It's a very historic area. Because it's such a traditional part of London. People are quite fascinated by it.'

'And I have a tour all of my own,' she says. 'Shall we go in here then?'

'No,' I answer.

She turns to me as we walk on. 'Tell me something else.'

'OK, well, you see over there, that's where I live, behind those flats. I once saw a map some guy in the last century did where he coloured all the streets of London, according to how rich the people who lived in them were. The highest was gold and the lowest was black. The black bits were where he said the vicious criminal class lived. Mayfair – that's a rich part of

60

London – was all gold. But exactly where my house is, that was all black.'

'And is it like that now, full of criminals?'

'Well, there are a few. But not really, probably it never was. The really vicious criminals lived in the gold bits.'

'They probably still do,' says Ana María.

I steer Ana María into a pub, through the pool area and over to a table. She looks around her. Over the upturned vodka and brandy bottles there are a couple of glass-eyed ferrets, all fur and muscle, tubular bodies curved up and tiny teeth bared, paralysed by the taxidermist into a snarling eternity. On the painting above our heads a fierce sea battle is being waged, puffs of smoke emerging from the cannon of the great sailing ships. In one corner sits a giant man, muttering angrily to himself, periodically sprinkling snuff on to the back of his hand and snorting it before returning to his monologue. Ana María glances at him slightly nervously.

'Don't worry,' I reassure her, 'he's always in here. Anyway, what are you having to drink?'

She looks at the couple sitting across from us who are sipping at pints of Murphy's, and points to their glasses. 'That,' she says.

I lean on the bar watching the barmaid carefully flattening the head of the Murphy's with a red plastic knife before turning the tap again so that the head rises perfectly to the top of the glass. Ana María sips at her pint, which leaves her with a white moustache. She wipes at her mouth and smiles like a child. 'Nice,' she says.

She tells me that for the first week she was here she was so homesick that she just lay in her room reading, only coming out to eat. Then she started drifting around the city, going to the cinema in the afternoons, visiting museums and sitting in parks. One day she got the wrong bus to go home and ended up in Homerton. Totally lost, she went to call Eduardo and a man decided that she was taking too long on the phone and started kicking the phone-box. When she still did not come out, he burst in and grabbed the phone and tried to hit her with it. In her struggle to get out of the phone-box, she dropped all her change and had to scrabble around on the pavement for it. She laughs as she tells me this story, but her tone is flat and she twists her ring round and round on her finger.

'Haven't you been out with Soledad?'

'Yes, once. She took me to a party, but I didn't like the music.'

'So what have you seen that you do like here?' I ask.

She sips at her beer, furrowing her eyebrows and thinking hard. Finally, she says, 'I like it when the sun shines. Even when it is just a little bit warm people go crazy, taking all their clothes off and lying in the park. Here, people are so happy to see even a piece of the sun. And then there are the little lorries that come round playing music . . .'

'Lorries playing music?' I look at her doubtfully.

'Yes. You know, the ones that sell ice-cream. They *do* play music,' she insists stubbornly in response to my first expression. 'To tell the children they are there.'

'Oh, right. Ice-cream vans.'

'Yes. And Soledad, she makes Eduardo go and buy us an ice-cream. He looks so funny, standing there with all the little children . . .'

I laugh as I imagine Eduardo with his grey cardigan and mournful moustache standing among the urchins from his estate and asking for three medium 99s.

The pub starts to get more crowded, filling up with students from the college in Suede T-shirts, and groups of medical students from the hospital wearing jumpers with the names of their rugby clubs on them. Some people start giving the students dirty looks and begin the ritual muttering about how they are ruining the pub. Nobody goes to sit down at the snuff man's table and he continues to mumble harmlessly, sipping his pint and throwing his hand back to his nose.

'I also like this beer,' Ana María smiles.

I look at the empty glasses. 'Well, it's your round.'

Her smile fades. 'What do you mean?'

'Oh, sorry, it means it's your turn, you know. To get a drink in.'

'I . . . I don't know if I have . . . wait . . .' she takes out a leather purse and empties out some change. She has about a pound.

We both look solemnly at the small pile of change on the table.

'That won't be enough?' she asks faintly, her cheeks bright red.

'No. But it's OK, don't worry, if you haven't got any money I'll get it.'

'I'm sorry,' she says. 'It's just . . . you see when you invite me to a drink I think . . . you see it's nothing to do with you being a man . . . it's just if I had invited you to a drink I would have paid for them but because you invite me . . .'

'Don't worry about it,' I say.

'No, but . . . that is normal here? First one person buys a drink, then the next person and so on?'

'It's quite normal, yes. But not always.'

'Ah,' she says, looking as if she would like to jot this down in a notebook. 'Well, next time I will buy all the drinks . . .'

'It's no big deal,' I say.

'Round,' she says as I move away, testing the word out. 'Your round.'

When I arrive back from the bar, Ana María is talking to the girl from the group sitting next to us. She has great waves of auburn hair, rings on every finger and is asking Ana María where she is from in a strong northern accent. When Ana María tells her, she nods wisely and says that she and her boyfriend Badger – she gestures over to a boy in a thick jumper smoking roll-ups – have just got back from Morocco.

She tells us that they are all from Preston originally but that she is temping down here, saving up more money to go away again. Badger has just got a job delivering plants to office blocks in the City and on their next trip they are either going to go to the Greek islands or Ibiza. 'Get the drinks in, Tammy,' shouts one of her friends, and she takes out a twenty-pound note. 'What are you drinking, honey?' she asks Ana María.

'No, thank you,' says Ana María, looking wistfully at her glass.

The girl cackles. 'Come on,' she says. 'Never turn down the offer of a drink from a stranger. Murphy's, is it?'

'But . . .' says Ana María, glancing at me, 'I will not be able to buy you a round.'

'So?' says Tammy. 'It's pay-day. As long as we've got some money left over for some blow. What about you love?' she gestures at my empty glass and I nod.

While she is at the bar, one of the group who has been staring at Ana María shifts up alongside her and starts asking her again where she is from, how long she is planning to stay here, and where she learned to speak English. 'Your hair,' he says, gazing at it as if bewitched. 'It's so . . . it's so fuckin' black. That's beautiful hair, man.'

Before Ana María can respond, however, Tammy is returning from the bar. 'Fuck off, Nicky,' she says, setting the drinks before us. He wriggles obediently back to his place, from where he casts sideways glances at Ana María. Tammy settles herself regally back down next to Ana María. 'Let me see your ring, ooh, that's gorgeous, lapis lazuli in't it . . . look, I got this one in Morocco . . .' and she spreads her hand next to Ana María's so that each of her elaborate silver rings gleams in the dim pub light.

After we have said goodbye to Tammy and left the pub, I walk Ana María to her bus stop. 'This will take you almost to your front door,' I say.

Ana María nods and we stand quietly at the bus stop, as we

seem to have suddenly run out of conversation. When the bus arrives, she turns and kisses my cheek. 'Thank you. That was a good evening.'

'Give my regards to Eduardo and Soledad.'

She nods and waves. I watch her move along the bus and climb the stairs, taking the seat at the very front. The bus swings round into the Cambridge Heath Road and heads away towards Bethnal Green. The Nat West tower continues its perpetual watch, its black helmet lit up now by a ruby triangle. Above the trees, a big full moon hangs in the sky, very close to the earth. I walk back to my flat, watching it all the way, the smoky patterns of its dry seas staining the brightness of its uninhabitable surface.

Tomorrow Belongs to Them

Mrs Khan is the first person in the office. A stone has been thrown through her window and shit smeared on her door. After putting on the repair for the window I phone Paula and we agree to meet at Mrs Khan's house after work. As I hold the door open for her to leave, I spot O'Leary in reception scowling at the floor and tossing a packet of Bensons from one hand to the other.

'Take a seat, Mr O'Leary.'

'I've seen an empty flat I want.'

'I'm afraid it doesn't quite work like that, you see . . .'

'You're not being very 'elpful, Mr Collins. It seems like I'm doing the council's job for 'em. Now I find myself a flat and you tell me I can't have it even though it's empty.'

His eyes have not left mine and I look down at my pad. Tenants seeking transfers are always pulling this little routine, telling you about empty flats that they have seen and demanding to know why they can't move in immediately. I have given the explanation so many times that the words always feel as if they are crawling from my mouth tugging a ball and chain behind them. I can't be bothered today.

'The thing is you really must deal with the allocations officer about this – I have no control over it once I've done your transfer application form.'

'I asked for him. He's not 'ere. Always on 'oliday. You lot spend all yer time on 'oliday when yer not on fuckin' strike.'

I start uncomfortably, remembering that there is a shop meeting scheduled for lunchtime.

'Well, I'll definitely leave him a note telling him you've been in and asking him to call you.'

'Listen, mate. I'm sleeping in my bleedin' car at the moment. There's some geezers I've gotta avoid. I've even been round to me mum's but I can't stay there. Now if I don't get a flat soon I'm in big trouble and ALL I'M FUCKIN' ASKIN' IS THAT YOU HELP ME.' He bangs the table with his hand. A frightened O'Leary is a startling development. He has even begun to blink. I dread to think what the people hunting for him must be like to have him in this state.

'Well, I'll certainly add to your form that there's a threat of violence against you. That will definitely increase your chances. What about your probation officer? Could he write a letter supporting your appeal for a transfer?'

'That useless cunt,' spits O'Leary venomously. 'He's not like the last one. He was good as gold, him.'

'Well, ask him anyway. These people. What are they after you for exactly?'

'Well, I fucked up didn't I?' He leans over and says in a tone which is half conspiratorial and half proud. 'I was turkeying the wrong bird, if you see what I mean. She was the missus of someone who was inside. But now he's out and gone garrity.'

'Turkeying?'

'Yeah, you know.' And he makes a gesture which leaves me in no doubt as to the nature of their relationship.

'I see,' I reply primly, wondering how 'Turkeyed the wrong bird' would look in the 'reason for transfer' section of his application form. Somehow, the balance of forces between us is changing and I look up and meet his eyes. 'Well, look, you know, you're not going to be able to just pick any empty flat but I'll leave a note for Bob Townsend asking him to give this matter his immediate attention. In the meantime, keep me informed of any new developments.'

'There's only gonna be one development. And when it happens I ain't gonna be around to tell you about it.'

He crashes out of the interview room in his normal manner, but as he leaves the office I see him look quickly up and down the street and then half jog to his car – a battered dark blue Granada – watching all the time as he puts the keys in the door.

When I return to my desk just before the shop meeting I am disturbed to find Adrian Thompson, the union housing convenor, sitting in my chair with his feet on the desk, wearing a red baseball cap and a baggy V-neck cricketing jumper. He is a housing benefits officer from Karen's office who dominates union meetings, making long impassioned speeches as to why the one-day strike he is calling for will be another mortal blow not just for management but for the Tory government. His speech is then repeated several times by those of his supporters who are not on paper-selling duty in the entrance to the Town Hall room where union meetings are held. Recently, there have been so many one-day strikes that several members in my office have got fed up and left the union. When I put this to Adrian Thompson, he seemed pleased and said that there was no room for the uncommitted in the union.

'Jamie, hi. I thought I'd come down and say a few words at the shop meeting about the strike.'

As people assemble for the meeting I can hear a hostile murmur at the presence of Adrian Thompson, who remains cheerfully immune. Joan, the receptionist, who always asks difficult questions, braces herself for the fray. She takes a Raffles superlong cigarette from her handbag, snaps the bag tartly shut and lights up, without once taking her eyes from Adrian, who is unaware of the beehived predator bracing itself for the most opportune moment to attack.

'Right, well, Adrian Thompson's come down to tell us about what's happening on Wednesday.'

Adrian explains that the written warning given to a member

of staff for taking three weeks off sick without notifying his manager is the start of a concerted attack on the union which must be met with immediate strike action. 'It's the thin end of the wedge,' he announces. 'Today Graham Willis, tomorrow . . .' he points around to various people '. . . it could be you or you or you.'

'Except that we're not stupid enough not to phone in sick,' mutters Joan, receiving a revolutionary glare from Adrian in response.

At the close of the meeting, Adrian makes the mistake of asking for a show of hands as to who is going to participate in the strike. The only hand that goes up is that of Michael the clerical assistant, who is involved in a militant animal rights anarchist group and whom Roy vainly tries to stop from coming to work in a dirty parka and assorted stained T-shirts depicting smoking beagles or Welsh punk bands. Adrian scowls at me and I quickly put my hand up as well.

'What a bunch of reactionaries,' Adrian says, replacing his baseball cap when the meeting is over. 'Leadership is critical on these occasions, Jamie. We've got to send a clear message to management.' Then he pats me patronizingly on the shoulder and smiles amicably. 'I'm off to Riverside office. I expect a better response there. Do your best.'

Paula arrives towards the end of the afternoon with Khaled. Nodding curtly to me, he says, 'What are you going to do when we identify these people? Are you going to evict them?'

'I'm not sure yet.'

'Typical council attitude.'

'Shut up, Khaled, let's see what happens first,' says Paula.

'He's all we need,' I grumble when Khaled goes to the toilet.

'Oh, he's OK, don't let him wind you up, it's all a big act. And he's really good in these situations actually. You know his brother was nearly killed in a racist attack in Oldham. He was stabbed fourteen times. Khaled got involved after that . . .' She tails off as he returns from the toilet.

'Are we ready to go then?'

'Come on then.'

Mrs Khan's neighbour peers out of the kitchen window as we approach her flat.

'I think I'll have a word with her. See if she might act as a witness.'

'Fat chance,' says Paula.

On the wall outside the front door somebody has written 'FUCK OFF SMELLY PAKIS' in pink wobbly letters.

Inside the flat, which smells of children and condensation, there is a clutter of toys. A tricycle lies on its side by the kitchen next to a tiny abandoned trainer with lemon and lime striped laces. Mrs Khan pours us all glasses of Coke while the children poke their heads round the door and stare at us. I gulp my Coke down quickly and leave Khaled and Paula to speak to Mrs Khan, while I try questioning Mrs Reynolds next door.

'It's Jamie Collins, your housing officer.'

'Yes, I know who you are.'

There is a sticker on the kitchen window with a picture of a blue slit-eyed foetus, its minute blue hands clenched together as if it is praying, which says, 'We vote pro-life.'

'Sit down,' says Mrs Reynolds. She is a well-built woman with a hostile gaze and a gleaming diamond wedding ring. I begin to feel, as she holds me in her gaze, that my eyes are starting to enlarge and spiral green and blue, like Mowgli hypnotized by Kaa the snake.

'You've probably heard, Mrs Reynolds, that Mrs Khan next door has been having some problems in the evenings?'

'Yes, I've heard.'

She does not sit down, but stands by the mantelpiece on which there is a large collection of china cats and a framed embroidery of a cottage which says 'Home Sweet Home'.

71

'I wonder if you've seen the people who come to make trouble.'

'It's usually dark.'

'But you have an idea who they might be.'

'I don't get involved in other people's affairs,' she replies firmly.

'Aren't you involved with the Tenants' Association? With Hilda?'

'Now and again.'

'So you must have some idea of who is behind all of this. You must have seen something.'

She picks up a white cat which is stretching and yawning, wipes a speck of dust from between its china ears, and replaces it carefully in its original position.

'Look, young man. I feel sorry for the lady next door. She's never done anything to me and I've never done anything to her. And it's a shame for those little children. But you've got to expect it, haven't you? There's people on this estate who've got kids as well and they can't get flats. Now I've got nothing against the coloureds personally but . . . well, what do you expect? We should be looking after our own first.'

'I'm not sure I quite understand what you're trying to say, Mrs Reynolds. The question is whether you have any information about a case of serious harassment against your neighbour. I'm not interested in anything else.'

She flushes with anger.

'You know what your problem is? You're supposed to represent all of us, all the tenants. But you're just like the rest of the council. You only care about *them*. Anything they want they can have straight away, but us – well, that's a totally different story. You should worry about some of the problems *we've* got.'

At the sound of the raised voice, a girl comes into the room from the kitchen. 'Calm down, Mum.' She is about seventeen or eighteen, with blonde hair tied back in a long plait. I stand up, wondering what Mrs Reynolds would do if I were to sweep the china cats off the mantelpiece and start jumping up and down on them.

'Well, I'm sorry you feel like that. I shall be speaking to Hilda about this matter as well.'

Mrs Reynolds snorts derisively. 'You do that, young man.'

As I am about to close the door behind me, Mrs Reynolds's daughter quickly slips out and tugs on my arm. 'Listen, two of the boys are Jason King and Dean Anderton. It ain't just the Pakis they make trouble for . . .'

'Karen?' calls her mum from inside. 'Have you got the door open?'

She looks at me urgently and repeats, 'It ain't just the Pakis . . .'

Back in Mrs Khan's flat they are still sitting on the sofa drinking Coke. Mrs Khan is laughing at something Khaled has just said. They look up as I come in.

'Well?' says Paula. I roll my eyes and she laughs. 'Told you so.'

'Mrs Khan, among the boys who are causing the problems, have you heard the names Jason King or Dean Anderton?'

She lowers her head.

'Have you heard their names?' Paula asks gently.

She nods and I see a tear drop on to her bare foot. She wipes her eyes quickly, not wanting to cry. 'This one they call Jason, he is a very bad boy. He is ringleader. It is not just him, his whole family very bad. He have brother in prison, his mother she is also bad person.'

'Yes, I know a little about the family. Is there anyone else who's seen things going on who might be prepared to give evidence?'

'No. They don't care or they're frightened.'

There is a knock on the door but Mrs Khan does not move.

'That's the door,' I say.

'They always do this. They send the little ones to start off.

73

Then they run away. For them it is just game.'

There is another knock, but this time Khaled springs up and has the door open so quickly that he is able to collar the culprit, who must be about six years old and whose face is as white as a diminutive ghost. 'Let me go,' he wriggles. 'It's not me. Jason told me to do it. Let go.'

Khaled shakes him. 'Don't you come back here. Do you understand me? And tell your mates. Now piss off out of here.' And he throws the boy free.

The boy scampers away until he has reached a safe distance and then he turns round and screams shrilly. 'Fuckin' Paki cunt, I'll get my dad and brothers on to you.' He sticks two fingers up, enraged, and makes a wanking gesture which is almost funny from a six-year-old in mud-stained, elastic-waist jeans.

'I think that might be a junior King,' I say. 'Either Billy or Tony.' He still stands at the corner of Keats House, a grotesque bonsai version of his siblings. Khaled lunges forward as if he is about to run towards him and the child dashes quickly round the corner.

Back in the living-room I make a note of the time. 'Right,' I say. 'Well, I think the first step is to get the parents of King and Anderton down to the office and get really heavy with them. Maybe if we raise the possibility of eviction they'll knock some sense into their kids.'

'It's a start,' says Khaled, 'but it sounds as if it might be more than just the kids involved.'

'Also, I think we should speak to the local beat officer. Bob Clarke, is that his name?'

'Yeah,' says Paula, 'good old friendly Bob Clarke, nice as pie and lazy as . . .' She kisses her teeth.

'Would you like some more Coke?' asks Mrs Khan, but I have drunk so much Coke I feel as if I have done two lines of speed and that my bladder has swollen to the size of an ostrich egg. We all shake our heads.

Throwing the House Out of the Window

Walking back through the estate my heart sinks as I see a group of four boys sitting on one of the benches on the pathway which runs through the estate. Their legs are stretched out across the path and they are staring at us, obviously waiting. Behind them, in the background, there is a group of younger kids among whom is Billy or Tony King. They are kicking an empty chip wrapper about.

'You see that?' Paula murmurs.

'Yeah,' Khaled replies. 'Walk on. We can't turn around.'

As we draw level, one of the boys, who I'm sure is Jason King, sneers, 'A dirty Paki, a nigger slag and a white gay-boy. Which one's the traitor?'

Khaled stops. 'You what?'

Another boy springs up. 'Yeah, Paki? You want some? You wanna know, do you?' His hand is in his jacket pocket. His other hand is clenched and has a huge gold ring on it like a coin from a treasure trove. He is skinny with gelled hair and sharp features, almost handsome, a gold hoop in each ear.

Khaled faces up to him. 'You on your own, scum, yeah.'

'Yeah, just me, Paki.' And a butterfly knife flies out of his pocket.

'Khaled!' screams Paula instinctively.

The boy's face is taut and stretched, his teeth covering his lower lip. His face is tight as if his bone structure is seeking to escape from his skin. He holds the knife high with the obvious intention of sweeping it down across Khaled's face. I am paralysed with fear. Suddenly a window opens. 'Oi you down there,' and the boy's concentration is broken. A middle-aged woman leans out. 'Pack it in, all right. I've called the police.'

Paula seizes the opportunity to grab Khaled's arm and lead him away as if she were a disinterested peacemaker breaking up a fight. 'Come on, leave it, it's not worth it.'

The boy makes as if to follow but one of his friends places a hand on his arm. 'Another time, Gary, the Old Bill might get here in a minute.'

Ben Richards

The boy stands in the path watching us go, the knife still in his hand by his side. 'I'll fuckin' 'ave you you dirty fuckin' Paki cunt. You're fuckin' dead next time I see you. And you, you poxy fuckin' slags, I know who you are.'

A few curtains twitch in the flats above us. Paula is still gripping Khaled's arm.

'My car is round the corner,' says Khaled. We sit quietly for a while in the car. Khaled is shaking, white-knuckled, with one hand resting on the steering wheel, but his eyes are hard and angry. He keeps glancing in the mirror.

'I don't know about you,' says Paula, 'but the pubs will be open now and I could murder a drink.' Khaled revs up the engine.

'As long as there's no Coke in it,' I say, and it is a relief to see Khaled laugh.

'That's what us Pakis don't understand about you lot,' he says. 'You have visitors in your house and you don't offer them anything. Not even a cup of tea.' And we drive off quickly, leaving the estate behind.

Soho Nights

Iona is standing outside the French Protestant church, which I don't have too much difficulty finding. She is wearing a black Adidas T-shirt and kisses me lightly on the lips as we arrive.

'Let's just walk about for a bit,' she says.

We wander down Frith Street, past the closed women's hospital with its sign requesting people to go quietly. It is a long time since I have prowled around Soho at night. This is one of Colin's favourite pastimes; he knows the pubs and bars, the private clubs where journalists and actors hang out, the dingy one-room desperation bars which stay open all night with their battered pool tables, Pirelli calendars, and fat bottles of lemonade on the counter.

The air is heavy with expectation, the search for pleasure, for excitement, an infectious ache, a longing. Skinny Japanese teenagers with tiny rucksacks are already out searching for the clubs, the boards outside Ronnie Scott's announce forthcoming Roy Ayers and Irakere gigs, the man walking ahead of us suddenly disappears into a doorway with a sign reading 'Maltese Social Club'. The smell of warm garlic drifts up from the basement kitchens of the restaurants.

In Old Compton Street, the boyz are out preening, loving themselves, watching each other, while cappuccino-drinkers sit beneath purple and red neon bar signs with their packs of Marlboro Lights on the table in front of them, trying not to shiver in the chill night air. 'Yeah, tell Rory I'll see him in twenty minutes inside . . .' A man in a black leather waistcoat and white jeans breezes past us, obliviously chattering into his mobile phone, trailing fragments of conversation behind him. A group of people call Iona's name and she stops to talk to them. 'There's a party in Farringdon,' says a skinny girl with a translucent face and cropped peroxide hair wearing a tight T-shirt which says 'Made for Pleasure'. Iona nods and smiles and says maybe and her friends look at me with bored curiosity as if they can tell that I bought my shirt in Top Man and are wondering what on earth Iona is up to.

'Well,' Iona says when they have gone, 'we could go to the Coach or there's a bar down there we could go to . . .' She looks at me as if expecting me to make the decision. Knowing that there is more than a slight possibility of bumping into Colin in the pub, I say, 'Oh this bar sounds OK.' Which is stupid because she hasn't told me anything about the bar and when we get there it is not at all OK but decorated in green and purple with high-backed uncomfortable chairs along the walls, red plastic stools and cheesy house music. It also has a neurotic clientele whose average age appears to be about sixteen. However, we find a corner and sit and make relaxed flippant conversation over bottles of Budwar and glasses of Absolut vodka. I learn that she went to York University where she studied History of Art and English Literature, that her flatmate is Sophie, who does PR for some big record company, that her mum and dad are rich and live in Hong Kong and that she works for a small video production company. She tells me about lots of clubs we could go to later, and I say maybe, because I'm not that into clubbing, and she smiles and says she could tell. When she goes to the toilet I listen to the conversation next to me which is an anxious debate between three friends about whether they have enough money to get half a gram of charlie.

We move bars but everything is really packed now and we end up jammed against the wall next to the toilets. I am

longing to get to a pub, so we get on a bus to Islington and go
to one with a lock-in and sitting in one corner with a group of
friends is Helen. Iona feels me hesitate as we go into the pub.
'What's the matter?'

'Nothing. It's just there's some people I know here.'

'Don't worry about them. Come on.' And she makes her
way to the bar. Helen sees us and looks down at her glass. I
can make out Claire and Neil who are talking animatedly. I
can't just ignore Helen so I go over and say hello.

'What are you doing here?' I ask stupidly.

'We're having a drink actually.'

'Oh, sorry, I thought it was a synchronized-swimming
practice.'

'We've just been to a film.' Neil turns to include himself in
the conversation.

'*Kickboxer Two*?'

It turns out that they have just been to see a French film I
saw the other day.

'What did you think of it?' I ask Helen.

'Wonderful,' says Neil. 'I thought it dealt really well with the
nature of obsession and the masculine gaze.'

I stare at him for a second. I haven't heard this gibberish for
some time now. To be fair to Helen, she never really bought
into it completely. On a good day she was even capable of
laughing at it, reading bits out that she knew I would find
particularly ridiculous. But now she is sitting silently, her face
like a blank page. I turn back to Neil.

'Really? I thought it was rubbish. Who's that director again?
Lecomte or something? Anyway, he's a pretentious bastard.'

'I think he's made some great movies.'

'Movies? Oh right, you mean films.'

'Aren't you going to introduce us to your friend?' asks
Helen suddenly, placing a subtly contemptuous emphasis on
the last word. Iona has arrived with the drinks. 'Hi,' Iona
announces cheerfully, 'I'm Iona.' She sits down and begins to

chat to Neil, leaving me to talk to Helen.

'How've you been?'

'All right.'

There is an embarrassing silence. I can hear Neil explaining to Iona that he has decided to change the title of his thesis from 'Discourse and Docklands' to 'Deconstructing Docklands', and if there were a competition to put a caption in the thought bubble arising from Iona's head it would not prove too challenging.

'. . . You know I think we have to get away from the idea that there is a single identity of place. Just like people have multiple identities so do places . . .'

'Right,' says Iona.

I look over the top of my drink at Helen. She is playing with a beer-mat and staring down at the table. She holds the beer-mat between finger and thumb, spinning it round in her hand.

'. . . And just as the spatial is sexual, so the reverse is of course true – the sexual is always spatial. You just can't untangle that knot . . .'

'Right,' says Iona.

'You really can't untangle that knot,' repeats Neil, looking sternly at Iona as if he has caught her attempting to do precisely that.

'No, I don't think you can,' agrees Iona, chewing her lower lip slightly and catching my eye over the top of Neil's head.

Helen looks up at me and for a moment our eyes lock. This is the last time, she is saying to me. And I know she is right. I know that I'll never phone her house again and put the receiver down, never wonder if the doorbell might ring one evening. Goodnight, goodnight.

After a few more desultory attempts at conversation, Claire looks at her watch and says briskly, 'Do you think we should be going, Helen?'

'Yes, I think that would be a good idea.'

'Oh, but they don't close for ages,' says Iona.

'Thanks for the tip,' replies Helen sharply, 'but I'm pretty tired.'

'Surely we've got time for one more,' Neil begins to protest, but receives a look from Helen with which I am all too familiar. 'Yes, well, maybe you're right . . .'

As they make their way out Iona says to me, 'She seemed a bit grumpy, your ex.'

I look at her surprised. 'How did you know she was my ex?' And she giggles.

'Feminine intuition, Jamie, you could have cut the atmosphere with a knife.'

'Why did you ask them to stay then?'

'I was misbehaving of course. I thought twice about it because I might have had to stay talking to that awful character who wanted to outline the chapter structure of his thesis. Well, listening to him actually because he was talking nonsense and I didn't get a chance to put a word in myself. He's writing about Docklands but it doesn't sound as if he's ever actually been there.'

'He doesn't need to, he's exploring the discourse around it. You're just using outmoded Fordist concepts. Listen, I don't really want to drink any more. Shall we make a move?'

'Is that an invitation?'

'If you like.'

Back in my flat Iona flits about looking at books and records while I make tea. Then we sit and watch a late-night recession TV programme which has a feature on a gun in the United States called a Desert Eagle – apparently *de rigueur* among gang members – so powerful that it can blow an armour-plated hippopotamus in half. They succeed in making it sound as innocent as a pair of Nike Air Jordans, interviewing members of street gangs who have blasted their opponents away with it and who testify enthusiastically to its awesome efficiency. I find it quite hard to understand the obsession with guns which these programmes have. Obviously, the researchers and producers did not spend their time at university roaming around with Uzis, and wasting people who were doing the wrong course or lived in a different hall of residence. But suddenly it is as if it is particularly important for them to know the latest trends in lethal weapons.

Iona is sitting in an armchair and I sit at her feet. I rest my arm on her leg and she strokes my hair gently. Then she takes my hand and brings it slowly up underneath her skirt. I press through her tights between her legs and she opens them slightly. Turning round so that I am kneeling between her legs, I lift her skirt. She arches so that I can bring it up around her waist and kicks off her shoes. I run my hands down over her breasts to her waist and slide down her tights. She giggles, 'This chair's dead itchy,' and moves herself forward to the edge of the chair. My hands move up her legs pushing them gently further apart. On the programme a top ragga artist is being confronted about his homophobic lyrics and the audience have all started shouting abuse at each other. I touch Iona and she closes her eyes as I tease her with my thumb, feeling her wetness. She puts her hand on my head and brings it down between her legs while bringing my hand up under her T-shirt and placing it on her breast. As I enter her with my tongue I push her bra up to free her breast and feel her nipple harden under my palm. Several times Iona appears to be about to come and then she does so without making much noise, just a series of short gasps and her body arching up to meet me. I wipe my mouth and Iona smiles at me. 'Shall we go to bed?' We go into the bedroom where we finish undressing each other and I open the drawer for the condoms and take out the packet and it's empty. 'Fucking hell.'

'What?'

'There's no condoms.'

'What do you want to do?'

'I don't know. I could go to the petrol station, I suppose.'

'Lie down here.'

I lie down and she takes me in her hand.

'I want you to fuck me. I think I'm pretty safe at the moment. But don't come inside me.'

'Yeah, but . . .'

'I've had a test before Jamie. And I'm negative. And I trust you.'

'You shouldn't.'

'I know.'

'It goes against all safe sex education.'

'I know.'

But I know that safe or not we're going to do it. After a couple of attempts to enter her without assistance she smiles and reaches down to slip me inside her. At the last minute I pull out and the sheet is all wet and Iona wriggles away from it, 'Uggh, it's all over my leg,' laughing.

I bring the TV into the bedroom and we lie in bed, finishing off the brandy and watching a film about a man in Los Angeles who is having an affair with a witch without realizing it.

'This is very strange,' says Iona.

'Yeah, you'd think he'd at least guess there's something a bit weird about her. Especially since his dog's been having a nervous breakdown ever since she arrived.'

'Not the film, you idiot.'

'What then?'

'Well, you know, I've really enjoyed tonight and everything but we haven't got much in common, have we? I know you wouldn't like my friends much and you certainly wouldn't like me a great deal if you saw me too often when I was, you know, off my face or whatever. I would like to keep on seeing you but not like a relationship or anything. I mean, I'd like to just go out sometimes or have a night in.'

'Well, I wasn't thinking of proposing marriage or anything.'

'Oh! You bastard. You know what I'm saying. And anyway,

you've just split up with your girlfriend. Lots of guys do start getting really heavy after that and some even start wanting to get married – make sure it doesn't happen again, I don't know.'

I touch the rose on her arm.

'When did you get this done?'

'About a year ago.'

'Did it hurt?'

'It probably would have done if I had been sober.'

'I really like you,' I say suddenly.

'Tell your friend Colin that. He'll die when he finds out. He thinks that I'm the ultimate shallow drug-fiend slag.'

'He's all right.'

'He's a man's man. That's why he's screwed up.'

'What about your artist friend? Whatsisname? Haven't you got something going with him?'

'Malcolm? Well, you know, we have our moments but basically he's searching for a Frida Kahlo or something. Some fellow tortured artist. Someone who matches his artistic talent.'

'And he is frighteningly talented.'

She looks at me quizzically. 'What are you talking about?'

'No, nothing.' I giggle. 'You wouldn't remember, I don't think.'

She punches me on the arm. 'Don't take the piss, you arrogant pig.'

'Sorry,' I say, taking her finger and tracing the outline of her tattoo with it. 'You are the rose and I am the invisible worm.'

'There's nothing whatsoever invisible about you, but you've got the worm bit right.'

'Ouch! Please leave me a tiny bit of ego to cling on to.'

'It would take a bigger professional than me to rob you of your ego.'

'I'm sorry, I didn't realize you were a professional. Will you take a cheque?'

'I'll give you credit and you can pay in instalments. Shall we go to sleep now?'

'Let's go to sleep.'

'You don't want to make love until the sun rises?'

'No.'

'Good. Nor do I.'

'Shut up then and go to sleep.'

'OK, goodnight.'

'Goodnight.'

We lie in the dark for a few minutes. I can smell the mixture of shampoo and cigarettes on her hair. The pillow will smell of it in the morning. I close my eyes. Paper wraps stone, stone blunts scissors, knife cuts flesh. You're dead you Paki cunt. I'll break your fucking jaw. Aren't you going to introduce us to your friend? Where are you going, I don't know where you're going any more Jamie.

'. . . Are you asleep?' Iona asks suddenly.

'Yeah.'

'Good. So am I.'

'You've been talking in your sleep.'

'Does it make your brown eyes blue?'

'You've woken me up now. What about until a few hours before the sun rises?'

'It's all one to me, sugar. You're the customer.'

'And the customer's always right.'

Boring Boring Arsenal

I am meeting Colin to go to the football. It is a perfect football day, slightly windy and grey, the threat of light rain, and Colin is moaning because he can't find a burger stall since the club and police started clearing them away from the ground, to make people eat official burgers I suppose. We go to the pub and drink double Bloody Marys as I can't drink pints before a football match.

'So, Jamie, is it true the gossip I hear that you and wee cocaine Lil have been making the beast with two backs? I am disappointed in you, Jamie. She's no your type. You should have stuck to the bluestockings.'

'Is that right?'

'Trust me on this one. She's a slag. When she's not getting on too great with that arsehole Malcolm, she's shagging somebody else trying to get Malcolm's attention and when she's not doing that she's got her nose buried in a coke mountain that would have made Scarface envious. All of which, of course, is financed by Mummy and Daddy who probably think their little darling still has a pony and goes to balls . . .'

'Listen, shut up, right.'

'Jamie, I'm your friend. I'm telling you this in your own interest. I don't want to see you get even more hurt because of some stupid rich slag who . . .'

'I mean it, Colin. Change the subject.'

'How? What's your problem Jamie?'

'Well, if you don't mind me being frank, Colin, and I feel that our years of friendship permit me that privilege, sometimes you're just a stupid, ignorant, frustrated Scottish prick and if you don't shut up you can just fuck off.'

He scowls at me, eyebrows descending so that they look like a bird from a children's painting. 'Oh aye, and you're going to make me fuck off are you?'

'Oh, for God's sake. No, I'm not going to make you fuck off. If it makes you feel better I couldn't 'cause you're just so hard. All right? But I'll do the next best thing. I'll fuck off. See you.'

In the street, I join the crush towards the ground. Despite the row with Colin, I still feel the familiar surge of excitement on approaching the stadium; the programme and scarf sellers, the stewards in their fluorescent orange tunics, the blue-helmeted mounted police. When I have taken my position in the ground I realize that I had forgotten that having bought seats together there is an empty seat next to mine. I wonder whether Colin will show up. Just before kick-off the answer comes barging down the aisle, carrying two cups of tea, little bags of Arsenal FC chips, and wearing a stupid grin.

'Listen, Jamie, I'm sorry. I was out of order. Dinnae walk off like that, Jamie.'

'Yeah, you were.'

'I'm not taking back anything I said 'cause I'm right, but I shouldn't have said it.'

'As gracious an apology as I have ever heard.'

'Your mouth will get you into trouble one day, Jamie.'

'You'll be dead before then. You'll pick a fight with someone in a pub and they'll come up behind you and stick a knife in you. And it will serve you right for being a wanker.'

'You're a cheeky wee bastard, Jamie. Luckily my patience is as long as my sense of humour is large.'

'And your mouth is big.'

'And your stomach is fat.'

'And your accent is stupid.'

'And your mum is . . .' But I never get to hear what my mum is because the crowd is rising to its feet as the teams come out of the tunnel.

Arsenal score twice in the first half and then start messing about, causing the crowd to get bored and start singing the theme to *The Adams Family*, what they're going to do to Tottenham in a month's time and how virtually every member of their family, including their granny and the cat, would not have squandered the last chance in quite the same clumsy way. Apart from a cynical foul which sends the man next to us into such paroxysms of rage that he would clearly only be contented if a makeshift gallows were to be erected and the offending player left to dangle in front of the North Bank for the rest of the game, little else happens.

Half-time comes and Colin turns to the kid sitting next to him and asks to borrow his programme. The kid has sandy hair and glasses, holding the case tightly in his hand. It is one of those old cases where the lid snaps up, with a soft felt lining. His name – Robert Johnson – is written in felt tip on the case.

'Go on,' says Colin, 'I'll gie it back. I just wanna look at the teams.'

Robert Johnson stares at Colin and then turns away, his programme squeezed tightly in his other hand like a relay runner's baton. Only he's not going to pass it on.

Colin taps him, half-laughing. 'Come on, I've told you I'll gie it back to you.'

The kid turns and stares at Colin again. His face is totally expressionless, not even frightened, but he is gripping his programme as if any release would cause it to explode like a hand grenade. Colin looks at me and shrugs in mock amazement at this silent defiance. He taps his shoulder again, and again Robert Johnson turns to stare at him. He doesn't even ignore him, just turns, stares and turns away again.

I laugh. 'Face up to it, Col, he's not gonna let you look at his programme.'

The kid stares at me in the same blank way. 'I'll gie you ten pee,' says Colin, but the kid is safe behind his wall of silence. If he doesn't speak nothing will happen. 'Stupid wee shite,' says Colin to me but not loud enough so that Robert Johnson can hear. 'That's the problem with all-seating Jamie, you have to sit with the weans.'

A third goal is prodded in just before the end, the sky begins to darken, and we sing 'going down with the City' and 'we can see you sneaking out' to the dwindling band of an already small contingent of away fans.

'Cheerio, Bob,' says Colin to the kid as we leave. He just stares back.

'Do you wanna go to a party later?' Colin asks when we have struggled across the flow making its way to the tube station and are walking down towards the Blackstock Road.

'No, I'm babysitting for my sister.'

'On a Saturday night?'

'She's got to get out as well sometimes.'

'Your lassie will probably be there.'

'She's not *my* lassie. And you'd better not say anything to her, I mean it.'

'OK, OK. Let's not start all this again. My lips are sealed.'

'That'll be the day. See you later.'

'Aye Jamie, but just tell me one thing before you go. What's she like, eh?'

'Go fuck yourself, you sad bastard.'

'I'll probably have to with the luck I've been having recently. I blame this selfish image-obsessed society. A young and talented artist like myself shouldn't be having any problems. But just because I'm a working-class boy from north of the border the lassies don't wanna know any more. I should have lived in the sixties or something.'

'Of course. I'm sure it's got nothing to do with you being an ugly, boring motormouth.'

'Well, I thought it might be that. But you provide a perfect control sample to show that there must be some further explanation.'

'Talk to your analyst about it. I'm off.'

'See you, Jamie. And Jamie?'

'What now?'

'I fuckin' love you.'

'Yeah right.'

I take the tube straight to my sister's in Wood Green. Her husband, Michael, who is a computer programmer, answers the door. 'Jamie. Great. Thanks ever so much for doing this.'

'That's OK. What's the big occasion again?'

'Oh, a group of people from Catherine's work, you know. They've organized this big party for everyone and it's kind of a three-line whip.'

Catherine appears, wearing a green dress and fastening a pair of earrings with bright emerald drops which brush her bare shoulders. She works as a counsellor in an abortion clinic, and I sometimes wonder whether a bit of self-counselling wouldn't go amiss as she is apparently pregnant again. A little while ago she nearly split up with Michael because he went to bed with a woman at a computer programmers' conference in Leicester. Then she decided that throwing him out just for the principle of the thing, when she didn't really want to, made very little sense. I was relieved because Michael – in spite of his beard and his total refusal to wear anything without a Marks & Spencer's label – is not as unbearable as some of her previous partners. How Catherine managed to move from some of the specimens she has been out with to somebody as straight as Michael is a bit of a mystery.

'You're looking very colour co-ordinated tonight.'

'At least someone notices. It's really nice of you to do this on a Saturday night. I've told Robbie he can stay up to watch

Match of the Day with you but after that it's straight to bed.'

'He'll be asleep already if they're showing the match I've just seen.'

'There's loads of food in the fridge, so make what you want and there's a bottle of wine.'

'Only one?'

She ignores me.

'OK kids, be good with Uncle Jamie won't you? You promise Mummy? We'll see you tomorrow. Give me a kiss now.'

Robbie and Sarah sit obediently on the sofa. Catherine likes to pretend that there is a risk of them being naughty but they are alarmingly well-behaved and serious children. They always go to bed when they're told and never beg to watch the horror film. I remember the hell that Catherine and I used to give babysitters after our mum had disappeared in a waft of perfume redolent of an exotic and mysterious adult world. On one occasion we managed to reduce our minder to such hysterical tears that we were both slapped and I was not allowed to play football on Saturdays for three weeks. I can't remember Catherine's punishment.

They seem strange, those days of childish certainty, and very distant from my current situation. I suddenly remember family holidays – the smell of petrol on the car deck of the ferry, the yellow light of paraffin lamps in camp-sites, padding down a sandy path covered in pine needles to buy breakfast and repeating over and over again what I have to say: 'Une baguette et quatre croissants s'il vous plaît madame.' On one of these channel crossings I remember that I had a small blue plastic boat and I dropped it over the side of the ship into the terrifying enormity of the sea. Instead of seeing it bob cheerfully away as I had hoped, it simply disappeared on contact with the water, and the memory of this collision with the gigantic greyness of the sea has always remained with me. Just the white rails between myself and the heaving waves. Even thinking about it now makes me feel dizzy. 'Where's your boat?' my mum demanded angrily, and I shook my head truthfully. 'I don't know.'

Our mum was a teacher, the first generation from her family to go to university, and Catherine and I – with the mixed fortunes which being the offspring of a certain type of teacher brings – were brought up on a diet of Puffin books and a series of strange restrictions. For a long time as children we were not allowed to watch ITV because my mum disapproved of commercial television. This caused me endless problems at school, where I had to pretend that I had seen episodes of *Planet of the Apes* when I really had no idea what it was about. Evading our mum's prohibitions also meant that we had an early training in duplicity and we both learned to lie efficiently from a very young age. We have always laughed at the heavy-handed puritanism of our mum, but Catherine seems to have absorbed some of it, since her children are not allowed to play Nintendo like all their friends.

Instead, they get read to every night, and tonight I have to read to them before Sarah goes to bed. Catherine has also kept all the books from her own childhood and at the moment they are reading *A Dog So Small*. Robbie and Sarah sit in their pyjamas and listen intently as I read them the story of Ben Blewitt; promised a puppy for his birthday but receiving instead an embroidered picture of a Mexican dog called Chiquitito, and compensating for this disappointment by imagining a dog so very, very small that only he can see it. They are almost at the end of the book, and as I read about a small boy's realization that however much you long for impossible things, you have to come to terms with how things actually are, I also see myself and Catherine sitting listening to my mum's voice. Although it is completely absurd, a lump rises in my throat and tears begin to spill down my cheeks. It is a cruel truth to have to learn. The children are disturbed by my tears and as I stop to wipe my eyes Robbie says, 'Why are you crying?' and I say, 'Your granny used to read me this story when I was little.' They look puzzled and Sarah says, 'But you shouldn't cry,' which is completely true because what, after all, would I have thought if my mum had started weeping while she was reading me the story?

Later I ransack the fridge for all the more expensive Marks & Spencer's food, setting out tubs of olives, luxury taramasalata, Parma ham and ciabatta bread. Robbie watches me earnestly.

'Can I have a sip of your wine?'

'Does your mum let you drink wine?' I look at him sternly.

'No.' He drops his eyes.

'In that case, yes. And when I'm well out of the way you must make sure you tell her that I let you.'

'No.' He shakes his head. 'Then she might not let you come round and look after us again.'

I pour him half a glass and we sit on the sofa, Robbie cupping his glass with both hands, waiting for the music to *Match of the Day*.

'What football team do you support?' I ask him.

'Manchester United.'

'Why do you support them?'

'Dunno. 'Cause they're good. Everyone at school likes them.'

'Yeah, but you live in London. You should support a club you'll be able to go and see later on. Sometimes it's boring to support a club just 'cause they're good. What'll you do if they stop being good? I speak from experience.'

'Would you take me to the football?'

'Yeah, of course. If your mum says yes . . . And pays,' I add quickly, wondering if I can get Catherine to pay for both tickets in return for me taking her son off her hands on Saturdays.

'Maybe I could support Arsenal then.'

A good angel hovers above my head wagging its finger warningly at me, but I ignore it.

'Yeah,' I say to Robbie, 'you should definitely support

Arsenal. They're a great team. Consistent, solid and professional.' The good angel rolls its eyes. 'Always remember that, Grasshopper, for you will meet many who will mock your wise choice and call you boring. They will then punish you with long and boring accounts of how much they hate Arsenal. But you will receive your reward and be able to laugh in their faces when their side loses to Arsenal through a goal in the ninetieth minute at Wembley . . . And we'll ask your mum about going to the ground.'

After Robbie has gone to bed I sit on the sofa flipping channels, thinking about the party, whether Iona will go with Malcolm, and whether Colin will open his big mouth. I am exhausted and fall asleep dreaming that I am trying to hold the door shut while people try to force it open and others are climbing in through the back. I hate this dream, which I have with depressing frequency. This time one of the assailants is the boy who tried to knife Khaled, but when he finally gets in he caresses my face and says that he is just looking for a light for his cigarette. The sound of the front door opening and Catherine laughing wakes me up.

'Check the sleeping babysitter. How much wine did you have?'

'I'm knackered.'

'Do you want to stay the night? We can make you up a bed on the sofa.'

I do want to but somehow I know I shouldn't. 'No, you're OK. Call me a cab though.'

'Michael, where's the cab number? Michael! He's completely bloody pissed. And he was meant to be driving, the useless adulterous bastard.' The fact that Catherine did not throw Michael out does not prevent her from using his night of lust as an insult, especially when, like tonight, she has had a bit to drink. 'We had to leave the car there. Listen, Jamie, take this for the cab.' And she gives me a tenner.

As I leave, Catherine looks at me accusingly and says, 'How

come there are two wine glasses on the table?'

'Are there? Oh yeah, I forgot where I put my glass so I got another one.'

'You shouldn't give Robbie wine, Jamie, he's far too young.'

'What are you talking about, he drank me under the table.'

Michael emerges bleary-eyed, holding a cup of coffee. 'Jamie, good man, fine brother-in-law, well, sort of brother-in-law, what an evening, gin and knitting needles all round . . .'

Catherine rolls her eyes. 'He's been making that joke all night. Go on, get upstairs, I'll wait with Jamie for his cab.'

Michael salutes unsteadily and disappears.

The cab-driver chain-smokes and plays Irish music. He has a fat gold claddagh ring on his finger which he taps on the steering wheel to the music. We drive down Commercial Street, where a couple of bare-legged young girls in white miniskirts stand arms folded on the corners waiting for trade. Behind them, in the shadows of a grimed recess by a bus stop, is a pimp. The cabbie squeezes through the narrow back streets, across Brick Lane, past the Chicksand Estate, and out into the lights and traffic of the Whitechapel Road. People are still straggling from the pubs and the first N98 night bus is heading out towards Essex.

Back in the flat there is a message from Ana María asking me to call her. I lie on the bed staring at the ceiling. Somewhere I can hear a thudding bassline and far-away shrieks – the faint sounds of a party in progress. I can smell Iona's hair on the pillow where she slept, see the flower stain of our mixed secretions on the sheet. My oldest adversary, loneliness, stands in the doorway grinning knowingly, mockingly, at me. I am close again, I think, back where I don't want to be in a place I thought I might have left for ever. I get up and stand in front of the mirror. There is a string over the top of the mirror where Helen used to hang her earrings. I look at my face, turn round and look at the profile of my body, and look at my face again. I smile, I scowl. 'You stupid ugly fucker,' I say to myself.

Throwing the House Out of the Window

I pull the string off the wall, yanking one of the little gold picture hooks it was fastened on out as well. It brings a tiny piece of plaster with it. I sit on the side of the bed, then slide down on to the floor lying on my back staring at the ceiling, still holding the string in my hand.

Spare Some Change

'Right,' says Roy, 'let's hear what's been going on.'

We are sitting in the office kitchen discussing the Mrs Khan case. Roy listens carefully, thinking hard about the issues and possible complications. As I give my account of the evening at Mrs Khan's house he alternately chews on his biro and sips coffee, eyebrows furrowed.

'That explains the Tenants' Association suddenly getting stroppy,' he observes, removing the biro from his mouth.

'Why? What's happened?'

'Well, I got a phone call from Hilda moaning about you. Asking for computer printouts of all the repairs orders that have been reported to you in the last month.'

'Well, that's no problem. They're all on.'

'I know, I checked. But she also complained about your attitude. Said you were rude and unco-operative.'

'That's bullshit. What she means is that I won't prioritize something just because she says it's important or because it involves one of her friends.'

'I know. This woman Mrs Reynolds you're talking about is a good friend of Hilda's. They might be starting a little campaign against you. They've done it before. Listen, don't worry about that, I'll deal with Hilda. You concentrate on getting the parents of Anderton and King down to the office and tell them we're going to serve a Notice on them. We'll see what that does. We haven't got much to be going on but it might scare

Anderton at least. Mrs King's another matter. I've dealt with her before and she's not going to get scared about a Notice. She's a really nasty piece of work.'

He leans back in his chair. There is a scar on his face where he was knocked off his bike once. People both admire and slightly fear him because he is so efficient and has an air about him which is not so much haughty as detached and controlled. He maintains office discipline while rarely losing his temper and can be kind to people who have real problems. At office parties he always joins in and drinks but never enough to make a fool of himself. One of the housing advisers once fell madly and hopelessly in love with him, so much so that she got ill and had to be transferred along with her unrequited passion to another office. It was an unfortunate choice on her part since Roy is gay.

'I hear you're single again, Jamie.'

'On the office grapevine?'

Roy laughs. 'I listen sometimes, you know, when I'm sitting at that desk. You'd be surprised how much I pick up. So have you moved house or something?'

'No. I kept the flat.'

'How're you coping? Living on your own?'

'It's good not to argue about the telly or doing the washing-up and everything. But you have to work hard at not getting lonely. Watch out for those bank holidays.'

'I know.'

Roy's boyfriend Danny died of Aids about a year ago. He was completely unlike Roy, startlingly handsome and arrogantly laddish. He was always rude to Roy in public, a fact which never seemed to trouble Roy at all. Behind Danny's brash and offhand manner, he was devoted to Roy and it was always quite obvious where the real power lay in the relationship. The strange thing about the illness was that, until the final stages at least, when he could hardly speak because of the thrush infection in his throat, it made him even more beautiful. Danny's family didn't want Roy at the funeral but he went anyway.

'Well, how do you feel about this case, Jamie? It's a difficult one, you know. You're going to get lots of hassle. I want you to talk to me about it, not just to keep me informed but, you know, if you feel the pressure's getting to you. In this department, people accumulate lots of stress and then they just crack up without talking to anyone about it. But this is really important. I'm not just sitting back and letting them establish a no-go area on the Estate or turn a blind eye like the Tenants' Association. We might have to go all the way on this one.'

'OK, thanks, Roy.'

'All right, Jamie.'

Back at my desk I sit and draft a letter to the parents of Dean Anderton and Jason King asking them to come and see me on the day following the one-day strike. Then I phone Karen and Colin and ask them if they want to come for a drink that evening as I have arranged to meet Ana María. Colin and Karen like each other in an aggressive kind of way and tend to spend most of their time teasing each other and arguing. Last time they were both round at my house they argued about German expressionism, whether Captain Scott died on the North or South polar expedition and whether you can use a Nat West service till card in a Bank of Scotland cashpoint machine.

When I arrive at Embankment tube where we have arranged to meet, Ana María is already there, wearing a bomber jacket which she has obviously borrowed from Soledad and a long black skirt. She is hopping between each foot and clapping her hands gently together. I kiss her cheek which is very cold and slightly blotchy.

'You're freezing to death. Have you been waiting long?'

'About half an hour.'

'Oh. I'm sorry.'

'It's not your fault, you are not late. I was stupid and thought it would take much longer.'

'I thought Chileans were always late.'

'Like the English are all cold and reserved.'

When Colin and Karen arrive and the introductions are over we make our way across Hungerford Bridge towards the South Bank. The bridge shudders under the weight of the trains pulling into Charing Cross, and pale faces peer from carriage windows to catch a glimpse of the river. The night is frosty clear and through the gap in the walkway the currents of the Thames plait around the supports of the bridge. We pause for Ana María to admire the great sweep of the river, leaning silently in a line against the railings. It is a rare stepping back, a momentary glimpse of the city's power and scope. There is the golden dome of St Paul's, no longer proudly defying the firestorm raining down from German bombers, although still faintly evoking that collective memory and nostalgic yearning for a finest hour. Now there is no need to conceal light, the bright glow is open to the cold sky, the glass-plated office blocks containing low humming computers tracking dollars and marks and yen across the globe. They have gone home now, the brash executives, the high-heeled secretaries, the baby-faced, coke-sniffing dealers and traders making their way from City bars to Liverpool Street station. They have left the building to bored security guards and tired cleaners who will clamber on buses in the morning along with the bedraggled clubbers hiding their wrecked faces behind cheap shades to protect them from the morning glare. And to the east, following the river's curves, is my flat – a tiny atom of the city – and further still the sprawling estate where I work. It is strange to think of it at night, people in their living-rooms watching TV, in their kitchens preparing food, groups of kids hanging around the football area intimidating the passers-by just by being there. It has nothing to do with me at night but in the morning people will pile in to complain about used condoms on walkways, cats pissing on their doorstep, and the noise from their neighbour's TV or barking dogs chained on balconies. Why do I have to think of that now?

'It is very beautiful,' says Ana María slightly wistfully.

'Does Santiago have a river?' asks Karen.

'Yes,' she laughs, 'but a little one. Not like this.'

Colin drops behind to talk to me, confined by the width of the bridge.

'She is gorgeous!' he whispers. 'Check those eyes, Jamie. Mad eyes. And that mouth. I'd love to paint her.'

'I'm sure you would.'

'No really, Jamie. I'm in love. If she told me to jump off this bridge right now I would. By the way, Jamie, you missed a great party.'

'Is that right.'

'Yeah, wassername was there you know. With Malcolm.'

'Mmm?'

'Yeah, you should have come. She was asking after you. I said you were babysitting. Made you sound really sensitive and . . .'

'Colin.'

'Yeah?'

'Shut up.'

Coming down the steps of the bridge a figure huddled in a grey blanket, dirty white trainers poking out of the bottom, mutters, 'Spare some change please.'

'I wish I could,' Colin snaps.

'Mr Social Conscience,' sneers Karen when we are out of earshot. 'Why don't you go back and give the lazy good-for-nothing a kick in the ribs as well.'

'Well, they get on my nerves with their spare-some-change and those stupid bits of cardboard about how the DSS won't give them enough money for a cup of tea and their scruffy wee dogs. Some of them should get Oscars for that looking-at-their-feet-because-it's-so-traumatic-asking-for-money routine. I wouldn't mind if they did something like, you know, dance or play 'Greensleeves' on the penny whistle or rob a bank, or even sell that magazine, but most of them are just a pain in the arse. I'm not giving my dole money to some grungy runaway kid who's probably had ten times as many chances as I did.'

Ana María has been trying to understand Colin's flow.

'Yes, charity is just to make the bourgeoisie feel better,' she intervenes. 'It doesn't change anything.'

'Exactly,' replies Colin complacently. 'Not only that. It actually keeps things as they are. Maintains the status quo.'

'Which you do an awful lot to change,' mutters Karen.

I watch the patterns of the river through the garlands of lights which loop slightly incongruously through the bank-side trees. Waves from pleasure boats form a widening V behind them, lapping at the shore, light stolen from the buildings texturing the river's surface.

'What would you prefer me to do?' growls Colin, glaring at Karen. 'What do you do that makes you so self-righteous? And stop acting like some Mother Teresa. When some dirty gadge with a can of Tennent's Extra lurches up to you and asks for money for a cup of tea, do you think oh poor guy, what terrible wounds this society inflicts on people? No. You think fuck off out of my face, I don't even wanna know you exist.'

'But they do exist,' says Ana María, realizing that she doesn't particularly want to be in agreement with Colin's world view. 'Even if you don't give money to them you should want to do something about it.'

'Do what though? I'll be honest with you, I couldn't give a fuck about them. They just annoy me. It's probably not their fault but they do. Like nutters annoy me. All right, I'm sorry that they exist. I'm sure it is a problem of society and not just warped personalities, I'm sure nobody *wants* to sit on a freezing night on Hungerford Bridge or go around stabbing people in the eye on tube station platforms. But that doesn't stop them getting on my nerves. And people who go on about them all the time are even worse.'

'Yeah, us bleeding-heart liberals are all the same,' says Karen.

'I'm not saying that. It's just when I walk down the street and get asked twenty times for the change that I need to get home, or I'm waiting for someone at Brixton or Whitechapel tube station and get twenty arseholes howling and waving their fists in my face and stinking of pish and vomit, why should I have to take a broad sociological perspective on it all? I haven't got a cottage in France like some of these wankers who go on about veal or Indians in the rain forest or make films about the homeless.'

'So go and form a vigilante squad then, Mr Charles Bronson. Buy some Zyklon B. Clean up the streets . . .'

We walk along in silence, past the useless thicket of coloured signs pointing vaguely to nowhere in particular. Somebody is playing the saxophone, leaning back against the railings of the river bank beneath the trees, letting the lazy notes drift mournfully into the chill air. A small dog lies on a blanket by his feet, its snout tucked between its front paws. Colin drops some money into the open case. 'Just to show I'm not a total fascist,' he says.

'Ahhh, you're a rough diamond, Colin,' mocks Karen.

Colin puts his arm around her shoulders. 'And you're a headnipper,' he says and then whispers something in her ear at which she cackles with laughter and pushes him off her.

We arrive at the NFT and decide to go in and get some drinks. When Colin has bought the first round he perches himself next to Ana María and recovers ground by talking about his past political activity in Scotland, his granny who participated in the 1915 rent strike, his fascination for the Aztec and Mayan cultures destroyed by the murdering Spanish and whether the peaceful road to socialism was just a naïve illusion. Colin can be fairly charming when he puts his mind to it and Ana María giggles from time to time at some of his more outrageous statements, especially when he claims to be a direct descendant of mad Lord Cochrane, the Scottish mercenary who launched a suicidal but successful attack on a Chilean fort during the war of independence against the Spanish. Karen rolls her eyes at me.

'He has no shame.'

'He says he's fallen in love with her.'

'Well, she doesn't appear to be completely stupid so I don't think he's got much of a chance. She's OK. How did you meet her?'

I start to explain about Eduardo but I am interrupted by Colin, who wants to play a game involving guessing the total number of pennies people have got in their hands in order to determine who will buy the next round. We play and I lose.

'Ha,' grins Colin triumphantly. 'I'll have a pint of lager and a large brandy.'

'A pint of lager for Colin. Karen?'

'I'll have the same.'

But as I move towards the bar, Ana María stops me. 'No, Jamie,' she says seriously, 'it is my round.'

When the bar closes we take a cab back to my flat. Colin sits on the fold-down seat, swinging round to argue with the cabbie about the route, and acting as a guide for Ana María by pointing out the sights and telling lurid stories about what Jack the Ripper used to do with the entrails of his victims. 'They say it was the King,' he tells her, 'preying on poor innocent working girls like all his parasite class.' When he finds out that Ana María has never eaten fish and chips he makes a huge song and dance with the cabbie about stopping at a chippy to buy some and tries to make her promise to go to Scotland with him at the weekend because the English don't have smoked sausage suppers with brown sauce. 'Oh how simply dweadful,' he says, examining his fish and chips through the greasy white paper. 'This fish isn't free range. Take it back Karen. In fact I've got a horrible feeling they've given us baby dolphin in batter. We must write to Anita Woddick. Alert that raggle-taggle army of women holding hands across the world.'

'I've had that brown sauce they give you in Scotland,' says Karen, trying not to smile, 'and it's crap. All watered down.'

'That's a national institution you're talking about.'

'Yeah, that's why you all die of heart attacks and have milk bottle complexions, 'cause it's a national institution to eat crap in Scotland. The only thing the Scots know to do with a vegetable is slice it up, deep-fry it and pour watered-down brown sauce on it.'

Colin turns to Ana María. 'Don't have too much to do with English people if you can help it.'

But Ana María is still comically astonished at the British custom of putting vinegar on chips. She tries one, wrinkles her nose, but then has to admit that she likes it. Colin goes into the Sima Tandoori with Karen to persuade them to sell him some wine, the kind of mission at which he excels. They come out with brown paper bags containing three bottles of wine, one starter portion of chicken tikka and several papadums. When we get back to the flat there is a message on the answerphone from Iona saying that she is just calling to say hello. Colin raises his eyebrows so ostentatiously that Karen notices and looks at me quizzically. We sit on the floor eating chips and drinking wine while Colin teaches Ana María to sing rebel songs and explains Scottish sectarian football divisions. He is greatly disappointed when she says that she would support Hearts because she likes the name. 'But you cannae,' he says, 'you're from a Papist country.'

'Yes,' Ana María replies, 'and there's nothing good about that. No divorce, no abortions, even adultery is technically a crime.'

'But you're still a Catholic, right?'

'Certainly not.'

'Well, I'm not gonna teach you "Roamin' in the gloamin'' then.'

'She'll live,' says Karen, opening another bottle of wine.

I feel strangely dizzy with happiness. I wish it would never stop, this moment, laughing and fishing for the last fragments of chips from the vinegar-soaked paper. Colin tries to explain to Ana' María that it would be far too dangerous to go to Clapton at this time of night and that she should share a cab with him and stay at his studio. She laughs and says that Eduardo will be expecting her and that she is not frightened of going home on her own. Finally, Karen shuts Colin up by saying that she will get a cab and drop him off and they depart bickering about which route would be quickest after Colin has extracted a promise from Ana María that she will go out for a drink with him some time and let him paint her.

When they have gone, I make some tea and we remain sitting on the floor, talking quite naturally for the first time. She talks about the scandal of her dad and Eduardo's wife, and about never having lived anywhere permanently. 'I liked Mexico,' she says. 'In Mexico I met some very strange people. But I was quite young . . . it was so hot . . .' she tails off irrelevantly. She tells me about returning to Chile during the 1980s and wanting to throw herself into everything that was happening but always feeling like an outsider, somebody who didn't really fit in. 'People resented me,' she says. 'They thought that exile was all an excuse to get on in the world, that I must have had a really easy time while they were struggling.' She laughs suddenly, 'But I was bad too, really convinced that now I was back I was going to show them how to do things properly, change things on my own . . .'

'That doesn't sound like you,' I say, pouring some more tea.

'No, it's true. I can be really . . . Oh, you are laughing at me.'

'You'll have to get used to it, I'm afraid. We may be useless at everything else but we're still world leaders in irony.'

'That can be quite boring sometimes,' says Ana María slowly. 'If you think every time you say something, maybe something that is important to you, people will be smiling inside and trying to think of some funny comment, trying to outdo each other.'

'It can be good as well, though. Apart from anything else, it can stop people from getting too self-important.'

The circles which Ana María is drawing on the floor get slightly quicker.

'But then they don't say what they really feel because they are frightened somebody will make them look stupid. It can be quite stifling, I think. For example, Jamie, what do you really care about?'

I wriggle awkwardly as she stares at me. The question annoys me. What makes people think that they have the right to ask you that sort of question? 'Well I . . . dunno really . . . anyway just 'cause I don't know how to answer that, doesn't mean I can't answer it.'

Ana María continues to regard me steadily. 'Well, try,' she says.

'OK, well, there's this case at work. A woman on her own with some kids. Every night people come and shout things and push things through the letter-box. Stuff like that. Well, in lots of these cases the easiest thing to do is just to move that person somewhere else. That would be the easiest thing and most people would expect you to do it.'

I pause. I don't want to go on with this, don't want to sound as if I'm trying to make out that I'm some kind of hero. Ana María is watching me, her expression unchanged. 'So?' she asks.

'Well, I sort of know that I can't do that. I want to try and do something about the people who are doing it. It's hard to explain, I don't know the woman well, don't really know what it is she's going through . . . she once said to me that she just represented a work problem for me and in a way that's right, that's true . . . but at the same time I do still care that something is done about the people who are doing it to her, that they shouldn't just get away with it time after time . . . I don't know . . . maybe I'm not making much sense. But you're not the first person who has suggested that I'm kind of cynical or whatever. And I really don't think that's true. I really don't.'

'It's just,' says Ana María, 'that you seem quite separate from everything sometimes. As if you don't really care very much. Like in that argument earlier, everybody was arguing but you didn't say anything really.'

'I didn't really have anything to say. Well, it's not so much that, it's just those arguments . . . they don't have much to do with anything really. But normally I do join in you know. I just didn't feel like it.'

She nods and there is silence. What I want to tell her is how strange I feel. Not just because of living alone but because of the different weave of things at the moment, a new and frightening vulnerability that I'm not sure I know how to confront. I look at Ana María and think how little time we have known each other and how strange it must also be for her – this new displacement, these people, this city.

As if she is reading my thoughts, Ana María suddenly says, 'You know, I don't really know what I'm doing here. It was just an idea to come and stay with Eduardo. I didn't want to go back to Canada and there was nothing for me in Mexico – I'm not that close to my mother. But really I am quite ridiculous here. What am I doing?'

I cup my hands around the warmth that remains in the teapot.

'Well, maybe sometimes it's better not to know what you're doing. The people that I know here who know what they're doing are all quite . . . well, it's not that they're boring exactly, but I can't say that they've hit on the secret of happiness. People get to a certain age and they start to anchor themselves down with partners and mortgages or children or whatever and they fill up their lives and follow routines. That's not bad, I'm not saying there's anything wrong with that, but you must just stop and think sometimes, is this what it's going to be like for ever? I'd rather be you, not knowing what you can expect, just leaving for a new place, than them knowing that it'll never be any different.'

'I say that to myself sometimes,' replies Ana María slightly mournfully. 'But then I get scared as well. I thought that Chile . . . for years I thought it was my destiny, my real country, that all the moving and instability would stop once I got back there, and it just didn't work out like that. It wasn't the country I had imagined. I'm not saying I don't miss it or that I won't want to go back ever but . . .'

She picks up a wine bottle and swigs the last drops from it, and then pretends to twist the neck as if trying to wring some more out of it. We are both silent for a little while. Upstairs, the front door slams, and steps creak across the floorboards.

'When I was a little girl and we were first in exile,' Ana María continues, 'I used to love our house. There were always people there, eating, drinking, arguing. We would get thrown out of our bedrooms so that people could have a bed. Some of the visitors would spoil us, give us presents. I had a *tío* – but he wasn't really my uncle – I was his favourite and he gave me a *charango* which is a little guitar made from the shell of an armadillo. Everyone was so jealous. There was nearly a big fight with my brother and sister because they didn't get one. I took it with me everywhere even though I didn't know how to play it. I never had a doll – I hated them – I just used to drag this charango with me everywhere.'

'And where is it now?'

'I think my mother still keeps it. That was the last time I saw it, in her house in Mexico in a box with some old photographs.'

The couple upstairs start one of their ferocious post-pub arguments. Doors start to slam, indistinguishable words are

111

screamed from one room to another.

'I should be going,' Ana María says suddenly, looking at her watch. 'How shall I get home?'

'I'll call you a cab.'

'But I have no money.'

'I'll lend you some.'

I phone the cab and when I have ordered it Ana María smiles at me. '*Tu me caes super bien,*' she says suddenly.

'What does that mean?'

'It means I like you. But it sounds better in Spanish.'

I start to tremble slightly. She likes me? What does that mean? Cancel the cab, whisk her into my arms and waltz into the bedroom? Like in what sense? My throat goes dry. If I make a move now she might just think that I am a typical man with only one thing on his mind. Which I suppose I am. But I don't want to mess things up. I do like Ana María – in both senses of the word.

'I like you too,' I say, certain that my face is burning brightly. Ana María picks up her jacket and smiles cheerfully. 'Good. I would like us to be friends. And your friends are funny as well.'

Oh.

The cab hoots downstairs and I see her to the door. 'I'll phone you,' she says. 'Thank you.'

I slump on to the sofa, the adrenalin of lust seeping away from me gradually replaced by a feeling of deep gloom. I can feel her absence from the room while the mugs and glasses and chip wrappers – previously invisible – start to moan about not being left until the morning. Suddenly, there is a knock on the door. She's come back. I leap up and open the door. Ana María is breathless from running up the stairs. 'Jamie, I'm sorry, but you forget to give me some money. Quick, the man is getting angry.'

Later, I lie in bed wondering whether it is a good idea to start getting a crush on Ana María. It could become obsessive.

Throwing the House Out of the Window

I once fell in love with a girl when I was fifteen who lived near a hospital. I did voluntary work for the hospital for the whole summer in the hope that I would meet her as I was walking past her house. I never did and she never knew about it. Much later, I met her in a pub and wondered why I had spent an entire summer of my adolescence attaching black strips to the medical records of dead patients in a vain attempt to be near her. It would definitely be better not to fall in love with Ana María, I think before falling asleep.

PART TWO

PART TWO

Unchained Melody

Mike, the senior social worker, is standing at my desk when I arrive one morning at work, writing me a note.

'What's up?'

'Ah Jamie, good. Mr Carmichael is your tenant, isn't he?'

'Why?' I reply cautiously, sensing trouble. When social workers start asking if someone is your tenant it is better to deny everything and leave work at once feigning sudden illness.

'He's been sectioned. There was a bit of trouble last night.'

'What happened?'

Mike explains how Mr Carmichael and his wife separated a few years ago. Last night was their wedding anniversary and he marked the occasion by drinking bottles of whisky and hurling the empties, followed by nearly all the contents of his flat, out of the window. Then he sat precariously on the window-sill cradling a photo of their wedding day while his neighbours – whatever sympathy they might have had banished by the fact that he had played *Unchained Melody* over and over again all night – scavenged what they could from beneath his flat, and a group of young Samaritans stood jeering and shouting 'Jump then, you stupid wanker.' Finally the police and social workers arrived and he was sectioned.

'I'll come with you if you want,' Mike says, 'to take a look at the place.'

'Why are you walking like that?' I ask as we make our way

towards Herbert House. 'Have you hurt your leg or something?'

'No, no, it's not that. It's just . . . I've got a pile the size of a bloody golf ball. It's agony.'

'Right,' I say lamely.

Emergency Services have already boarded up the smashed windows of the flat. As we are about to enter, an elderly woman peers out of her door. 'Are you the council?'

'That's right.'

'Ooh, it was terrible,' she says, 'such a racket you'd never believe. And quiet as a dormouse most of the time. You know he just went mad. Threw his entire house out of the window. Bed, video, record player, plates . . .' She shakes her head. 'The whole house just went flying out really. I'd been round earlier to ask him to turn the music down and he wasn't nasty, you know. Just stared at me like I wasn't there and shut the door again. Poor soul.' She shakes her head again.

Mike nudges me and my heart sinks as I see Hilda Connolly striding purposefully down the walkway. I sometimes wonder whether she has planted a homing device on me. 'Shit, it's Big Sister. What does she want?'

'She wants more parking spaces, she wants no blacks, she wants gates . . .'

'. . . With *Arbeit macht Frei* on them.'

'She wants YOU Jamie, oh no, she's coming out of the sun, I can't see her, careful squadron leader, bandit six o'clock.'

'Well, Jamie?' she demands as she arrives, 'what are we going to do about this then? He can't come back here. There's too many old folk. You'll have to move him, because we're not having him back.'

I can feel Mike edging away behind me.

'I don't want any excuses this time, Jamie. Poor Mrs Galvin here was absolutely terrified. Weren't you, dear? If he comes back we'll be getting up a petition . . .'

'Wait a minute,' I say impatiently, 'the guy's only just been taken into hospital. It's a bit early to start going on about petitions. And from what Mrs Galvin was saying he doesn't cause any trouble for the other three hundred and sixty-four days of the year.'

'You'll sign the petition, won't you?' Hilda turns to Mrs Galvin, who ducks quickly into her flat and closes the door. 'I must say, Jamie, I've not been entirely happy with your attitude recently. Now I don't want to do this but I'm considering writing a letter about it to Tim Broadbent.' This is the area manager, who Hilda likes to pretend is a deep personal friend.

'You do that,' I reply sharply and turn to Mike. 'Shall we go in?'

'I heard that,' Hilda snaps.

'You were meant to,' I answer and turn the key in the door.

'Tim Broadbent will hear all about this,' Hilda growls and Mike takes my arm and steers me into the flat before the Houdini words in my head, which are struggling against their little straitjackets, can liberate themselves and really give Hilda something to complain about. I shut the door before she can push her way in behind us.

There is a terrible hush over the flat and smashed plates and broken glass lie everywhere. There is no need to take an inventory as it seems that everything throwable is either broken or did indeed go flying out of the window. Glass and china litter the floor, the nicotine-stained wallpaper is streaked with HP sauce and other items of food which were flung against it, and the mirror is smashed. The only objects which remain are an empty whisky bottle and the photograph of Mr Carmichael's wedding day with a cracked frame, which he was obviously holding when the police stormed in.

'Blimey,' says Mike. 'This is all a bit country and western.'

I pick up the photograph and stare at the picture. Mrs Carmichael is grinning broadly, clutching the arm of her new husband. He is wearing a grey suit with a carnation in the buttonhole. His best man looks as if he is about to burst out laughing.

'Was he known to social services before?'

'Well, yes. He had a drink problem. That's why his wife left home. The kids weren't on the at risk register or anything though. But he took it very badly.'

'He sure did.' I imagine Mr Carmichael on that particular day, the self-pity and self-disgust boiling inside him, driving him mad, turning inside out the ruthless cell of loneliness that his flat had become.

'Well,' Mike says. 'There's not much we can do here.'

I hand him the photo and he looks at it for a moment. 'Poor soul indeed,' he says. 'Wait a few minutes, Jamie. *Obermeister* Connolly is still outside – I feel it in my fingers, I feel it in my pile.'

Pudú Watch

I have absolutely no intention of mounting a one-person picket line outside my office on the day of the strike and phone Ana María to find out what she is up to. Eduardo has given her some money to buy warmer clothes so she is going shopping in Oxford Street. 'Come with me if you want,' she says, 'but I warn you that I do not like shopping and will get in a very bad temper.'

We meet at the ticket office of Tottenham Court Road station. 'Warm clothes,' she says. 'First I need warm clothes.' Oxford Street is at its most unappealing: mysterious people with clipboards conducting strange surveys; grinning Italians handing out leaflets for language schools; tatty shops where men with microphones are auctioning electric knives and Sony Walkmans; stalls selling plastic policemen's helmets, Beefeater money boxes and football calendars; groups of tourists who stop suddenly in the middle of the pavement forcing you into the road and the path of oncoming double-deckers. Ana María buys a black jumper and tights in Marks & Spencer's. Then we go looking for shoes, which is more tricky as she is definitely not taken with British shoe fashions. 'They are so ugly,' she says, picking them up and turning them round and round in her hand. 'And they must be really difficult to wear.' She starts to drag her feet sulkily. Finally we find a pair of boots that she quite likes. In the next shop Ana María tries on a pair of Levis while the assistant hovers irritatingly around her. She scowls at him several times but he just grins back at her, clicking his fingers in time to the shop music. Finally she snaps 'Go away' at him and he retreats looking aggrieved.

'How do I look?' she asks, peering at herself sideways in the mirror. 'Beautiful,' I say jokingly in Spanish but meaning it. After paying for the jeans Ana María says, 'No more shopping now,' so we go and drink cappuccinos to which she adds virtually half the bowl of sugar. It is a backstreet Italian café which is empty, sticky sugar on Formica tables, the chiller cabinets stacked high with tuna and chicken sandwiches trailing pale green lettuce leaves. Ana María is cheerful now that the shopping is over.

'Do you want to go home now?' she asks.

'Not especially.'

'Take me somewhere then. Somewhere English. You choose a place. Somewhere outside though, because it is so fine.'

'We could go to the zoo.'

'Animals in cages?'

'Come on, don't get all moralistic. It's great.'

She laughs. 'I like zoos really.'

The zoo is, in fact, something of a let-down. Half the most interesting animals seem to be on loan to other zoos. The last time that I was here it was on a school outing and I was clutching the packed lunch my mum had made for me of cucumber and Marmite sandwiches and Club biscuits. Ana María likes the reptile house and laughs at the kids busily banging on the cobra's cage in vain attempts to make it rear up and show its hood, despite the sign warning them not to and the cobra's weary indifference. I tell her about the kids in America who got eaten by polar bears after swimming the lake to the enclosure where the bears were kept, and the subsequent shooting of the culprits, a retaliation I have never entirely understood. We find the animals from Chile: a sleeping chinchilla, a gloomy condor in an undersized cage and, to Ana María's delight, some stubby short-legged deer-like creatures called pudús. They are both fragile and faintly ridiculous, with tiny furry antlers, fat stomachs, and delicate feet – like pot-bellied ballerinas.

'They are very rare,' Ana María says, 'practically inexistent in Chile now.'

'Extinct.'

'What?'

'Extinct. Not inexistent.'

We leave the pudús for the Moonlight World section, where the animals which are supposed to come out at night appear completely scornful of the attempt to persuade them that it is night, as cage after cage seems completely free of any animal life at all. Maybe they are so cunning at blending with the foliage that it makes no difference whether it is day or artificial night.

'There are a few animals where I work that only come out at night,' I say. 'I'd gladly donate them to the zoo.'

Outside again, we stumble across giraffes, monkeys, penguins and sea-lions. A baby delightedly throws its hat into the sea-lion's pond, as they burst grinning and exhaling out of the water and into the sun.

'Oh,' cries the mother, 'your new hat. Roger, go and get the hat back.'

Her partner turns to her in dismay. 'Don't be stupid. I'm not getting in there.' Ana María starts to giggle without trying to conceal it.

The mother flashes her a dirty look and then says, 'But it's a new hat. You could get on to that rock bit. Or at least go and find the attendant.'

'Christ almighty. Wait there then.' The baby chuckles and clutches fistfuls of air as its father disappears to find the attendant.

We try to find the tigers but eventually discover that they are on loan to a Spanish zoo. Finally we sit in front of a cage containing a scruffily comatose wolf which lies on its side, the wind ruffling its fur, its nose covered in dust. We assign animals to people. According to Ana María, Eduardo is a gnu, Soledad an ostrich, Karen a falcon and Colin a chimp.

Crowds of children with clipboards and fluorescent rucksacks troop around, policed by their haggard-looking teachers. 'Paul, I've told you before, leave Chelsea alone. Paul! Come here right now! No, Natalie, you've just been to the toilet. Where's Tamara?'

Two of the kids stop in front of the wolf's cage. They peer through at the sleeping animal.

'That wolf's dead,' one announces.

'It's not dead,' says the other.

'What's the matter with it then?'

'It's just a crap wolf. It's rubbish.'

'I bet you wouldn't get in there with it.'

'I bet I would.'

Ana María smiles at me. 'Poor wolf,' she says.

We sit silently for a time, watching the snoring wolf and the children disillusioned by its lack of ferocity.

'Jamie,' says Ana María suddenly, 'you remember that conversation we have in your flat about what I am doing here.'

'Oh yeah?'

'I have been thinking that maybe I should go back to Chile soon.'

'Oh,' I say dully. 'Right.'

'Sometimes I get quite homesick. And . . . I don't know . . . I'm not really doing anything here.'

There is another silence. 'What do you think?' she says, turning her face towards me. I can't think of anything to say though. All I can hear are animals chattering and shrieking, a sudden low bassoon-like moaning from a distant cage.

'I don't know,' I say slowly at last. 'You have to do what you think is best. But maybe you should give it a bit longer. Lots of people aren't doing anything particularly. And what would you do back in Chile that's so different?'

Very high above us in the pale sky, a tiny bullet shape makes its deceptively slow way over London, leaving a white trail behind it which begins to fade and break up and finally disappear in the thin cold air. I don't want Ana María to go away, but I am utterly at a loss when it comes to offering convincing reasons as to why she should stay.

'Maybe you are right,' she says. 'I'm just thinking, that's all . . . shall we go home now?'

'Let's go. Have you got all your bags?'

'Yes.'

We make our way back to Clapton. On the bus Ana María yawns several times and then closes her eyes and rests her head slightly against my shoulder. I am filled with an almost irresistible urge to put my arm around her and draw her closer. Instead, I stare straight ahead, gripping one of the bags tightly in my hand. When we get home, we sit and drink wine in the kitchen while Ana María shows her clothes to Eduardo. He tells us that the next week there is a fund-raising salsa night. While I am glad of the opportunity to see Ana María again I am slightly unnerved by the idea of dancing, since I have an unnatural lack of rhythm. 'Where is it?'

'Oh some community centre in south London. We are trying to get a representative from the Cuban embassy to come along. Half the money is going on medical aid for Cuba. Here, there is a leaflet.' Ana María smiles at me. 'You'll come won't you, Jamie?'

'Yes.'

'And tell your crazy friend.'

'The chimp? Yeah, he'll like that.'

Soledad wanders into the kitchen. 'Oh, hi Jamie. What have you been up to?'

'We've been at the zoo.'

'Mmmm . . . Very romantic,' says Soledad mischievously, 'no cierto, Papi?'

'Somebody phoned for you,' replies Eduardo, ignoring her but smiling slightly. 'Lenin Ramirez.'

'Lenin Ramirez?' I start to laugh.

'Sad, isn't it?' says Soledad. 'He went to school in Stockwell and had to call himself Lenny. These Chilean parents who call their kids after their political heroes. There's Ernesto Vladimir as well. Ernesto for Che Guevara and Vladimir . . . well, it's obvious really.'

Ana María laughs. 'I knew someone called Juan Stalin Gonzalez in Chile.'

'It must make it easy for the secret police,' I say, 'when it comes to rounding people up. It's a bit of a giveaway, isn't it? The British just do it with football players, kids named after the entire team sometimes.'

'It might all get mixed up in a few generations,' muses Eduardo. 'You know, Fidel Gazza Contreras.'

'It's a shame for his parents . . .' says Soledad '. . . I bet when they called him Lenin they never thought he would end up nicking cars in Stockwell.'

On the bus on the way home I rest my head on the window, which is steamed over with condensation, my cheek against the cold, wet glass. Suddenly the thought of the empty flat is almost unbearable. I think of Eduardo, Soledad and Ana María sitting at the kitchen table chatting, drinking wine and making up names. Then of the dishes in my kitchen lying in a sink of cold greasy water, the carrier bag so full of rubbish that the tins have spilled out on to the floor, and the washing basket from which I will have to try and find the least smelly pair of socks tomorrow morning. When I get in, the mess lives up to my expectations and there is nothing to drink. There is a Vietnamese film on Channel Four so I lie half-watching it, thinking about Ana María and how best to deter her from going back to Chile.

Duelling Banjos

Mrs Anderton is painfully thin, with shoulder-length tightly permed hair and several gold necklaces. She sits with her hands on the desk playing nervously with an expensive lighter. Her expression is not exactly hostile, more wary. There is something strange about her, as if some fundamental part inside is not quite working properly. She does not look at all at Trevor, who is acting as a witness and taking notes. The letter I sent her, slightly torn and crumpled, lies on the desk like a reproach.

'So you're saying that Dean is responsible for causing trouble?'

'Yes. And it's not just causing trouble. This is serious harassment of a family on the estate on a regular basis.'

'And he's doing it on his own, is he?'

'No, there are other people involved, but he appears to be one of the ringleaders.'

'And what do you want me to do about it?'

I explain that, as the tenant, we could take action against her for breaking the tenancy conditions. She listens with an emotionless face, fingering one of the gold chains around her neck, which has small red nervous blotches on it.

'Yes, but you can't hold me responsible for him. You think there's anything I can do about it? He's out of control. He won't listen to me.'

There is something almost desperate in the flat tone of Mrs

Anderton's voice, as if she is possessed with some tremendous crushing misery which she is quite unable to communicate adequately.

'Well, he lives with you and forms part of your household. In that sense you are responsible, because the tenancy is in your name. That's why I'm talking to you.'

'Well, what about the others though? I mean Dean's not the only one, and he's easily influenced. You're just going to pick on us. Typical.'

'No. I know that there are others involved and I'll be seeing them as well. But I'm not picking on you, Mrs Anderton. There's a family on this estate living in terror because of the activities of your son. And it's got to stop.'

She looks at her nails. 'But it's me who suffers in the end.'

'Well, I'm hoping that you'll be able to talk to Dean and explain that if he carries on like this his family could be without a home.'

She laughs abruptly and takes a cigarette from her packet. The lighter is tortoiseshell and clicks out its tiny blue flame at the touch of a golden button. 'You really don't get it, do you? You don't understand at all.'

'What don't I understand?'

'You think I wouldn't stop Dean doing things if I could? You think I wouldn't stop him hanging around with the King kids? A long time ago I would have liked to stop him taking money from my purse. And there are other things I would have liked to stop him doing . . . that girl . . . I know about that as well. Sometimes I feel people looking at me and . . . well anyway . . . I would stop this business with the Paki family as well. People who don't bother me, I don't bother them. There's a lot you don't know. You think you're a big shot threatening to kick us out but there's a lot you don't know.'

'At the end of the day, Mrs Anderton, there's a lot I do know as well. I know there's a family that can't leave their house or spend an evening in peace because of a gang of kids which includes your son. Now I understand what you're saying to me . . .'

'No, you don't understand.'

'. . . But my priority in this case has to be the victim.'

She blows smoke out. A drooping grey finger of ash hangs from her cigarette. Trevor passes her the ashtray and she smiles at him for the first time. She plays with the letter on the table, tearing off little pieces of the envelope flap and rolling them between her fingers.

'But you know, Mr Collins, maybe you'll evict us 'cause I can't promise you that I can stop Dean. But do you think that will stop all of this? You think people on this estate will just settle down and start living happily together? You're pissing against the wind.' I start to speak but she continues regardless. 'You know when he was little he was such a timid little boy, wouldn't go nowhere without me, had to have the light on and the door open at night, he was a right little coward, kids used to pick on him, steal his toys. God almighty, look at him now. Something happened, I don't know, something happened, maybe it was my fault, you don't know really, you think you know but you don't, Mr Collins,' and she shudders involuntarily.

Trevor looks down at the floor and there is a moment of heavy silence. I can't let up on her just because of her visible suffering. Somehow, her assertion of my ignorance frees me to play the role of cold-hearted bureaucrat which I have been assigned. It is curious, because my sympathy for her is detached and slightly tinged by irritation. I suppose it is because all of her sorrow is for herself. Mrs Khan is still just the Paki family. I could be telling her that Dean has been vandalizing the football area.

'Well, that may be the case. Unfortunately, however, you are the tenant and not Dean. And we can't just sit here and do nothing about it. You must speak to Dean because, as I've said, I won't hesitate to go to court over this.'

'I'll speak to him all right.' She gets up and stubs out the cigarette. 'Oh, one more thing, Mr Collins. Good luck with Susan King. You think we're bad . . . you just wait.' And she laughs bitterly as she walks out of the office.

Trevor looks at me and raises his eyebrows. 'Bwoy, I don't envy you this case. Sounds like this King woman gonna be vex when she comes in. She's going to be pleased to see me in here as well.' He breaks into exaggerated cockney. 'No fahkin' coon's gonna tell me wot to do.'

'Have you ever met her?'

'No, but I've heard about her. When Jean used to have your patch there were all sorts of problems over rent arrears. They were on the point of getting evicted. Loads of hassle. But then just when it seemed like we really had them and we were about to open the champagne bottles, she walks into the office with three thousand pounds in cash and pays the whole lot off. Roy was mad, guy. But he'd said that the only way they could avoid getting evicted was to pay the whole lot off and that's what they done so he couldn't do anything about it. Had to stick by what he said. The funny thing was about a week later the cashier's office got done by armed robbers. Roy's always been convinced it was just the Kings getting their money back. There are some right villains in that family, Jamie. In and out of the nick. And they're like those things in that film, *Gremlins*, they just seem to multiply. Try flicking some water on Mrs King when she comes, I bet about four more will appear.'

I change the subject, as I am beginning to get nervous. 'Did you come into work yesterday?'

'Of course not. I don't go against union decisions.' This is totally untrue, but I ignore it.

'Who was on strike then?'

'Me, you and Michael. Michael's pissed off with you 'cause there was no picket line. Apparently Adrian Thompson came down and wasn't too pleased either.'

'Tough. I wasn't going to come in but that was my limit. And I want to resign as steward. These one-day strikes just so that Adrian Thompson can pretend to be a revolutionary are a total pain in the arse.'

'Nobody else will do it. You can't.'

'So all the offices were open?'

'Is Hilda Connolly an evil Nazi?'

'What a waste of time.'

'It was quite handy for me. Lorraine's gone to see her mum in Leeds and it's half-term.'

I look at my watch and feel a flicker of hope.

'Mrs King's late.'

'Maybe she won't come.'

But I can see a woman at the reception desk and, although I've never met her before, I know it's Mrs King.

'Is that her?'

'Let's see . . . yep, bad luck, Jamie.'

Mrs King has brought one of her sons with her but it is not Jason. He does not sit down but stands at the door watching me steadily from little watery blue eyes with his arms folded. He has a squint, as if one eye is trying to look at the other. Mrs King is a small wiry woman with short stringy dyed hair which has gone a kind of orangey colour. She is wearing white track-suit bottoms and trainers with pink edgings and tiny glass chip diamonds. On her wrist there is a charm bracelet with a silver clog, a golden heart and a miniature padlock. She slams the letter I sent her on to the desk and then stares at me aggressively without saying anything, drumming her fingers ostentatiously on the table, the charms jiggling on her wrist. I can see the *Yours sincerely, Jamie Collins, (Housing Officer)* on the bottom of the letter.

'Right,' I say. 'Well, you know what this is about. This is Trevor Campbell, another housing officer who will be sitting in on the interview.' The boy at the door snorts derisively. Mrs King curls her lip slightly.

131

'You're not Jason, are you?' I address the boy directly.

'Nah.'

'So who're you?'

He pauses before replying and then looks up at the ceiling. 'Paul. His brother.'

I repeat what I have said to Dean Anderton's mother. Mrs King watches me as I talk and, when I mention the broken window, a slight smile plays around her lips. I look at her eyebrows, her nose and ears, thinking how strange that someone who has all the features of a human being, who must have felt most of the normal range of human emotions at one time or another, can be so calmly vicious. I can feel the uselessness of my words, the hollow formality of the threat, and I know that she knew about all of this anyway, does not care and is completely unmoved by the possible sanctions against her. She glances at her son and grins at him.

'Got witnesses, have you?' she says drily when I have finished.

'What?'

'You heard. Have you got someone who will be prepared to stand up in court and say it was Jason.'

'I can't disclose that sort of information. My more immediate concern is for you to talk to Jason to get him to stop this behaviour. Explain to him that there is a serious risk of you becoming homeless if . . .'

'Homeless! Don't make me laugh. You think this is the first time the poxy council's tried to throw us out? And as for talking to Jason, why should I? He's not doing nothing wrong as far as I can see.'

I resist the temptation to make some smart-arse comment about her use of the double negative.

'Breaking people's windows. Making them scared to go out. There's nothing wrong with that then?'

'Maybe those people shouldn't be there in the first place.'

I pause and stare at her. She meets my gaze coolly with a

blend of amusement and contempt. It is one of those moments when I wish I were the international crime-master, the bald one with the white cat from the James Bond films. I would murmur, 'You are beginning to irritate me, Mrs King,' before pushing the red button that opens the trapdoor and drops her into a pool of open-mouthed starving sharks. Except the sharks would probably come off worse.

'So what you are saying to me is you see nothing wrong with what Jason is doing and that you're not prepared to make an effort to get him to stop?'

'I think she's saying,' says the boy suddenly, 'that it's *us* what's getting aggravation getting called down to this poxy office. And it had better stop. 'Cause I'll tell you what mate. You're well out of your depth.'

'Is that a threat you're making?' says Trevor suddenly. The boy looks at him for a second and then straight back at me as if to deny Trevor's right to address him at all.

'Read it how you want, mate.'

I stare at him. Unspoken, unspeakable words bubble inside me. Playground taunts. 'Your mum's a slag and she lives in a baked-bean can,' or 'Paul King is illegitimate, he ain't got no birth certificate . . .' I almost laugh as I imagine their faces if any of these insults were just to burst, involuntarily, from my lips.

'Look,' says Mrs King, suddenly adopting the pacific tone of one who is simply seeking a reasonable solution. 'This is the first time I've met you, isn't it? I don't want to get off on the wrong foot. We've never had no reason to meet before and that's how I like it. Live and let live is my motto. Nobody interferes with me, I don't interfere with them.' And she smiles benevolently at me. This game is getting stupid, it is just meaningless words again, irrelevancies.

'Oh yeah, I've been hearing that line a lot recently. But somebody's interfering with someone. And it's got to stop. Now, let's put our cards on the table. I will be serving you with a Notice of Seeking Possession on the basis of you breaking your tenancy agreement and we'll go to court. Maybe you're right and we won't win, I don't care. But I'm going to give it my best shot and no amount of veiled threats is going to change that. Do I make myself absolutely clear?'

Trevor stares at me amazed, as I have always had a reputation for being a wimp with difficult tenants. The boy looks at me and smiles slowly. 'Yeah?'

'Come on, Paul,' says Mrs King, getting up out of her seat. 'There's no use talking to these . . .' and she looks straight at Trevor '. . . monkeys. All right mate, do what you want to do, it won't get you nowhere. You won't find a single person on this estate will get up and give evidence.'

The boy holds the door open for his mother. Then he turns back inside the room and, staring at me as directly as is possible for someone with a squint, says, 'You've just made a very big mistake. See you later.'

We sit in the interview room in silence for a few seconds.

'Fucking hell, Jamie,' says Trevor. 'Can't you just get the person a transfer or something? You're putting your neck on the line a bit here. And you haven't got any witnesses, have you? I don't think the legal department will even touch it.'

'Roy thinks we should go ahead.'

'So? He's not the one who's having threats made against him, is he? These are rednecks, hillbillies, po' white trash. Years of interbreeding, mate. You saw his eye didn't you? They'll whup your arse, boy.'

'Yeah, but Roy's right. What happens if we move Mrs Khan? They've got what they want and we won't be able to put anyone but white families on the estate without worrying about them facing this type of problem. Fair enough, if Mrs Khan wants a transfer then I'm not going to stand in her way. We can't make her suffer in the interest of the wider issue. But even if she gets a transfer I'm still going to serve them with a Notice.'

'I know what you're sayin', Jamie. But you're gonna get aggravation off this lot. Do you get paid enough to fight battles you're not going to win?'

'Would you say that if it was an Afro-Caribbean family and not Asians?'

'That's out of order, Jamie. And yeah, I would. I'd get them a transfer and that's it. I ain't some Sidney Poitier. Think about what you've just said, Jamie.'

'All right, I'm sorry. But I don't care, I don't think people should just get away with things. I'm sick of these bastards. Most people on the estate are too. You know you can get really embittered by this job because most of the people you meet are either pathological moaners or twisted psychopaths. But they're not the only people who live here. I think we might be able to get a witness. I mean, Mrs Anderton, I can see she's got problems and everything and maybe we'll be able to do something without evicting her. But that other family. I never thought I'd say this but it must be in their genes or something. They're just evil bastards and I want to get them out. I couldn't give a shit where they go. I just want them away from here.'

'Just be careful,' says Trevor seriously. 'That family's nasty, Jamie. I ain't joking now. They carry their threats out. They've got relatives everywhere as well. There's Kings in West Ham, Canning Town . . . you name it. You know what I'm sayin'.'

'I'll wear my garlic necklace.'

'I think silver bullets might be more effective.'

Roy is not at his desk when I get back upstairs. I leave him a note telling him what I am going to do and fill out the paperwork for the Legal Department and the Central Race Unit. It is beginning to spit with rain outside, speckling the skylight above my head. The light is fading into a gloomy yellow and the office lights are switched on. It gives the office an almost holy feeling. Apart from myself, only Eileen, the administration officer, is upstairs sorting papers into trays for filing.

'Had a hard day, Jamie love?' she says, seeing me staring out of the window with my chin in my hand.

'You might say that.'

'Here,' she says, 'have a Jaffa cake. I've just put the kettle on so I'll make us a nice cup of tea.'

'I was kind of hoping for a nasty cup of tea.'

She shrieks with laughter, as she always does when anyone makes a joke, however lame.

'All right then, Jamie, I'll make it nasty especially for you.'

'Too rye aye Eileen.'

And she roars with laughter again, disappearing into the kitchen with a bundle of yellow tenancy files under her arm.

I make a real effort, when I get home, not to collapse in front of the TV and get drunk. I take the rubbish to the chute. From next door, the familiar sound of Phyllis shouting at Harold is clearly audible. I put some washing on, change the bed sheets and sweep the kitchen floor. Then I wash up and try not to cheat by pretending to myself that the pans need to be left to soak. I even force myself to clear the mould-spotted courgettes, saucers of left-over discoloured tuna and old tubs of yoghurt out of the fridge before wiping it down. Finally, I collapse in front of the TV with a can of beer to watch a Tory minister explaining why single mothers are responsible for everything from rising crime to the decline in religious observance; succeeding joyriders, devil-dogs, trade-unionists, ravers, new age travellers, social security scroungers and ram-raiders in the hierarchy of moral outlaws. I throw my empty beer-can at the TV and pick up the guide. Fuck all on TV apart from *The Bill*, a nature film about Arctic foxes and an 'above average' TV movie based on a true story about twins separated at birth. I kneel up on the sofa, looking out of the window. Starlings swirl in a black pointillist mass around the post office, and the blades of the orange helicopter from the London Hospital begin to thwack-thwack as it prepares to take off. This is the noisiest place in the world. I wake up most mornings to the shuddering clash of metal on tarmac as workmen drill up the road yet again, sirens wail continually at night, car alarms whinge intermittently. Even the pensioners around here are unbelievably loud: Phyllis competes with the drills by yelling at Harold every morning, and in the evenings they troop out of their bingo sessions in the community room yelling goodnight to each other at the tops of their voices. Goo'night Vi, ta-ta Ron. I smile to myself. It's all right really. The helicopter rises, nose dipping, from its pad and races away. I wonder about the person waiting for it, perhaps a motorist trapped in a heap of twisted metal on the M25 or a building site worker who has slipped and tumbled from scaffolding. My breath makes clouds on the window and I put my hand on it, making a skeleton print. You could just get Mrs Khan a transfer and leave it at that. No you couldn't. It's all right really. Don't worry, be happy.

The telephone rings but I leave it as I have the answerphone set. After the bleep I hear Iona say, 'Jamie, I'm beginning to suspect that you listen to these mess . . .' I pick the phone up.

'Well, you're wrong.'

'Ah, I'm flattered. Listen, Jamie, I'm near your house in a pub in the City. Shall I come round?'

'OK, that'd be good.'

'I'll see you in half an hour.'

When Iona arrives she is wet from the rain which is thudding down insistently outside. 'It's really horrible out there,' she complains. 'Look, I bought a bottle of brandy since we drank all of yours last time.' I give her a towel to dry her hair and pour two glasses of brandy.

'What have you been up to? How's your job?' she asks.

'Fine. How about you?'

'Oh, the same as ever. I saw your friend Colin at a party.'

'Yes, he said.'

'What did he say?'

'That he saw you.'

'Nothing else?'

'No, why?'

'Oh, nothing. I just wondered. Give me more brandy, Jamie, I'm still freezing.'

She stands in front of me patting her hair with the towel. Her face suddenly looks quite pale and small. I reach up and pull her by the thick buckle of her belt towards me so that she is right in front of me. I begin to unfasten the belt, tightening it to loosen the buckle pin, feeling the sudden release as it is undone. She laughs. 'Aren't you meant to say "I can think of how to warm you up." '

'I can think of how to warm you up.'

She takes a sip of brandy as I undo the buttons of her jeans one by one. I put my hands on her waist and slide the jeans down until they are round her knees. She edges closer to me still shivering slightly. 'Wait,' she says. 'I'll have to take these trainers off. I've only just paid a ridiculous sum for them and the rain's made them go all funny.' She puts her glass down and bends awkwardly to unfasten her purple Pumas, which are matted by the rain. She kicks them off and steps out of her jeans. I pull her towards me holding her hips and she puts her hands on my shoulders. Then she moves me back on the sofa so that she can kneel on top of me. We spin round so that we are lying the length of the sofa. I push up her top over her breasts and put my hands round to unfasten her bra while she unbuttons my jeans. I reach to her shoulders and pull the straps of the bra free of her arms, feeling it loosening, falling away, becoming just material. She brushes her hair away and kisses me, her arms round my neck.

'What about . . .'

'Shhh, it's OK, I've put my cap in.'

Afterwards I bring the duvet into the living-room. Iona lies with her feet on my lap and I play absent-mindedly with her toes.

'Jamie,' Iona says suddenly. 'You know I was asking you about Colin.'

'Mmmm.'

'Well, at the party on Saturday I was there with Malcolm, you know. And Colin was like acting as if I was betraying you or something. But you know that I carry on seeing Malcolm, don't you?'

'Yeah, I know that.'

'Like the way we talked about it last time and everything, maybe I made it sound as if it were over between me and Malcolm.'

'No, I never thought that. I never really thought anything, to be truthful.'

'Do you mind about that?'

'Not really.'

'Just one thing, Jamie, Colin said to me that I was just doing this to get Malcolm's attention. And that's not true. I'm not even sure if he knows. It's because I like it. And I really like you.'

'And do you like Malcolm?'

'Like? That doesn't come into it really. You're very different.'

'I should hope so. And next time tell Colin to mind his own business.'

'Don't worry, the compliments always fly thick and fast when our paths cross. Anyway, what about you? Is there anyone else?'

With perfect timing at this moment the telephone rings. The voice on the answerphone says, 'Hello Jamie. Phone me. It's Ana María.'

'So is that your other woman?'

'No, of course not.'

'OK, it was a joke actually.'

I listen to the sound of the tape clicking and whirring,

resetting itself. I think, slightly guiltily, that I would be mad with jealousy if I knew that Ana María were sleeping with someone else right now. And that I am not telling Iona the entire truth. Then again, I don't know if Ana María feels anything for me at all. I am just doing Eduardo a favour, showing her the city, her alternative tour-guide. And it is not as if Iona and I have made any commitments to each other. Anyway, it's been a long time since my life has been interesting enough to have that kind of dilemma to ponder over, so I can't pretend that I feel that bad about it.

'Oh, my God,' yelps Iona suddenly.

'What? What's the matter?'

'My leg's gone to sleep.' And she gets up and begins to hop naked round the living-room trying to get some life back into it. I get up too and wrap the duvet round us like a cloak. 'Come on, let's go to bed.'

'Bring the brandy and the TV.'

Arctic foxes scamper around the tundra in their brilliant white coats searching for nests to snatch eggs from. Their numbers are decimated in the winter. They lie with their legs smashed by the cruel serrations of traps, splashing bright red blood on the snow until frosty-mouthed hunters arrive on snowmobiles to sling the pelts into sacks. Failing this they starve, because all the other animals have done the sensible thing and migrated to warmer climates. That's what I need at the moment – the snow goose strategy – taking my place in a neat soaring formation, heading for the sun and thinking of nothing while gazing down at a world in which Mrs King and her family of predators are just mere dots on the surface. Ana María migrated, but went the wrong way, crossing mountains and pampas and the ocean to land clumsily in cold and miserable London. And now she's talking about going back again and who can blame her? A fox cub stands shivering on the windswept arctic plain. 'Winter has arrived on the tundra,' intones the commentator in that mellifluous voice reserved for nature commentators. 'Now, only a few of the foxes will survive the harsh months to come.'

'Ahhh,' coos Iona, 'poor little thing. Did you see that brilliant one last week on hyenas? They're mad, they eat broken glass.' And she bites my shoulder.

Yellow with Pink Spots

Before taking the first steps against the Anderton and King families, Roy calls a meeting in the office. Khaled is worried that the Notice of Seeking Possession will lead to an upsurge of activity against Mrs Khan in the month that follows.

'I've thought about that,' says Roy, 'and I'm making her a Category One case. She should get the next available offer. I've spoken to Bob and hopefully we'll have her out of there pretty fast.'

'As long as she doesn't get offered some rubbish flat on the twenty-fifth floor of a tower block,' Paula replies. 'It's happened before. Especially with Bob Townsend. In the meantime, we've organized for somebody to be with her most nights this week. When are you going to serve the Notices?'

'Tomorrow. And Jamie, I don't want you to actually serve them. I've arranged for a housing officer from Riverside office to do it. I think we should reduce your profile a little.'

'What about Mrs Khan?' I ask. 'Is she still prepared to give evidence even if she gets moved out before it goes to court?'

'I've spoken to her about that,' says Paula, 'and she is. But that raises the whole question of other witnesses.'

'We could do with some witnesses,' Roy agrees. 'We've got Mrs Khan and what you lot saw when you were round there that night but we need some neighbours who will positively say that it is Anderton and King who are instigating this. I want Jamie to speak quietly to some of Mrs Khan's other neighbours. Just because we didn't have any luck with Mrs Reynolds doesn't mean that nobody will be prepared to say something.'

'I've found something,' I say. 'A letter I got some time back which I'd forgotten about. It was from someone in the facing maisonettes complaining about kids at night banging on doors and throwing things. It must be the same lot because the house backs right on to Mrs Khan's. I'm going to go and have a word with them this afternoon.'

'Good. Right, well I think you're all aware that this is going to be very difficult. There's certainly no guarantee that we'll even get to court if I know our legal department. Also, we can expect aggravation from the Kings. I don't want any housing officer to see them unless it's in a screened interview room and myself or a senior officer is present.'

In the afternoon, I make my way to the address of the complainant. From the spindly handwriting on his letter, and the name Walter Peters, I assume that he is a pensioner. It is starting to drizzle as I make my way around the estate. Mr Peters lives in a maisonette which backs on to Folkestone Road and the front of Keats House, where Mrs Khan lives on the ground floor. He is on the first floor, perfectly positioned to see from his back window everything that is going on. I have been trying to get these maisonettes shifted on to Trevor's patch for some time, on the grounds that I should have nothing south of Folkestone Road, which is a kind of equator between the two halves of the office's jurisdiction. I pass in front of Mrs Khan's house, where somebody has tried to scrub off the graffiti about Pakis, cross Folkestone Road and walk through the arch which is stinking of piss and littered with chip wrappers, to ring on Mr Peters's buzzer.

'Yes?'

'It's Mr Collins, your housing officer.'

'Who?'

'The housing officer. From the council.'

'All right, wait a minute.'

He buzzes the door entry system and I pull the heavy silver door open. As I climb the stairs I can hear him still buzzing and shouting down the intercom. 'Are you in yet?'

The front door is open on the chain when I arrive at number 16.

'Can I see some identification, young man?'

Shit. I always nag the tenants to ask for ID cards and today I've come without it.

'Listen, Mr Peters, I've left it in the office but honestly, I'm Mr Collins the housing officer. I've come about your letter. About the disturbances.'

'But that was about a month ago.'

'Yes, I'm really sorry but I haven't had time to come earlier.'

'All right, come in.' There is the sound of scraping metal as he releases the chain. Mr Peters is wearing slippers and a cardigan. He is still quite a broad man, with bright blue eyes and a nose that appears to spread across his face. The flat smells slightly – but not unpleasantly – of age.

'Would you like a cup of tea?'

'No thanks.'

'I'm making one anyway.'

'Go on then.'

I sit down on the sofa in the living-room and look around while Mr Peters busies himself in the kitchen. The heavily embossed wallpaper makes the room seem smaller, the light switch is encased in a decorative piece of scallop-edged plastic. On the wall there is a painted picture of a Spitfire among the clouds, and a photo of three gap-toothed little girls in pale pink J-cloth school uniforms grinning. Another photo shows a young Mr Peters with a woman who looks like she has just stepped off the set of *Brief Encounter*. Beside what has obviously always been Mr Peters's special armchair, which is turned to face the TV, lies a copy of the *Radio Times*, a *Daily*

Mirror and a heavy glass ashtray with a pipe in it.

'They're my granddaughters,' remarks Mr Peters, coming in with the tea. 'Sandra, Sarah and Samantha. Biscuit?' He hands me a saucer with a mixture of gingernuts and custard creams on it. I take a gingernut and dip it in my tea.

'Thanks. So, Mr Peters, about the problems you've been having . . .'

'Now, why haven't you come before? I bet you just got the letter and thought, "Oh no, not another moany old git," and binned it.'

I can't help giggling guiltily.

'See, young man, you shouldn't jump to conclusions. But seriously, it's no laughing matter, it's shocking what's been going on around here lately. It's all hours and my bedroom's at the back. Not that I sleep much anyway these days.' He glances at the photo of the woman.

'What exactly has been going on?'

'Those bleedin' kids. Breaking things, shouting, swearing. And it's all against that poor woman over there in Keats House. She's got little 'uns as well. Now, I'll tell you something young man. Somebody's colour don't mean nothing to me.' He pauses to take a biscuit but does not take his eyes from mine. 'Black, white, yellow with pink spots, it's all the same to me. No, I'm being serious now, it's wrong what they're doing, they're torturing that poor lady.' He takes a custard cream and begins to eat the biscuit bit off the top.

'Do you know who they are?'

"Course I know who they are. The whole bloody estate knows who they are. Listen, young man, that King family is nothing but trouble. Always has been, always will be. I'll be truthful now, when Michael King got stabbed that time, there were more than a few people around here who breathed a big sigh of relief, I'm telling you.'

'You've seen the people who are doing it then?'

'Of course I've seen them. There's lots has seen them. But

they pretend they haven't. Ain't you going to do something about it, Mr Collins? It's shocking, it really is.'

'Who have you seen?'

'Who have I seen? I've seen that young Anderton, Dean it is, Peggy Saunders's grandson. I've seen Jason King. Now he really is trouble. Just like his brother. Sometimes other Kings, the younger ones. I've seen the boy they call Gary. I forget his surname, he's not from round here. Oh, I know 'em all. And I'll tell you something else, it ain't just them. There's others as well.'

'Mr Peters, we are doing something. We're taking the King family to court for racial harassment to get them evicted.'

'Well, about bleedin' time. I don't care what it's for, just get 'em off the estate and you'll be making a lot of people very happy.'

'But we need witnesses, Mr Peters. If the case went to court and we had to get people to come forward and say they'd seen Anderton and King, would you be prepared to do it?'

'No.'

'You see, Mr Peters, that's our problem, isn't it, it's all very well saying . . .'

'Not for Anderton. I know his grandmother. They're not a bad family. The boy's wild, he's done some bad things, but deep down he's not as bad as the other one. Now, for the King boy I would. That family's scum.'

'You would be prepared to stand up in court and say that you had seen Jason King outside Keats House, you know, doing those things?'

'I would, yes. I've seen it all. I saw them break the window that time. It was the King boy who done that. I'm not frightened of the Kings. I'm not frightened of anything except something happening to my granddaughters.' He touches his head with his finger.

'Mr Peters, if I leave you some diary sheets would you make a note of the time and take details of any further incidents?'

'All right, Mr Collins.'

'That's brilliant. Now let me get this completely straight. You are prepared, if the case goes to court, to appear as a witness for the council saying that you saw Jason King?'

'Yes. But not the Anderton boy.'

'OK. Now here are the diary sheets. Don't forget the date and time.'

'Yes, yes, I heard you. Now listen, Mr Collins, there's another thing. How long is it going to be before we get a gate on that arch? It's shocking that alleyway what with the kids in there at lunchtimes and all the rubbish. Then there's the drunks using it as a toilet and the junkies with their syringes and whatnot. I don't want my grandchildren seeing that, do I? They live out in Brentwood now with their mum, but I feel terrible them coming here through that. Now all it wants is a gate and a padlock. Surely the council could stretch to that. I mean, you read about some of the things they spend their money on, sending the councillors to Pakistan and all that nonsense to learn what it feels like to be an Asian or whatever, free bloody holiday more like it, now I've always paid my rent, not once have I been in arrears . . .'

'All right, steady on, you don't want to start being a moany old git.'

This is a calculated risk which fortunately works. Mr Peters laughs and says, 'You cheeky monkey! There's a time I'd have given you a good hiding for that. Used to box in my time. Down Bethnal Green. Next time you come I'll show you the photos, I can tell you don't believe me. You ever boxed? No, doesn't look like it, you wanna get in shape, you've got the face for a boxer, too old to start now I suppose. Anyway, I'm serious about that alley. Put a gate on it. You'll look into it for me?'

'Yes. I will.'

I walk back towards the office. A group of kids are kicking a ball against the wire fencing of the football enclosure. I see

Mrs Reynolds's daughter walking arm in arm with another girl. They are almost identical except that her friend has dark hair. Karen Reynolds ignores me as I move out of the way for them to pass, but as I glance back over my shoulder I see that she does the same.

Back in the office I tell Roy what has happened. 'Excellent, excellent,' he says, chewing on the plastic bit from the end of a Bic biro and holding it between his teeth.

'But what about Anderton?'

'To be honest, Jamie, I'm more worried about King. I don't think we're going to get Anderton. We can focus now on King, that's the main thing. We'll serve a Notice on Anderton anyway just to make them think we're serious. How reliable is this witness?'

'Wally? He's cool. He might demand a gate on the alley of Folkestone Road in return.'

'Oh, the famous gate. I don't know why we've never done that. It's been an issue for long enough. You should try getting some money out of the Crime Prevention Fund. You can usually get something if you dress it up enough. Trevor's wangled some outrageous things. Anyway, Legal will need to speak to this guy once we've served the Notices.'

'OK.'

'Well done, Jamie. Oh yes, and Jamie, don't take this to heart or anything but we both know your paperwork isn't always what it should be. Like your rent arrears sheets and those lost insurance claims. Now we need really good documentation on this case. I know it's boring but you can do it if you put your mind to it. And it's important.'

'Yes, sir.'

Ice Swans

Looking back on an argument, I often find it hard to remember the point at which it moved through its various levels from conversation to heated conversation to full-blown argument to prolonged sulk. The point at which I could have stopped it, laughed, agreed to differ, changed the subject. Especially when it starts off as idle chatter about some topic of mutual interest. Sitting in Eduardo's kitchen, before going to the salsa evening in Kennington, the conversation turns to the execution of some general in Cuba, a hero of the Angolan war, subsequently revealed to be a drugs trafficker. Somewhat suspiciously, in my opinion, one of Ana María's principal arguments in favour of his execution is that he emerged from his trial agreeing that the firing squad was the only punishment appropriate for his crime. I say that I do not think that it was necessary to execute him and thus take my first step on the ladder of a major battle with Ana María.

I do not have the advantage of absolute rejection of the death penalty on moral grounds to strengthen the logic of my argument, since I tend to think that Nazi war criminals and violent paedophiles are beyond rehabilitation. I am not sure, however, that logic would be much help, since we are arguing at such cross purposes and Ana María is not actually listening to half of what I am saying. The mention of anything which might be construed as a criticism of Cuba brings out a streak of fanaticism which leads her to treat me as if I were an apologist for everything the United States has ever done in Latin America, from the economic blockade of Cuba to the murder and rape of nuns in El Salvador. Meanwhile, I am starting to shout, because if there is one thing that drives me crazy it is someone who keeps switching the terms of the argument and whose logical process resembles a ball of tagliatelle. Eduardo tries to soothe the rising tempers but it is too late.

'The thing is you're not listening to what I'm actually saying. I'm not saying that what he did was right, I'm not saying that there might not be a time where execution was the right thing. I just don't think from what you're saying that it was justified in this case.'

'Yet, in the midst of all the crimes being committed against Cuba, you want to speak out on this one case. Typical Western liberal attitude.'

'Well, I'm not addressing the United Nations about it for God's sake or picketing the Cuban embassy. It's a conversation around a kitchen table about a certain issue and I'm giving my opinion. We weren't actually talking about crimes against Cuba. We were talking about a specific case and whether the sentence was correct or not.'

Eduardo raises his hand as if he wants to say something, but nobody pays him any attention.

'General Ochoa was a traitor and a counter-revolutionary,' announces Ana María pompously, folding her arms as if she herself were the counsel for the prosecution, 'and for that he deserved to be shot.'

'That's not an argument, that's just boring rhetoric. Why don't you add running dog of imperialism. You should have lived in China during the cultural revolution, you would have made a perfect Red Guard.'

Ana María's eyes widen indignantly as Soledad wanders into the kitchen and opens the fridge. She is dressed up to go out, wearing tight black velvet shorts with a gold belt and knee-length lace-up boots. She gives an exaggerated yawn. 'Oh God, you're not all arguing about politics again, are you? Boring. What's the matter with you lot? Are you frightened of enjoying yourselves?'

'Fuck off, you bastard,' snaps Ana María, who has not yet learned, when swearing, to make the response appropriate to the provocation encountered. Patrick bursts out laughing.

'You see how she cuss you, Sol.'

His laughter makes Ana María even more angry and she glares ferociously at me. Soledad swigs a mouthful of milk from a bottle, puts her hand on her hip and fires at Ana María. 'Maybe people take you seriously in Chile because they're used to listening to a lot of crap. But here you're just another immigrant, not any hotshot revolutionary. If you want to talk about the working class all the time then go and clean offices like my dad had to. Otherwise, shut your mouth.'

Ana María shoots back something in Spanish which I don't understand, but Soledad's eyes narrow and she is about to come back at Ana María when Eduardo puts his hands up and says sharply, '*Basta ya!* Enough, Soledad. Come on, we're supposed to be getting ready to go out.'

'Yeah, but I didn't call her *huevona,* did I? I never said she was *una hueca*. I didn't start cussing her in the first place. I wasn't even talking to her.'

'I said enough!'

'Oh right, blame me, yeah. Don't say anything to little Miss Stuck-up Bitch. Fuck you lot. Get a life, Ana María. *Andate a la chucha* yourself. Come on Patrick.' And she storms out. Patrick follows her, eyebrows raised in a comically resigned way as if he knows he is going to get an earful.

We sit at the kitchen table in a dense silence waiting for Colin, who has borrowed a car and is going to pick us up. I realize I am now implicated not only as an enemy of Cuba but as an accomplice of Soledad and apoliticism. Ana María is a model of pure silent fury and is studying her hands, as if searching for her destiny in the lines of her palms.

'Have you been to any events like this in London yet?' I say, for the sake of saying something and as a peace offering. She does not look up but she just shakes her head slightly. Then she gets up and silently leaves the room. Eduardo puts his hand on my wrist. 'Jamie, you are in the house of the dog I think. Don't worry. She'll get over it. You are her friend. She know that.'

'Does she?'

'Yes.'

Colin arrives, wearing an old Brazil football shirt and exuding energy and good spirits. 'Where's my favourite Chilean?' he roars. 'I need a crash course in salsa dancing, it's all in the waist movement they tell me.' And he cavorts crazily across the kitchen wiggling his waist, putting a bunch of grapes on his head and pretending to be Carmen Miranda. Ana María emerges from the bathroom. She has tied her hair back into a pony tail and is wearing the clothes she bought when we went shopping. 'Caramba!' Colin shouts, putting his hand on his heart and pretending to fall against the sink. Ana María flashes a smile at him but continues to ignore me completely, which is beginning to become very irritating. It also makes me feel miserable and I contemplate going home. I don't want to argue with Ana María but I'm certainly not going to grovel to her. 'Let's go then.' Colin produces his car keys. 'Everybody salsa.' His cheerfulness is starting to get on my nerves.

The event is being held in a community centre in Kennington which has been decorated with a massive Cuban flag and a picture of Che. It is fairly easy to tell the difference between the Latin Americans and the British because while the former are smartly dressed, the majority of the latter are sporting a variety of T-shirts with topics ranging from Guatemalan Indians to red-eyed tree frogs. Children dash around shrieking, chasing each other through the legs of the adults. Before the DJ starts, we listen to a boring speech from a representative of the Cuban embassy, at the end of which everybody gets up and cheers their approval and somebody shouts 'Viva Cuba libre.' Eduardo buys a bottle of Havana Club rum and Ana María softens a little, even going so far as to look at me while she is saying something, which is a definite step forward. She dances with Colin, whose antics provoke surreptitious giggles from the Latins present. I buy another bottle of rum. But then the slight thaw is ruined by a tall Cuban with a moustache who comes over and invites Ana María to dance. He stares at her like a child with a brightly wrapped sweet. He also dances fluidly and expertly, whispering occasionally as they move across the dance floor, and she throws her head back and laughs. Afterwards, he comes to sit at our table and talks to Eduardo for a while. From what I can understand he has served in the Cuban army in Angola. Ana María asks him admiring questions about this and then they return to the dance floor. The Cuban is holding Ana María by the waist and gazing into her eyes.

This is a disaster and I am getting drunk. The music stops, but as Ana María is making her way back to the table the Cuban takes her arm, imploring her to continue, and she laughs and stays on the dance floor. People give mock shrieks and whistles as the lights go down and the DJ puts a romantic song on. Somebody shakes a bucket in front of me and I drop a pound in. Colin sits down beside me, shaking his head as he watches Ana María and the hero from Angola.

'Bastard.'

'Yeah.' I pour myself more rum.

'Look at that moustache, and those trousers. At least Che had a bit of style.'

'He's still a hero of the revolution though.'

'And he's not a bad dancer either.'

'In fact, he's an all-round diamond geezer.'

'We could still take him to the bogs and give him a kicking.'

'Oh, that's a good idea. The man who probably master-minded the defeat of the South African Defence Force won't know what's hit him when a failed artist from Edinburgh and a local government bureaucrat sort him out in the bogs.'

'Jamie. You've got to have a higher opinion of yourself than that. Actually, there's some pretty nice-looking girls here tonight. I was dancing with a Colombian. She's a fox. Why don't you have a wee dance, Jamie? You've been looking like you're about to start greetin' since I picked you up. What's up, Jamie?'

'I've got a lot on my mind.'

'It wouldn't have anything to do with Ana María by any chance, would it? You've been staring at her like your eyes are fixed with magnets and you haven't said a word to each other all evening. Forget it. The Cuban wins for now. He's playing at home though, isn't he.'

'No, don't be an idiot. It's work actually,' I lie. I haven't been thinking about the Mrs Khan case at all, but pretending that I have serves to give an air of moral superiority to my rum-fuelled jealousy and self-pity.

As we speak, Ana María and the Cuban come and sit at our table. They are both flushed and laughing and Ana María seems to have forgotten all about the argument.

'Jamie, you haven't danced at all. Come and dance with me, Jamie.'

'No,' I say ungraciously, knowing anyway that I would make a complete fool of myself.

'You've got to dance,' she laughs. 'Come on.'

'Why? Is it an order from the Central Committee?'

'No, I just want to dance with you.' She reaches over and takes my wrist but I shake it off.

'Find someone else.'

She stares at me for a moment, her eyes wide like a child, as if I have slapped her, and I want to bite my tongue. What did I do that for? It is as if the whole evening is on a fast track to complete fuck-up and I can do nothing about it. I open my mouth but she has turned back to the Cuban, who shrugs dismissively in a what-do-you-expect-from-these-stupid-gringos? way and leads her back on to the dance floor. I pour myself more rum and don't put any Coke in it. Colin claps me on the back.

'Excellent, Jamie. You handled that quite brilliantly. Maybe you should ease up a little on the rum. I say this for your own good, not out of any moral objection, you understand.'

The bucket is waved at me again and I put another pound in.

'You're going to solve the financial problems of the entire island at this rate. And end up with fewer friends. Slow down, Jamie . . . And see you, speccy, that's the third time you've been round with that bucket trying to take advantage of the fact my pal's a wee bit pissed, so take it away and ask somebody else or you'll be wearing it home, OK?'

The man with the bucket stares at him indignantly. 'It's not for me you know, the money, it's for the Cuban people.' I had spotted him earlier on the dance floor, waving his arms about joyfully to the salsa, with a happy disregard for the rhythm. He is wearing a brightly coloured T-shirt which says "Democracy in the country and in the home". I can see how everything about him would annoy Colin, especially the way he said Cuban people with the earnest drawing out of the last syllable. Still, that doesn't mean Colin can start picking on him.

'Colin, let's go.'

'Now? I promised that Colombian she could have the next dance.'

'Please.'

'OK, let me just go and get her name and number.'

I finish my rum and say goodbye to Eduardo, who has been arguing most of the night with some fellow Chileans who are all pot-bellied with leather jackets and moustaches. Eduardo flaps his hand impatiently at his opponent as I approach. He can see how drunk I am and looks at me with concern.

'Your friend is taking you home, yes?'

'I hope so.'

'OK, Jamie. Jamie?' He looks like he wants to tell me something but then thinks better of it. 'Don't worry. Another time.'

As we leave, I turn to see Ana María and the Cuban sitting alone at a table. He is holding her hand across the table, playing with her fingers, examining her ring, and she is laughing. She looks across at me as we leave but her expression does not change. That's it, I hate her now.

'Carlita,' says Colin, fishing for his car keys, 'Carlita from Peckham. She's going to teach me how to dance. Shame about Peckham really.'

I slump into the passenger seat. 'Colin?'

'Yeah.'

'I don't want to go home. I want to go for a drink.'

'Pubs are closed, Jamie. D'ya wanna go to a party?'

'Where?'

'Shoreditch.'

'Yeah.'

We drive through south London, past the pink shopping centre at the Elephant, on to the drab Southwark streets. We take a wrong turning and end up on the Old Kent Road, where baggy-jeaned white youths eating kebabs stare us out at the traffic lights. 'Millworl,' mocks Colin, staring straight back at them. 'No one likes you . . . I can't think why.' I want to go back and say sorry to Ana María and tell her that I am in love with her, but Kennington is getting further and further away, and the feeling of misery and humiliation stronger and stronger. Colin gathers speed as we approach Tower Bridge. 'This bridge . . .' he says, waving a contemptuous goodbye to south London, '. . . is mad.' I nod in drunken agreement, because it *is* mad, this twin-towered icon repeated in silhouette on countless ash-trays and mugs and plastic table-mats. A bridge that can suddenly stop being a bridge, a road that is no longer a road, that can split in two – and not just for any old ship – causing the kind of excitement that children feel at a railway level crossing when the barrier is down and the red lights are flashing and they know that a train will come rushing past, that *something strange and exciting is going to happen*. But there is no show tonight, no great ship to force the elaborate machinery into action and we are almost over the river, passing the Tower of London where traitors languished before being led to the block. I suddenly remember an argument which seems to have taken place weeks rather than hours ago and I vaguely wonder whether having your head chopped off would be worse than being dragged before a firing squad and waiting for the bullets to smash into your body.

At the traffic lights a motor-cycle draws level with us, the woman passenger is clinging to the waist of the driver who has spectacles and a sandy moustache, Colin is singing along to *Burn Rubber on Me*, and this is mad and I really . . . I really . . .

. . . I feel sick. Perhaps I should tell Colin to stop the car, and lean over the barrier to gaze down and gift my rum-soaked insides to the swift-flowing Thames. Or better still, stand up on the barrier, wave cheerio to Colin and take the plunge, feet first like an arrow into the river's blackness. Because this is a bridge too fucking far. I should drop to the bottom, slowly expiring in the depths of the dark river, sighing for love, gurgling for love, love bubbling from my mouth, the choir of love among the mud and the fish and the detritus of Old Father Thames: the turds and the condoms, the unwanted Christmas puppies stuffed in rucksacks, the unlucky gangsters with their feet snugly embedded in a concrete plinth like a sculpture park or trophy display on the bottom of the river, perhaps even a couple of O'Leary's relatives hanging out down there after lazy housing officers messed up their transfers. But the river is clean now. They say that the variety of fish in it has multiplied astonishingly. Maybe smiling dolphins glide through its crystal waters, maybe a ray of moonlight illuminates a golden-haired cockney mermaid singing upon a shell, a fishy tail curled around her, maybe even the spotty flounder – that dismembered cardboard fish we used to piece together as children. And I could have stopped it. I never think that things are my fault but maybe they are. I didn't need to stand up for some dead drug-dealing general and if I hadn't it might have been me holding the hand of Ana María across the table instead of the Cuban, although still not dancing with her because, as well as not being able to drive, I can't really dance salsa. I did get my bronze medal for swimming, but I don't know where it is now. I heard the whistle and splashed obediently with all the others into the pool in my red pyjamas, doggy-paddling while my arms and legs puffed up with chlorinated water like an astronaut's suit. What am I doing? Maybe I should just go home, maybe I should go back to Stepney, get Colin to drop me at the top of Sidney Street and go wandering until I end up in some Twilight zone, transported to a Dickensian London of fog and gas-lamps and ladies of the night shivering behind their shawls. But no, see you later Pip old chap, because I'm going to a party to join in what may or may not be among the most morbid symptoms of this dreary interregnum, when it should be me sitting holding Ana María's hand before leading her on to the dance floor, while people stop in amazement at the sheer beauty of our perfectly co-ordinated waist-swaying salsa movements and then driving her home to Stepney (when will that be, chortle the cynical bells) instead of being driven away, far away, from Kennington towards Shoreditch by ma best fuckin' pal Colin who would be hurt if he knew that I would happily haul him out of the car and chuck him straight into the Thames if I could replace him with Ana María. And I do still have a question to ask, a last request concerning the price of that doggy in the window, the very small fat one with the waggly tail, the real furry whimpering doglet that pees on the carpet and cries at night, yes that fucking doggy, not the bold borzoi hunting down wolves, because the real wolf is still probably face down snoring in its cage in the London Zoo. It's too expensive for you, chime the cynical bells of Stepney, you rum-swilling moaning drunken bastard, it's out of your reach the doggy with the waggly tail, it's gone off with a dancing Cuban. Take a leaf, my son, out of the book of Colin the best fuckin' pal in the world, better than any doggy invisible or otherwise, the Celtic Obelix who fell into the magic potion and is now very kindly driving you to a party so that you can drown even further in your stupid drunken self-pity. Because meanwhile, Mrs Khan listens to the taunting wails and the hideous shrieks of the local youth and she couldn't give a fuck about the size, price or waggly tail of the doggy in the window because she's more worried about the brick shattering the glass in her own and, yes, I am very very very pissed heading across Tower Bridge with my cheery Scottish pal who is not nearly as drunk and I'll tell you what: I'm glad I'm not in a mini-cab with one of those traffic light air fresheners or the dangling pine trees, and some cabbie bastard pretending he doesn't know the best route. And I love my friend Obelix too, he's all right, he's got the bear necessities . . . Ah shut up, cry the bells of Stepney, you'll never grow rich, so just shut up you drunken wild bore. And they're gonna 'ave their clappers pulled out soon those bells 'cause they've bin givin' it the big 'un all right, the poxy slags, 'cause now what is it they're chiming? Is she really gonna take him home tonight. So give me a sov, a butterfly knife, I'm a plane losing height, because I'm drunk and I tend to repeat myself when I'm drunk I tend to repeat myself when I'm drunk. Oh please just take me home.

The party is held under some railway arches and bullet-headed bouncers in bomber jackets are scrutinizing the entrants. 'All right Colin,' one of them says as we approach and we go in without paying anything. There are three rooms and a bar for which you have to pay in cloakroom tickets purchased from another room. Colin troops off to find some E. 'I'd offer you one, Jamie, but you're mashed enough as it is. Now, where the fuck's Scott got to, it's imperative that I get some drugs . . .' I stand swaying slightly. Light is splintering off the ceiling and walls, flickering crazily across the floor. On the wall is a huge white sheet with THE UNEXAMINED LIFE painted in black letters. There is a slide of a blue Cadillac with no wheels. Why hasn't it got any wheels? I watch a couple dancing, clutching bottles of water, playing at trying to stamp on the fragments of light racing around the room. A desperately pretty girl is dancing by the speakers, dry ice swirling around her as if she is in the clouds. My eyes are full of the lights, my ears stopped by the hardness of the music which is making my throat tremble.

As Colin seems to have disappeared I buy a ticket instead and go to the neon-lit bar area where a series of slides flash up: a fly feasting on a sugar cube, a Buddhist monk in flames in Vietnam, somebody falling from a window, a couple in a 69 position. I don't like the slides but I can't think straight enough to decide why and anyway this is no time for analysis. An angelic-faced boy is holding his head in his hands and muttering to himself while a girl in a tiny pink dress whispers in his ear. Somebody starts yelling loudly at the barman about wanting a bottle of Jack Daniel's. The barman who is skinny and pale explains that they only do shots and not bottles. He grows impatient when the man keeps moronically repeating Jack Daniel's over and over again and eventually says, 'Nash, ya cunt,' and turns to serve somebody else. The man mumbles some abuse at the barman which, even in my condition, I can see is probably an error. The barman stares at the man as if he is recording his face for a future moment and then turns and smiles at the next person. 'What can I get you darlin'?' Standing in the queue will give me a purpose, so I squeeze in behind the last couple waiting. The girl turns to look at me and I realize that it is Iona and that by her side is someone who can only be Malcolm.

'Jamie. Hello sweetheart,' Iona murmurs spacily. She looks different from when we normally meet, wearing a very short flimsy red satiny dress. I open my mouth to say that I don't want to be called sweetheart but then close it again because I like Iona. She smiles dreamily and dances slightly on the spot, shaking her head from side to side, appearing to look right through me.

Malcolm is very tall and high-cheek-boned, with closely cropped hair, a white jumper and tartan trousers. He frowns down at me.

'Do we know each other?'

'I don't think so.'

'This is Jamie,' says Iona. 'He's my friend. Jamie's my friend. Aren't you darling? Oh . . .' she breaks off enthusiastically as she hears a record she obviously likes – but which isn't significantly different from all the previous records – and starts to dance around us, waving her arms in the air.

Malcolm looks me up and down in a condescending manner and then laughs and shakes his head slightly. 'A friend of Iona's,' he says slowly, and then repeats, 'A friend of Iona's. The thing is, Iona doesn't have friends as far as I know. You see, Iona knows two types of men. Those she gets her drugs off and those she's fucking.' He leans towards me slightly. 'I don't quite see you in the first category, but I must confess that I would be slightly disappointed with Iona if you fell into the second.'

I stare at him. OK, so he is definitely being rude to me. Which means that I am entitled to be rude back. In fact it means that it is essential that I am rude back. I spend too much time dodging arguments, smiling at people, deflecting aggression. Well, I'm not at work now and I'm not taking it from the Malcolms of this world, however elegant his bone structure is.

A sudden image flashes in my mind. Colin once told me about a party he gatecrashed for some opening where there was an enormous ice swan in the middle of the gallery. All my drunken fury at the disastrous evening is about to burst loose. I remember Malcolm's exhibition and the swastika in its triangle of neon tubes. I imagine the ice swan slowly melting in the midst of the bad art and the drug patter, water dripping from its disappearing beak like tears. I think of Ana María and the Cuban foxy gentleman.

'You know something?'

Malcolm arches an eyebrow expectantly.

'You're a wanker.'

Malcolm smiles. 'Very good. I didn't expect you to be quite so articulate.'

'No, but wait a minute. Let me explain why. You go to parties with ice swans. That's what I hate about you actually. And you call yourself an artist. But how can you be an artist when you know nothing?'

Images flicker crazily across my mind like slides: the boy who tried to knife Khaled, the cracked photo inside Mr Carmichael's house, the misery of Dean Anderton's mum, tears dropping on to Mrs Khan's foot.

A sneer crosses Malcolm's face and he turns to Iona. 'You really must introduce me to your friends more often, Iona. You've surpassed yourself this time, darling.' And he gives a nasty shrill little laugh.

I can't remember deciding to do it but I swing my arm at his face. I flail at Malcolm, managing to catch him round the ear even though the plan was to go for his nose. He grabs me easily and pins me up against the wall. 'You are stupid and incoherent and drunk. Now get out of here,' he says.

'What? Who do you think you are? Fuck off, you pretentious

wanker,' and I spit in his face since my arms are pinned against the wall.

'Stop it, Jamie,' wails Iona. 'What are you doing?' Malcolm is raising his arm to strike me, but fatally pauses to wipe his face, just allowing enough time for an all too familiar figure to hurtle through the crowd, catch him by his upstretched arm, spin him around and, stretching cobra-like to his full height, strike him full in the face with his head. Malcolm drops to the floor, clutching his face, blood dripping on to his white jumper. Iona cries out and bends down to him but he pushes her off. 'Leave me alone, you stupid bitch. This is all your fault anyway.'

'Don't call her a bitch.' I kick him hard on his leg, using the wall to support me so that he topples over. I have dropped my bar ticket somewhere.

'I've wanted to do that for some time, Montgomery,' snarls Colin at Malcolm as he picks himself up again, 'but I could never quite find the excuse. And if you ever go near Jamie again . . .' A group of people stand like dummies staring at us. Malcolm's face is more incredulous than pained. Fortunately, the bouncers are nowhere to be seen. A woman's voice in the background of the record is saying PLEASE DON'T BE ANGRY WITH ME over and over again and the slide has changed to an image of goose-stepping Nazis, arms stretched before them in a rigid *Sieg Heil*. The next slide reads: Our moments of joy are planned with military precision.

'It was him,' says Malcolm, 'he just went crazy. What do you mean go near him again? I never wanted to go near him in the first place. He spat in my face. He tried to punch me. Didn't he?' He appeals to the watching group, who turn away shrugging disgustedly at the entire scene.

'You're a wanker,' I say, feeling I had better not change my line of argument. 'You go to parties with ice swans, you put swastikas in your paintings just because you feel like it, and you know nothing.'

Iona starts to laugh manically. 'The stupid thing is,' she says suddenly, 'he's right.'

Malcolm casts us a look of utter contempt. 'You're such a bunch of losers.' When Malcolm says the word losers, his glance lingers provocatively on Colin. I suddenly understand something about the world they inhabit and why Colin must hate him so much.

Colin steps closer to him. His body is stretching and tensing again. Iona pulls his arm. 'Stop it now,' she says. 'Just stop it please, Colin.'

Although Colin is not as tall as Malcolm he seems to be looming above him. 'Losers?' he says slowly. 'Yeah, maybe I'm a loser. But I'll give you a bit of advice. See those trousers of yours. I don't like them. Us losers can develop some irrational prejudices and one of mine is about the English wearing tartan. And I especially don't like it when it's a cunt like you. So keep them away from me or next time you won't be standing up to call me a loser. And if you ever, ever go near Jamie again I'll fucking kill you. Know what I mean?'

Malcolm stares at him silently.

'I said, do you know what I mean?' repeats Colin, edging nearer.

'Yeah,' says Malcolm sullenly.

'So you know what I mean then?'

'Yes. I know what you mean.'

'Good.' Colin turns to me. 'Come on Jamie, let's get you home.'

'Wait Colin, I've dropped my ticket. Excuse me . . .' I say to Malcolm '. . . I think you might be standing on my ticket.'

Iona and Colin start to laugh. 'Come on Jamie,' Colin says. He pushes through to the bar. 'Stevie. Give us two bottles of Becks. I'll sort you out later.'

'And a bottle of Jack Daniel's,' I say, but Stevie doesn't seem to find this funny and just hands Colin the beers.

'If you find the ticket,' I turn to Iona, 'you can have it. It has number 47 on it. Or Maybe it's 74.'

'Yeah, thanks, Jamie.'

Colin strides through the party, brushing people out of the way while I try and keep up with him, watching his back anxiously like a lone duckling in flapping pursuit of its mother. The bouncers are talking to a young policeman, the blue light of the car is pulsing off the walls of the arches. Another policeman sits in the car talking on the radio. The bouncers are joking now with the policeman and wink at Colin as he passes. 'Excuse me please, officer,' says Colin as we squeeze out of the door and into the cold air of morning.

We drive through the back streets. Spitalfields is like an abandoned film set, no sign of movement behind the darkened windows of the restaurants and Halal butchers. Yet at the corner of Commercial Street there is a flash of white miniskirt and bare legs as a young girl stands with her face turned bravely to the headlights of the oncoming traffic and it seems as if she might just be swept away into the slipstream of the lorries which thunder past her. A young rubber-legged drunk abandoned by his mates in the grimy, claustrophobic streets turns and shouts 'Cab!' as we pass and then flaps his hand disgustedly after us.

'I'm sorry,' I say.

'What the fuck for?'

'I've really messed things up.'

'Stop feeling sorry for yourself. And don't worry about that radge Malcolm Montgomery, he deserved that totally.'

'I don't believe in fighting really.'

'Aye, right. And next time don't kick him on the leg. Go for the ribs at least. Jamie, I'm starvin'. Have you got any money? I could murder a couple of bagels. Don't worry, you stay in the car. What do you want? Cream cheese? Tuna?'

'I gave all my change to Cuba. Here, I've got a tenner. I don't care. Anything.'

I sit in the car gazing transfixed at a poster peeling off the wall which says 'Drive the Nazis out of Brick Lane.' Colin returns with the bagels.

'I got you cream cheese, OK?'

'Fine. Colin?'

'Mmm?'

'We've got to drive the Nazis out of Brick Lane. It says so.'

'I'm not driving them anywhere. It's bad enough having some love-struck idiot who's just caned two bottles of rum in the car.'

'Do you think I'll have a chance with Ana María?'

'Well, not tonight, Jamie. But who knows what tomorrow will bring.'

'I do actually. It's gonna bring me untold embarrassment and a terrible hangover. Colin?'

'What is it? I'm trying to drive and eat a bagel at the same time for fuck's sake. The cream cheese won't stay in the bagel, it keeps coming out of the hole. There's more on the steering wheel than in my stomach.'

'You can sleep on the sofa if you want.'

'Yeah, I think I will. Fuck, I forgot. I paid for that E and I never got it in the end because of that shenanigans.'

'Oh no. Sorry about that. Colin?'

'Jamie, just ask the question. I cannae see anyone else in the car so I'll assume that it's directed at me, OK?'

'Right. Sorry. Colin?' I start to giggle helplessly. 'No, that was a joke. No listen, right, what's she like, Carlita from Peckham?'

'Very nice. She's gonna teach me how to dance merengue. And I'm going to teach her that, when it comes to sexual technique, there's a few things we Scots can show those Latin lovers. She is going to find out how undeserved their reputation is once she's experienced the Broomhouse lovin' machine. Jamie?'

'Yes, Obelix?'

'What's pretty in Spanish?'

'*Bonita.*'

'Excellent. It even rhymes. Oh Carlita you're so *bonita.*'

'It was really nice to meet yer.'

'I'm glad you're not called Peter.'

''Cause your name's much neater.'

'You have the grace and poise of a cheetah.'

'I want to get my hands in your sweater.'

'That doesn't count.'

'It does if you say it in Scottish like I just did.'

'You sounded like Ian Paisley actually and anyway, Jamie, don't lower the tone.'

'I think I'm going to be sick.'

'Wait till we're out of the car. It's not mine. Is this Vallance Road coming up?'

'Could be.'

We turn into the Whitechapel Road, still full of the garbage and piled cardboard boxes from the market and I know that we're nearly home. I manage to fall over at least three times on the way upstairs to the flat. Finally, Colin drags me inside and dumps me on a chair. We finish the bottle of brandy that Iona brought the other night, watching and re-watching the video of Arsenal winning the championship at Anfield. At some point, in the middle of Colin explaining the voyage to unknown levels of sexual pleasure that awaits his new admiree, I fall into dark, dreamless oblivion.

Never Apologize

A ray of morning sunshine breaks through the gap in the curtain and falls on my face like a spotlight. I open my eyes with some difficulty and stare for a while at the window. Dust particles spin in the bright morning glow.

Rehydration before remembering. I get up, still wearing the shirt from the night before, and make my way to the kitchen. Colin is lying on the living-room sofa on his back, his arm dangling from the side of the sofa, fingers almost touching the empty bottle of brandy lying on its side on the floor.

The water is very cold and hurts my throat but I carry on drinking as if to wash away the nausea which is rising up in me and the memories of last night. I go to the toilet and piss, supporting myself with one hand on the sink by the side of the toilet, gazing through still blurred and sticky eyes at the changing colour of the water in the bowl. I must still be slightly drunk; all that alcohol cannot have left my system by now. My head is thumping and I have a horrible twitching feeling in my arms and legs so I stagger back to bed, take off last night's shirt, wrap the duvet tightly around me and fall asleep again.

When I awake it is early afternoon. The sky is a very clear cold blue with a bright pale sun and a few high white ribbings of cloud. There is music coming from the living-room; Colin is up and dressed, drinking a cup of tea, smoking a cigarette and listening to an old Grace Jones album.

171

'I always forget how great this record is,' he says on seeing me. 'The kettle's just boiled if you want some tea and I'm gonna make some scrambled eggs. Fuck, Jamie, you're a frightening sight.'

I slump into a chair and listen to the comforting sound of him busying himself in the kitchen, singing along to *Pull Up to the Bumper*. The lingering cigarette smoke increases my feeling of nausea. When Colin re-emerges carrying the pan of eggs and a plate of toast, he grins at me. 'What a night, Jamie.' We eat ravenously, tearing the toast to use for chasing pieces of egg around the pan and cramming it in our mouths, competing for the remaining food. I realize that one of the reasons I was so drunk yesterday was the fact that I had hardly eaten anything.

'Can you speak now?' asks Colin and I shake my head. After a silence, I say, 'I don't think I've got any friends left.'

'Ah bollocks, Jamie, you've got me. You've got Karen.'

'What about Ana María,' I say, 'what about us beating up Iona's boyfriend?'

'Yeah, that was brilliant. Dinnae worry about that, Jamie. The majority of people who know Malcolm will consider you a hero. It's probably not the first time it's happened either. And I'm sure you'll be able to make up with Ana María. She's a tough girl. Don't mix the two things up. Remember that Ana María didn't see the last bit, she'll get over your little tiff, you're one of *her* few friends.'

'Do you think I should phone Iona?'

'What for?' Colin begins to pick up the tiny remaining pieces of egg with his fingers.

'Well, to apologize, you know.'

'Never apologize, Jamie. Wait and see if she phones you. Remember, she was off her face, she probably won't remember that much about it. And Malcolm's not going to be that quick to remind her either. Listen Jamie, I've done some disgraceful things when I've been pissed. I just forget them and in the end everybody else does as well. The only way people remember is if you start phoning up and apologizing and saying you don't know what came over you and all that crap. Relax, enjoy your hangover, have a drink later on. It's much better in my opinion to get drunk and behave badly than be one of those boring bastards who takes a bottle of wine to a polite dinner party and only drinks a bit of it because they've got to drive or get up early the next day for work. I hate those fuckers.'

Images of some of Helen's dinner parties flash across my mind and I laugh. Colin is contentedly licking the wooden spoon from the saucepan. I wish I had his supreme self-confidence.

'Your problem is, Jamie, that you've fallen for Ana María in a bad way. I did at first but, you know, it was purely physical and I realized I didn't have a chance. I just like flirting with her. But you're a bit more serious. That's what's really bugging you if you're honest.'

'I don't think I've got a chance either.'

'I dunno. I think you should hang in there for a bit. She likes you a lot, I can tell. Otherwise, why did she get so worked up about a disagreement about shooting drug traffickers? . . . That reminds me, I'm gonna have to see Scott about that E I paid for . . . Plus, I saw her face when you told her to fuck off when she was asking you to dance. I don't know if she fancies you though.'

I change the subject and tell Colin about what is happening at work and my fear of some kind of retaliation from the King family or their accomplices. He offers to get some guys together to go down to the estate and sort them out. 'Most of them are Orange Lodge Jambo bastards who would probably vote BNP anyway but they'd still give these guys a kicking for you. The difficulty would be getting them down here . . . I'd give Blackie a ring but he's gone fuckin' weird lately. Started talking about getting back to nature and going to live in Libya, pure shite. I don't even know where he stays right now. Probably in Colonel Quadaffi's tent.'

'Yeah, thanks anyway Colin, I don't think that's the answer right now.'

'It's always the answer with those bastards. Taking one of them to court's gonna do fuck all.'

We sit and drink more coffee until Colin decides to go to his studio. I watch him from the window walking briskly down the street, his arms swinging, until he turns the corner to where he left the car. The kids in the flats opposite race around on bicycles. One little girl, pedalling furiously, does not notice the child moving across at right angles and they smash together, sending girl and bike skidding across the tarmac. She gets up brushing her knees, her jumper torn at the elbow, and picks up the bike which is slightly too big for her and wheels it away. She dabs at her eyes as she walks while the child responsible for the collision claps his hand over his mouth in mock laughter, shoulders shaking like a little Muttley. I lie on my back on the sofa with my eyes closed, allowing waves of fury and self-hate to wash over me. Why am I so clumsy? Why do I always make a mess of things?

The Sunday afternoon sky begins to darken and I feel a horrible, terrifying loneliness and depression descending upon me. It is the *Antiques Road Show* time of day. I dial Eduardo's number but hang up when he answers. Then I phone Helen's house but there is no reply. Finally I call Karen. Her flatmate answers and says she will not be back until late. The day continues its slide into evening. I have no energy for anything but lying on the sofa. The record finishes and I cannot be bothered to change it over. The TV remote control lies just a few inches from my hand but picking it up seems a terrible exertion. In these strange moments of failing light I fall asleep. When I wake again I force myself to have a bath and begin to feel slightly better as the hot water splashes over my stomach. My head under the water, I lie in a state of almost trancelike relaxation watching the condensation dripping from the ceiling. I wonder if it is true that having water dripping on to you would drive you mad. Suddenly, dimly, I hear the phone ring and leap out of the bath, splashing water chaotically and leaving Man Friday prints from bath to phone. I hold the receiver to my wet ear. It is Iona.

'How are you, Jamie?'

'Terrible. How are you?'

'Worse.'

'Did you stay long, you know, after we . . . erm . . . left.'

'I can't really remember. Malcolm was pretty angry as you can imagine and decided it was all my fault and wouldn't speak to me again so I came home on my own.'

'Have you spoken to him since?'

'Yeah, I phoned him but he was still furious. Saying he never wanted to see me again and threatening to press charges against you and Colin and that sort of crap.'

'He won't do that.'

'No.'

There is a pause and I watch a small puddle forming by my toes.

'I didn't expect to see you there,' she says.

'No, well, I wouldn't have gone but I was so drunk and I just wanted to go on drinking.'

'Didn't you think I might be there?'

'No. It never crossed my mind.'

'Oh well . . . what are you up to now?'

'Nothing, you know, just watching telly and stuff.'

'Do you want to come round?'

I look out at the dark cold night and think of the Sunday tube and getting into work on time tomorrow.

'I'd better not actually. I've got a big day ahead of me tomorrow at work and I feel terrible still.'

'OK. Jamie, phone me in the week won't you?'

'Yes.'

'We're still friends, right?'

'Of course.'

'I'll speak to you later then.'

She hangs up and I get back into my lukewarm bath and turn on the hot tap with my toes.

Rights for Whites

There is always something agreeable about the day after a terrible hangover; the sensation that it has lifted and that you can go about your normal business. I get to the office early so that I can catch up on some of the work that has been neglected because of the Mrs Khan case and ignore the copies of the Notices on King and Anderton which have been left on my desk. I write letters for overdue rent, a stern demand for the removal of a CB antenna which has been precariously set up from a top-floor flat window, and process minor repair requests. People begin arriving and feign astonishment at seeing me already seated at my desk, studiously going through my in-tray and drinking a cup of coffee.

Roy arrives. 'How's things, Jamie?'

'Fine.'

He sits on the edge of my desk. 'Well, it's all starting now. I've been on the phone to Legal about it and they'll probably want to talk to you. Also, the Monitoring Group phoned. Mrs Khan's had paint poured over her front door so you had better go and take a look at it. Take the polaroid camera. I think Jane had it last. We may need to give her bed and breakfast accommodation until her offer comes through. See what's happening and talk to the Monitoring Group, they've been round there a lot . . .'

The telephone rings and Roy pauses to let me take the call. A man with a strangely muffled voice says, 'Is that Mr Collins the housing officer?'

'Yes.'

'I'm just phoning to say that if you think sending court letters is going to change anything around here you're mistaken. Also, we know how to deal with traitors and we're watching you. We know where you live Mr Collins so keep looking over your shoulder. Be seeing you.' And the phone clicks down. I replace the receiver.

'That was my first threat.' I am shaking slightly.

'Right,' says Roy, 'write down exactly what was said to you. I'll get on the phone to the police.'

'What can they do about it though?'

'Not much. But we have to log every incident with them. And Jamie, I don't want you out on the estate too much on your own. I'll come with you to Mrs Khan's. We'll go about eleven, OK?'

'OK.' My calm paperwork mood has evaporated completely.

I feel confident walking briskly through the estate with Roy, even though there is no reason to think he would offer a great deal of protection if we were attacked. He has worked on the estate for some time and commands a certain amount of respect as he is both fair and impossible to intimidate. Once a lunatic tried to strangle him in the reception area after claiming that Roy had ordered a black angel to hide inside his flat and whisper atrocious urgings in his ear. The caretaker is out sweeping leaves from the pathway and nods at us as we pass.

'There's something strange about Mrs Reynolds's daughter,' I say to Roy. 'It's like she wants to talk to me but doesn't know how to. She was the one who first gave me Anderton and King's names as the principal culprits. She might have said more but her mum was calling for her.'

'Well, there's not a great deal you can do about it. Maybe she'll get in touch with you.'

178

Throwing the House Out of the Window

'I don't know, she's had the chance but she hasn't taken it up.'

We arrive at Mrs Khan's house. The front door and the step are covered in green paint. On the path to the house somebody has used a stick to write 'Paki Grass'. Roy takes a couple of photos from different angles. The pictures slide out, gradually emerging from nothingness to take form and colour before our eyes. We knock on the door and I call through the letter-box until the door is opened. It is not Mrs Khan who opens the door but a young man who turns out to be a nephew from Leicester. He is angry. 'Until we come down she wasn't even putting the lights on. They used to be in the dark at night so that they would think they weren't in. They were using candles, the bloody house could have burned down with the kids and everything. You know they've got dogs, they bring dogs with them sometimes.'

Mrs Khan emerges looking tired, one of her children dragging around her leg. 'Hello Mr Collins, Mr Tomlinson, come through.' We go into the living-room and one of the children is dispatched to bring glasses and juice. She comes back carefully carrying a large tray then stands shyly in front of Roy, holding out the glass with both hands. 'Thank you very much.' He takes it and sets it down equally carefully on the table in front of him. 'Now Mrs Khan, you know that securing an eviction is going to take some time. A month has to go past before the case can even go to court. We have now made you a Category One case so you should be getting an offer very soon. In the meantime, I have approval to offer you bed and breakfast accommodation if you wish to take that up.'

'A hostel?'

'Yes.'

'I was in hostel before they offer me this flat. I do not want to go back to hostel. Very bad place.'

'It would only be for a short time until we have a proper offer sorted out. We could have done it quicker but we don't get many four-bedroom properties at the minute.'

'No, I don't want to go to hostel. Now Akhtar is here with me I would rather stay here. And the people from the Monitoring Group have been very good. I wait here until flat come.'

'OK, if you're sure.'

'Yes, I do not want hostel. Very bad place for children. We will have same problem in hostel,' she shivers.

'Yes, it's not very good for children.'

I say that I am going to check whether Mr Peters has been keeping his diary sheets over the last few days.

'OK,' Roy says, 'but come back via Folkestone Road, not through the estate.'

As Mr Peters opens the door I hold out my ID card like a police badge and he laughs. 'Good lad. You're learning fast.' He shuffles over to the sideboard and picks up the diary sheet. He holds it out like a script and clears his throat. 'Thursday October 24th, 10.30 p.m. Group of youths outside Keats House with pitbulls. Youths making dogs bark. Knocking on door of 8 Keats House and throwing objects at windows and shouting. Saturday, October 26th, 11.45 p.m. Same youths plus others outside Keats House. Shouting and swearing. One youth who I can identify as being Jason King throws can of paint at door of Keats House. I phone police at 11.55. Police arrive at 12.25 by which time youths have dispersed. Is that OK Mr Collins?'

'That's perfect. I'll take that back to the office.'

'Sit down, I'll put the kettle on.'

'No, it's OK, I've just had a drink.'

'What, no time for a little chat? Don't be silly, go on, they won't miss you back at the office.'

'All right then, you twisted my arm.'

We sit and drink tea while Mr Peters tells me about his time in the Navy and working in the docks. 'They used to sound a siren,' he says, 'when the ships come in.' He shows me more photos of his years boxing and the various stages of his granddaughters' development. I sit lulled by the recounting of his stories: memories of the Blitz, his brother Ted whose boat was torpedoed at sea and whose wallet, containing the letter he was writing to them before the ship went down, was washed up later and returned to the family. He tells me about moving into the new estate. 'Used to be lovely this estate, even won a prize,' he says and I listen and murmur assent from time to time, happy to just let him talk, his old man's voice strangely soothing, almost hypnotic, as I cup my mug of tea feeling the warm china against the palms of my hands.

Back in the office I phone Eduardo's house and swallow nervously as Ana María picks up the phone.

'It's Jamie.'

'Oh, hello Jamie. How are you?'

'Fine. I wasn't too good yesterday but I'm OK now.'

She laughs. 'Yes, I imagine yesterday you have a bit of a bad head.'

'You could say that. Anyway, what are you up to?'

'Oh, not much, reading, writing to my stepmother. I go now to buy some food. Are you at work?'

'Yes.'

'Would you like to come and eat tonight? I am cooking.'

'Yes, I'd really like that.'

'OK, come after your work.'

'See you later then.'

A shiver of happiness runs through me as I return to work. I am going to see Ana María tonight. It is still *before* seeing her, a long way from *after* seeing her. I will leave the office at five o'clock and take the bus to Clapton. There's plenty of time.

A letter has arrived from Mr O'Leary's probation officer, supporting his application for a transfer on the grounds that he is under threat of extreme violence. There is even a letter from the police backing this up. As O'Leary is only in need of a one-bedroom flat and will go absolutely anywhere in the borough, this makes his move much easier. I get Roy to sign my request for him to be upgraded to Category One and pass it on to Bob Townsend. Then there is the question of the gate for the Folkestone Road maisonettes and I fill out the required forms for an application to the Safer City Crime Prevention Fund. Later in the afternoon O'Leary comes in to see me.

'Did you get the letter from my probation officer?'

'Yes. And the police. We've upgraded you to a Category One. Given that you're so flexible about where you go, you should be out very quickly.'

'It'd better be quick. It's not comfortable sleeping in a car. You should try it, mate. I don't care where I go, as long as it's off the estate.'

Although his eyes are still unblinking and he maintains his aggression, some of the overt hostility seems to have gone out of him. He no longer terrifies me.

'And you don't mind if it's a tower block?'

'Prefer it. Top floor if possible. The higher the better. Also, I want you to deal with it, not that useless wanker Bob Townsend.'

I feel like a mob lawyer deemed capable of sorting the legal problems of the Godfather. Since it makes little sense to enlighten O'Leary as to the actual functioning of local authority housing departments, and given that he will very shortly be somebody else's problem due to his lack of fussiness about where he goes, I nod solemnly, accepting my responsibility. As he leaves he makes the completely astonishing gesture of turning to shake my hand.

'What's up?' Trevor asks as I return to my desk.

'O'Leary just shook my hand.'

'You'd better not mess up his transfer or it will be your neck he's shaking you by.'

'He's as good as gone.'

'What if the people looking for him start coming after you?'

I can see Trevor is on his positive tip again. He can get to be a real pain at times, pointing out everything that is likely to go wrong for you. He is at his worst if you buy anything, because, with total inevitability, he has seen it for at least a tenner less somewhere else. He has one fatal Achilles' heel, however.

'Did you find out who did that to your car?'

'Did what?' His head jerks up.

'I thought you must have seen it. Some kids have snapped the aerial off and scratched up the paintwork. I saw it this morning and thought it must have happened yesterday.'

'Fucking bastards! I'll find them, I'll find them and kill them, I know who it'll be.' And he leaps from his seat and charges down the stairs towards the car park.

As he leaves the office, Bob Townsend turns round giggling. 'I can't believe he's fallen for it again.'

Roy wags his finger at me, laughing. When Trevor comes back in puzzled, everyone bends over their desks studiously.

'What are you talking about, Jamie, there's nothing wrong with . . .'

But somebody cannot restrain a splutter of laughter and the penny teeters on the edge and finally drops. 'You bastard, Collins. I'll get you back, you know that.'

Bob swings round on his chair. 'How can you fall for it every time, you dozy sod?'

'How come you're so crap at your job?' Trevor shoots back. 'The world is full of such unsolved mysteries: the identity of Jack the Ripper, crop circles, whether the CIA shot Kennedy and why Bob Townsend can't perform a perfectly straightforward task like getting someone a transfer.'

'This is what I like in the office,' Roy intervenes. 'The gentle hum of contented, industrious staff, the sound of biros on rent arrears sheets.'

'The ebb and flow of Campbell's bullshit,' growls Bob, stung by the reference to his professional failings.

'Sorry Bob,' Trevor replies, 'I'm sure you just appear to be completely rubbish. Deep down there's probably a really efficient allocations officer just bursting to get out. I know you're only a victim of the system really.'

'Right, that's enough,' says Roy, spinning round on his chair. 'Trevor, go and buy some biscuits, Bob, make everyone a cup of tea.'

'What about Jamie? He started all of this.'

'Jamie can answer both your phones.'

At this point, however, there is the sudden and terrifying sound of glass shattering downstairs followed by a car screeching away. Everybody rushes down the stairs. The window next to Housing Benefits is completely smashed and Maggie is sobbing and picking shards of glass out of her hair. The brick which came through only just missed her head. Jagged pieces of glass lie like transparent fangs all over her desk and the cheese plant that the brick did hit has fallen to the ground spilling soil and leaves in all directions. Joan leads Maggie off to the kitchen to make her a cup of tea. I pick up a jagged piece of glass which curves into an evil point and touch it against the ball of my thumb.

'Do you think . . .?' I turn to Roy, who is trying to get through to somebody on the phone. He shrugs.

'I don't know.'

But the question is soon answered by Rosemary McKee, who is in charge of reception.

'Come and have a look at this.'

We troop out shivering into the cold evening air. On a wall round by the side of the office is a huge newly painted swastika and the words 'RIGHTS FOR WHITES'. Using a different spray can, somebody has written in smaller letters 'exept Paki lovers'. We stand for a few seconds shivering, our breath making clouds in front of us. A police car arrives, parks carelessly and two officers get out, their tiny radios crackling. 'I understand you've had a problem with vandals again,' the first officer says to Roy as we all file back into the warmth and light of the office. 'Bloody kids.'

Sleepless in Stepney

Ana María opens the door and smiles at me as I stand stamping my feet in the bitter cold. She kisses me lightly on the cheek as always.

'Jamie! You are freezing to death, no?'

'I am freezing to death yes. Here, take this.' I hand her a bottle of wine.

'Come into the kitchen. You can talk to me while I cook.'

I sit at the kitchen table watching her chop an onion. She does it in a strange way by slicing the top off and then hitting the surface very quickly and hard with the knife. Tiny pieces of onion cascade on to the plate in front of her. Tears stream down her face and she brushes her hair away to wipe her eyes.

'Jamie, please pass me the . . .' She points to a roll of kitchen towel. 'I hate chopping onion.' I tear off the kitchen roll and hand it to her but her hands are full of knife and onion. 'Could you . . .?' I carefully dab at the tears on her cheek with the paper and she smiles suddenly. I feel that someone is using my stomach as an accordion. What if I just did it? What if I just kissed her? What if the smile disappeared suddenly and she said she thought it would be better if I left? I sit down again. The onion sizzles as she sweeps it into the oil. I tell her about the attack on the office, the painted swastika.

'That sort of threat, they are the same the world over. And you never know when or where they will do something next.' She begins to chop fiercely at some coriander. I can't help

185

wondering, as I watch her, whether she slept with the Cuban, and what went on while I was disgracing myself at the party. I bring that thought to a halt with a lunging two-footed tackle, forcing myself back to the idea of what would have happened if the brick had hit Maggie's head.

Ana María suddenly looks at me slant-eyed. 'So how is Colin?'

'He's fine.'

She drops a tomato into some hot water. I watch its skin crack and open, curling up from the heat like a Chinese fortune-telling fish in the palm of a hand.

'What did you . . . I mean did he take you home afterwards?'

'We went to a party.'

'Oh,' she says coldly, lifting the tomato out with a spoon and pulling off the skin.

'It wasn't very good.'

Ana María waves the knife in the air as if this is of no interest to her whatsoever.

'What did you do . . . you know, afterwards?' I say, feeling my cheeks reddening. She ignores me for a second, digging out the core of the tomato and starting to cut the red pulp into pieces.

'We went home,' she says, glancing at me.

'Right,' I say, wondering who 'we' means and which 'home' she is referring to. 'Look, I'm sorry we argued and everything. I didn't want that to happen. I was looking forward to it and everything.'

'Yes,' she replies. 'That was a pity.'

There is a desperate silence. Ana María sweeps the tomato into the pan with the onion and turns up the heat. After a while it begins to bubble fiercely, juice from the sauce flying out of the pan and flecking on to the cooker. She snatches her hand back as a bit spits out on to her wrist.

'Shouldn't you turn it down a bit?'

'No,' she says, but then does.

Eduardo comes into the kitchen. 'Ah, Jamie,' and Ana María says quickly, 'I have forgotten something important, I am going to the shop.' Eduardo sits down opposite me and pours himself a glass of wine.

'How are you, Jamie?'

'I'm OK. Sorry about the other night, Eduardo. I kind of messed things up.'

He swallows his wine. 'Not all of the blame is yours, Jamie, Ana María did not behave so well. She has got to learn that somebody disagreeing is not . . . how do you British say it . . . high treason. But Jamie, you know that I notice many things and I suspect that you are falling a little in love with Ana María?'

I feel as if I am going scarlet. 'What makes you say that?'

He raises his eyebrows. 'It does not matter. What I want to say to you is to be careful and remember a few things. Ana María has had many problems, she is very unsettled and confused. She is in a strange place, she is quite lonely and homesick. But it is more than that, she has a very unclear future. What is she going to do in Chile if she went back? She does not have any job. What is she going to do here? She have no papers. So she is terribly confused, quite unhappy. You have been good for her, but I'm not sure if it is entirely wise to go further than that at the moment.'

I feel a surge of anger. 'What, is it not included in the five-year plan then? Look, it's a bit late for this sort of talk Eduardo. Even assuming that you're right in your diagnosis which I don't admit for a moment, you can't go around telling people what they should feel. Did she ask you to say this to me? Is that why she went out?'

Eduardo looks genuinely surprised by this question. 'Don't be ridiculous, Jamie. You underestimate her if you think that. As far as I could see she went out because the topic of your conversation had upset her.'

'Yes, maybe. Anyway, I really don't think you've got any worries on this score. What about that Cuban? Shouldn't you be doing the concerned stepfather routine with him?'

Eduardo laughs and slaps my shoulder. 'I can see I have made you angry, Jamie. I am not terribly good at this sort of thing and it's the last time we'll talk about it. Believe me, I would be very happy if things could work out properly for you. As for the Cuban . . .' he roars with laughter '. . . that *pobre huevón* has been phoning about fifty times since he met her. Well, this is all quite flattering for Ana and he is very nice person. But really . . .' he laughs again and wipes his eyes '. . . one of the terrible things about jealousy, Jamie, is that it also makes you a bit of a *huevón*.' And he goes on laughing.

'Yeah, thanks a lot, Eduardo. Go on, enjoy yourself, have a good laugh.' But the howl of laughter with which he meets this wounded statement forces me to laugh as well. Ana María comes back into the kitchen with a box of eggs from the little shop downstairs.

'What are you two laughing at?'

'Men's talk, *mi hija.*'

'Well, I don't know about that. They say Chilean men are *machista* but English men are just as bad. They say really disgusting things to you. I just pass men on the stair and they say really terrible things to me.'

'You should be glad you are young and beautiful,' says Eduardo. 'Some women will never have things said to them. It would be worse to be ugly and nobody ever say anything to you. *I* wouldn't mind if women . . .'

Ana María throws the dirty washing-up cloth in his face before he can finish. 'I was wrong. Chilean men *are* worse.'

The atmosphere improves as we are eating. Soledad comes in and winks at me. Then she sits down beside Ana María and opens her mouth imploringly for some food like a puppy. Ana María smiles and holds out a fork to her mouth but as Soledad moves open-mouthed towards it she pulls it away. They repeat this game several times, giggling, until finally Soledad grabs her hand and forces it towards her mouth. 'You win,' says Ana María and Soledad grins. 'I always win.' When she gets up she stands behind Ana María gathering her hair in her hands into a pony tail. The phone rings and Soledad picks it up. 'I said no,' she snaps straight away and puts it down again.

'Who was that?' I ask.

'Oh, it could have been a few people. But it applies to all of them.'

'I hope it wasn't someone from Chile,' frowns Eduardo.

'Oh, especially them,' replies Soledad.

Later that night, when I am leaving, Ana María accompanies me to the door.

'Thank you for phoning, Jamie. I hope everything goes well at work.'

She leans forward to kiss me, but instead of my cheek, as if by accident our lips meet. I reach out my hand to her shoulder but she pulls back quickly, shaking her head slightly. She smiles at me from the hall. 'Bye, Jamie. Call me.'

The door shuts behind me. It is starting to snow lightly, the tiny flakes melting immediately on contact with the ground. The windows of all the flats are steamed over and cars are covered with a light film of frost. 'Lovely weather,' says a man as we pass on the stairs. The streets are deserted and there is nobody standing at the bus stop. I look at the timetable in the way that one does at night even though it is completely pointless. A posse of youths suddenly emerges from behind me, hoods pulled over their heads. I tense slightly but a voice from under one of the hoods says, 'Yo Jamie, you're gonna freeze to death man,' followed by Patrick's unmistakable giggle.

'All right Patrick,' I say, relieved.

'Looks like your spar think we was gonna mug him Patrick,' says his friend, to which I don't have an answer.

'Shut up man,' says Patrick. 'Soledad up there?'

'Yeah.'

'All right, I'll catch up with you,' he says to his friends. 'I'm gonna wait with Jamie for his bus.'

At that moment the bus swings round the corner. 'You're in luck,' he says. 'Later, Jamie.'

'Yeah. Thanks anyway, Patrick.'

That night I lie in bed with a tape playing, thinking about the evening. I think of our lips meeting at the door, the shake of the head as she withdrew into the flat and Eduardo's words – very unhappy and confused. The words run round and round my mind. Lonely, unhappy and confused. I turn my head to the window. The snow has got much thicker now, swirling around the orange glow of the street lamps. It is obviously going to settle.

Retribution

Throughout the next week, small incidents occur at the office. Superglue is put in the lock of the door, air rifle pellets are fired at the windows and all the cars in the car park have their tyres slashed including, ironically, Trevor's Sierra. 'Even I'm not going to fall for that one twice in a week,' he says when he is told, and it takes him some time to be persuaded that it is true. Fortunately the rise in this activity is mirrored by a decline in that taking place outside Mrs Khan's house, although it is difficult to know how much this has to do with the snow and bitterly cold weather deterring late night activity. People become paranoid. Trevor chases a group of kids who throw snowballs at him, even though this is a familiar occurrence whenever it snows. Everybody is tired and pissed off and the number of people on sick leave rises sharply. The Crime Prevention Fund approves the bid for a gate in Folkestone Road and work begins on measuring up, so I write to all the tenants explaining that they will soon have to come and collect keys, one of those tasks which should be relatively straightforward but always degenerates into an administrative nightmare.

The low-level warfare waged against the office in general lasts until the end of the week. On the Friday, I have arranged to meet Karen and Ana María at the cinema, working late as it is not worth going home. Only Rosemary McKee is still in the office as I leave. It has started to snow again lightly and there is a sharp chill wind blowing against my face. As I walk away from the estate towards the station, huddling into my jacket, two men step suddenly out of the shadows and block my path. I do not recognize them at all and they are a good deal older than Jason King and his mates. They are both stocky with thinning hair. One is wearing a green combat jacket. He has stubble on his face, a nicotine grin, and clearly marked jowls. 'We've been waiting for you,' he says, stepping forward and pushing me against the wall. 'You're the one who wants to get rid of white people and give their houses to Pakis ain't you?'

'I don't know you,' I say stupidly. 'What's this about?'

'Oh, I think you know,' and he punches me in the stomach so that I double up and slump down the wall. They stand over me as I try desperately to get air back into my lungs, making the most terrible gasping noises. I cannot speak and just look up at them. Maybe if I look at them the right way they won't do this. The street is totally deserted. The other man kicks me hard several times in the ribs, my body making a spasm with every blow. Then he lifts me up by the hair. 'Look at that,' he says 'the little shitter's wet 'imself.' He punches me on the side of the head and again in the stomach so that I go down again. Then I feel an explosion in my head as the first man kicks me in the face. Blood drips on to the snow. It is my blood I think. That is my blood on the snow.

'Please,' I manage to say, 'Please stop now.'

They laugh. 'Please stop,' one mimics me. 'We're only just warming up, you little Paki-loving slag. They're not going to recognize you at work. Your girlfriend's not going to want to know you. Or maybe it's your boyfriend. You like it up the arse do you? Do you?' he screams and the kicks fly in again to my ribs and face while I try vainly to get into some kind of foetal position and cover my face with my arms. I hear the click of a knife opening.

'Get him up and hold his arms,' one of them says. 'We're

going to leave you with a souvenir, something to remember us by.'

I am hauled up again, blood dripping from my mouth and nose and one of them stands behind me trapping my arms behind my back. The man in front of me sneers. 'You gettin' excited? You think he's gonna fuck you, gay-boy? No, bad luck, but we're going to give you a pretty little swastika tattoo,' and the man behind me pulls my head down to one side so that my cheek is exposed for the blade. Tears and blood run down Jamie's face. Fear and hatred and pain form into a sob of protest at what they are about to do to him. But then he hears a car coming slowly round the corner and struggles to cry out. 'Hold him still for fuck sake,' says the first man. The car stops opposite and the front door opens, the engine still running. Through his tears he sees a recognizable figure, a person he knows. Tony O'Leary gets out and takes the scene in for a second, leaning over the roof of his blue Granada. Then, 'Let him go,' he says.

'You've got some front, O'Leary, showing your face around here. There's a few geezers looking for you.'

'Let him go. That's my housing officer.'

'I don't fucking care if he's your mother-in-law, O'Leary, you mad cunt. Now fuck off.'

O'Leary reaches into his car under the seat and takes out a short baseball bat. 'You what? I didn't quite catch that. What was that again?'

The man behind me lets go of my hair. 'Leave it out, he's a fuckin' nutter. Let's leave it.' I drop to the ground as he stops supporting me. There is blood on the snow. The first man looks at O'Leary, who is patting the baseball bat against his palm and smiling slightly.

'You know I'll kill you, you fuckin' nonce. But if you wanna know, just step forward,' O'Leary sneers.

'Come on, let's go,' says the man who was holding me up. His partner laughs.

'From what I've heard, O'Leary, you're not long for this world anyway. But if you want to protect this little piece of Paki-loving shit I can't be bothered arguing about it.'

He bends down and looks at me in the eyes and then spits full in my face. I wipe my eyes and look up at him, still crying. He turns away. 'All right, let's go. But remember, this was only Round One. You've got a lot more coming to you if you stay around here. And you, O'Leary, let me know what flowers you like for the funeral.' And the two men walk away, the first staring out O'Leary who stands impenetrable with his base-ball hat.

When they have gone, O'Leary replaces his baseball bat, switches off the engine and shuts the door. A car behind, trying to get through, honks its horn. 'Fuck off,' O'Leary shouts menacingly and it reverses away. He lifts me up. 'Can you walk?' and I shake my head. He puts my arm around his shoulders and I howl with pain from the kicks I have received to the ribs. 'Shut up,' he says. 'It's not that bad. We'll get you to the office.'

As we gradually make our way to the office he says, 'Any news about my flat?' and I can actually feel myself want to laugh.

'Not yet,' I managed to mumble.

'We're closed . . .' says Rosemary McKee sharply as she finally opens the door to O'Leary's repeated banging. 'Oh dear God, Jamie, what have they done to you?'

'They've given him a good hiding,' says O'Leary. 'You'd better get him to the hospital. I can't stay around here. I've gotta get back to my car,' and he walks away.

'Wait!' Rosemary screams. 'Wait, for Christ's sake. What the hell happened?' But O'Leary has gone.

I slump on to a chair in the reception area while Rosemary phones first a taxi to get me to the hospital and then Roy. I can hear her speaking to him at home. 'Yes, I'm going to get him to Casualty now. Yes, badly. I don't know, he hasn't spoken yet.

All right, I'll see you there. OK, thanks Roy.' She comes to me and touches my forehead.

'Jamie love, can you hear me? Just nod. I've called a taxi because I think it'll be quicker than an ambulance. And you're not going to die.' She smiles anxiously.

'My friends,' I say, 'they'll be waiting for me. They won't know where I am.' Blood trickles from my mouth as I speak.

'Don't worry about that. We can sort that out later. Don't talk for now.'

'But they'll be worried. They'll think I've let them down.' And I begin to cry again thinking of Ana María and Karen trying to decide what to do when I don't turn up.

'Shhh, Jamie. I think that's the taxi.' Two circles of light shine on the office door and a horn sounds.

With enormous difficulty, Rosemary and the cabbie manage to get me into the car. Whatever position I sit in, the pain from my ribs is almost unbearable. And every time I try and shift slightly to relieve the pain, another surge of pain wrenches through my side. I catch a glimpse of my face in the mirror. One eye is swelling up and closing, my nose is a strange shape and my lip is open. Dried blood covers my face and shirt. My jeans are clinging and sore where I urinated as they kicked me. 'They tried to carve a swastika on my face,' I whisper.

'Shh, Jamie. We're going to get you to the hospital.'

'Christ almighty,' the cabbie exclaims, 'what's it all coming to?'

We pass over some speed humps and I cry out as I am jolted. 'Sorry, mate,' he says, and takes the rest very slowly.

Roy is already standing outside the hospital when we arrive. 'My God,' he says when he sees me. 'Oh Jamie, I'm sorry.'

My jaw is really aching but I try and smile at him. 'It's not your fault.'

It is still early so the casualty department is not full up and I am taken through and put on a trolley bed. I can only lie on my back because of the pain in my ribs. Somebody in another cubicle is crying softly to themselves. Roy stands by the bed drinking a cup of coffee from a beige plastic cup. 'Do you know who it was?' I shake my head slightly.

Finally a nurse comes to examine me. She takes my blood pressure and looks at my pupils as well as asking me for my full name, what day of the week it is and how many fingers she is holding up. 'Were you unconscious at any point? No? That's good. The doctor will be along to see you in a little while. You've probably got a couple of broken ribs. There's not much we can do about that except strap you up to make you more comfortable. We'll do a chest and a skull X-ray anyway and keep you here a little while longer. Your face is a mess so we'll clean you up a bit as well.'

'It hurts,' I say.

'Yes, broken ribs are very painful. The only thing you can do is get lots of rest. I'll get someone to bring you some pain-killers. Do you have anyone at home you can call to come and get you?'

'No,' I say. 'Roy. If I give you a number could you call it? I was meant to meet somebody tonight. They might be a bit worried.'

'OK. Don't worry about getting home, Jamie. I'll give you a lift. But if you don't want to be on your own you can stay at my house tonight.'

'Thanks.'

I close my eyes as Roy goes off to phone Eduardo's house. The pain in my side is horrible and insistent and I cannot move into any position where I am not in agony. Even trying to move brings spasms of pain running through me. Roy returns. 'I got through. You didn't tell me it was Karen Metcalf you were meeting. I used to work with her in Portland office. She's a really good housing officer. Anyway, they'd gone back to the house when you didn't turn up. Karen's coming down now to see you, she said.'

'Oh her own?'

'She didn't say. She just said she was coming down.'

I close my eyes. Probably Ana María will not come. The doctor comes to see me with a nurse. He asks the same questions and touches my ribcage with cold hands. He is brisk and efficient, wearing Eau Sauvage and a gold wedding ring. 'OK,' he says, 'we're going to take a couple of X-rays. If there's no problem with those you can go home in an hour. If you start feeling poorly at all you must ring your GP's emergency number.' Everything is becoming too much for me now and I just close my eyes and let myself be wheeled around. Despite my insomnia, I have the capacity when under serious pressure almost to hypnotize myself. After being X-rayed, I am wheeled back to the cubicle where Roy is still waiting. 'Karen's here,' he says, 'I'll just go and get her.'

She comes into the cubicle on her own. I feel a tremendous disappointment and then feel guilty for this. 'Well, James, you're looking pretty horrific.'

'Thanks.'

'And you made us miss the film which I really wanted to see.'

'He's always been a bit inconsiderate that way,' Roy joins in, but I can't take teasing and once again a tear rolls down my cheek.

Karen takes my hand. 'Sorry, Jamie. Don't put salt in your wounds, it'll hurt more.'

'Where's Ana María?' I say. 'Couldn't she be bothered to come?'

'Is that the girl waiting outside with her dad?' Roy asks Karen.

'Yes. We all came with Eduardo. They didn't want us all coming in at once. Don't make a fool of yourself, Jamie, even if you do have an excuse for once. Hold on, I'll just go and get her.'

When Ana María comes in I feel a tremendous ache in my

chest and want to start crying again but manage to stop myself. She stands beside me and takes my hand. '*Pobrecito*,' she says with a far-away smile, looking down at me and stroking my hand. 'They have really hurt you, no?'

'They have really hurt me yes.' I can't help saying and she smiles again sadly.

'Jamie,' Roy says, 'Karen says that she'll take you home and stay with you tonight. But if you want to stay at my house the offer's still open.'

'Thanks a lot, Roy, but I'd quite like to go home when they say I can.'

'All right then. Listen Jamie, I'm going to leave you with Karen and . . . sorry I've forgotten your name . . . they've said they can stay until you get discharged. But I'll come round tomorrow to see you. You're going to be a bit immobile for a while. Can you tell me your address because I've only got it in the office.'

As I am dictating my address, two policemen arrive to take a statement and description of the two men from me. Roy must have called them. The one asking the questions has cropped ginger hair and pulls at his ear as I recount what happened.

'You say they were about to cut your face with a knife? What stopped them?'

I do not want to bring O'Leary into it. 'It was a passing motorist. He stopped and shouted at them so they got scared and went away.'

As the policeman gets up to leave, Roy touches his arm. 'Can I have a word outside? See you tomorrow, Jamie.'

Karen comes back into the cubicle. 'You're a lucky devil, Jamie, having two adoring females to wait on you. I'm going to stay with you tonight and then Ana María's going to come round and relieve me tomorrow. Don't leave it too late . . .' she turns to Ana María, "cause I'll have had quite enough of him by tomorrow.'

After about another hour, the nurse comes in. 'We'll get you cleaned up and then you can go home,' she says, smiling at me. 'Have you got a lift?'

'Yes,' says Ana María, 'Eduardo will take us in the car.'

It is snowing again when we finally leave the hospital and a stream of casualties is limping in with assorted black eyes, stab wounds and whiplash from car accidents. One youth looks at me as he helps his mate in through the doors and laughs. 'Blimey mate, you've been in a battle haven't you?' There is something oddly comforting about the way in which he makes this cheerful observation as if lurching into Casualty on a Friday night after the pub is as routine as buying a kebab. His mate, who appears to have been hit over the head with a bottle, grins at Karen and says, 'Yeah but he's got someone much tastier helping him. 'Ere love, do you wanna take my other arm?'

'No, you keep it, I think you might need it. I've got two perfectly good ones of my own.'

'Yeah, I can see you've got two perfectly good ones,' and they roar with laughter while the first opens the door for us with mock gallantry.

'Thanks,' says Karen. 'You behave yourself with those nurses now.'

'That's the only reason he brought me here,' says the one with the head injury, 'to try and chat up the nurses.' He grins at me. 'Take it easy, mate. Don't do anything I wouldn't do,' and they head for the registration desk still laughing.

I sit in the back of the car, my face turned to the window. Some children in the street are scraping the snow from car windscreens for snowballs, shrieking with laughter. The car hits a pothole and I yelp. Ana María takes my hand and I turn to look at her. Her eyes are sad but she smiles at me. I feel like I am going to burst if I don't say something to her. She looks away but does not let go of my hand.

Fortunately the flat is not too much of a mess, although it is as cold as the street since the heating is switched off. Gingerly,

I try and ease myself on to the bed without crying out. The pain is making me feel sick and Eduardo says, 'You've gone completely white, Jamie.' There is really not much for them to do and I want them to go.

'I'll come in the afternoon,' Ana María murmurs to Karen, and they disappear out into the still lightly falling snow.

'Right, Jamie, what have you got to drink in the house?' demands Karen, opening cupboard doors. 'Aha,' she finds a bottle of Jameson's and waves it triumphantly. 'I bet you haven't got any ice. Oh, I'm wrong, we've got everything now.' She pours two glasses of whisky and comes back into the bedroom. 'Don't get any ideas, Jamie, but I'm going to get into bed 'cause it's bloody freezing. Wait though, I'm just going to bring the telly in. How do you unplug this thing from the video? Oh, that's it.' She hauls the TV in and sets it precariously on a chair. 'Where's the socket?' and I point to where the light is plugged in. Karen gets into bed beside me, sitting with her knees pulled up to her chin.

'I knew you wouldn't be able to resist it in the end. That's why you were top of the list,' I say.

'You've got enough on your plate as it is from what I can see.'

'What?'

'Well, James, they say that the age of romance is over but from the way the air starts crackling when you and somebody whose name I shall not mention are together I'm not so sure. Carefully weighing up the available evidence I would say that you are head over heels for a certain señorita. L.O.V.E., love.'

'Yeah yeah, remember I'm an invalid. I'm not sure I can handle these lashings of sarcasm.'

'OK, Jamie,' says Karen. 'If you don't want to talk about it . . .'

She sips at her whisky, smiling enigmatically. I know that she will be able to hold out for far longer than I will.

'Talk about what, though? What is there to talk about?' I ask impatiently.

Karen turns her face to the window. The lights from the block opposite are glowing through the snowy night.

'It's funny, isn't it,' she says, 'there must be about fifty flats in that block and you don't really know anything about what is going on in any of them. You just watch the lights going on and off. You don't know what any of those people are doing. And they don't know anything about us.'

'Karen,' I sigh, 'don't start getting deep about a block of flats. I'm not in the mood.'

'OK,' she says. 'Look Jamie, it's really obvious you've fallen for Ana María, I mean its obvious to everyone . . .' She looks at me significantly.

'What? Have you been talking about it? Has she said something to you about it? Like tonight . . .'

Karen sips at her whisky, cupping the glass in her hands. She glances at me as if she is carefully considering what she is prepared to say to me.

'Well . . . you weren't completely absent from our conversation tonight.'

'And?'

'And nothing. Look Jamie, Ana María she . . . well you know I think the idea of a fling with somebody wouldn't have been entirely distasteful to her, but that's not exactly what you offer is it?'

'What do you mean? I mean if she only wants a fling I can live with . . .'

Karen laughs. 'I should have expected that one. Be realistic, Jamie. You know that's not the deal here. And Ana María, she's not some little party-babe you're gonna phone up once a fortnight for a drink and a shag.'

'That's not fair . . . she isn't just . . .'

'I don't care about that,' Karen flaps her hand dismissively. 'I'm just telling you what I think. I might be wrong.

I'm not a bloody relationship adviser, it's just that Ana María's been through a bad time recently what with one thing and another. And I think, Jamie, that you're a bit of a puzzle to her, well, you're a puzzle to everyone, but especially to her . . .'

'What do you mean?' I almost shout, jerking up so that pain rips at my side. 'What are you talking about? What's so puzzling about me? And anyway, you can't have it both ways. One minute, if it was just a fling it would be OK, the next you're saying that it can't just be a fling.'

'No,' says Karen patiently, 'I'm saying that's not what it would be like between you and Ana María. Oh Jamie, I don't know really. You should sort it out with her.'

I am not sure what is making me more miserable, the pain or the nature of this conversation. Karen senses this and takes my hand suddenly.

'I didn't mean puzzling in a bad way . . .' she says. '. . . And Ana María likes you a lot as far as I can tell. But you've got to deal with reality, Jamie, you can't just identify her as your heart's desire and forget the real person.'

'Maybe. But that's also part of the process. Everyone invents a little. Harsh reality can come later.'

'Well, that's all very romantic, Jamie, but you should maybe bear in mind that in your case, the harsh reality might be waving goodbye to Ana María at the airport.'

This isn't what I wanted to hear at all. I wanted some kind of confirmation, a green light, the go-ahead. But I sense that Karen is not going to respond to much more probing and that the conversation will just begin to go round in circles, so I decide not to ask any more questions.

There is a long silence and then Karen pours some more whisky. 'God, I love this stuff. Look at the colour of it. Drink a little, Jamie, it'll do you good.' She holds the glass to my lips and I take a small sip, feeling the sting of it against my cracked lip. 'Anyway, that's enough about your personal life. This is a bastard case you're involved in. You'll have to think about transferring to another office.'

'No. I may be a complete coward normally but there's no way now I'm doing that. Trevor will just have to give me lifts to the station every night. Anyway, I'll have a few weeks to think it over but at the moment there's no way I want to do that.'

Karen laughs suddenly. 'You see, Jamie, that's what's puzzling about you. One minute you're kind of drifting along, just getting by, and the next you've got this pitbull-like commitment to tackling one of the most notorious families in the borough.'

I shift my position and pain judders through my body. 'Speaking of notorious, I didn't tell the coppers everything. You know who it was who saved me?'

She shakes her head.

'It was Anthony O'Leary.'

'Not *the* O'Leary? The psycho's psycho?'

'That O'Leary.'

'Why? How?'

'I was lucky. He was driving past. He basically lives in his car now, hiding from some villains, and he saw what was happening. He thinks I'm single-handedly dealing with his transfer so he didn't want anything to happen to me. Also, funnily enough, he's not as big a bastard as he makes out, although he is a maniac. You remember the kid at school who was dead hard and a bit of a nutter but didn't actually do much fighting because of their reputation, like they weren't the real bully or anything, but still got blamed for everything . . .'

'Yeah, in my school it was Paul McKenzie. I fancied the knickers off him.'

'Well, O'Leary's not particularly fanciable, but that's him. And because I'm dealing with his case I'm on his side and he has to protect me. I mean, he helped me to the office and everything. He didn't just stop them. And it meant showing his face round there, you know . . .'

'And you didn't tell the police?'

'No. I just knew not to. He's not going to want to be hauled in. He knows who they are though. The two guys.'

'But you could find out.'

'He won't tell. Anyway, that's not the point. He saved me from having to walk around for the rest of my life with a swastika-shaped scar. I can't just involve him with the pigs if that's not what he wants.'

'No, I suppose you're right. It's pretty funny though, isn't it? Rescued by Tony O'Leary.'

'Yeah, it was a real scream.'

She gets out of bed. 'Can you lend me something to wear, I can't sleep like this.'

'There's some pyjamas in the drawer.'

Karen goes to the bathroom to change. 'I'm gonna use your toothbrush, I hope you haven't got herpes or anything.' When she comes back, the oversized striped pyjamas cover her feet. She clambers into bed and switches off the light. I watch objects gradually emerging from the darkness, the shape of the jacket hanging behind the door.

'Jamie,' says Karen suddenly.

'Yeah.'

'Talk to Ana María. I think you should.'

I lie on my back, arms by my side like a toy soldier packed in its box for the night. Karen curls into a ball, wrapping the duvet over her head. As she sleeps she growls and murmurs slightly to herself. It is hard to sleep. Images of the two attackers keep flashing before me, the thought of the knife cutting into the soft flesh of my cheek, O'Leary gently patting the baseball bat against his hand. I get little bursts of sleep with bright vivid dreams – one of which involves trying frantically to get on a plane to Dublin but losing bag, passport and ticket at various intervals. When I finally do get on the plane, it embarks on a nightmare voyage, unable to gain the necessary height and desperately dodging buildings and flying under bridges. Why am I dreaming of flying to Dublin – a city I have never visited in my life? Karen stirs in her sleep and mutters something which sounds like 'Mind your manners.' Tomorrow when Ana María comes, I am going to say something to her. Comforted by this moment of resolution and certainty I close my eyes again and allow myself to sleep.

PART THREE

A Declaration

'Karen, wake up.' I flap with my left hand and manage to slap at her back. 'Karen, I can't move. Wake up, you've got to help me.' She groans and tries to pull the duvet over her head.

'Karen, wake up.'

'What do you want me to do?'

'Help me to try and get out of bed.'

Sleep arrived accompanied by paralysis. My body is locked, jammed, stuck. I can't move. When I do manage to shift a little, a terrible pain grinds from my ribcage and I cry out again.

'You're just stiff from being in bed. It will get better.' Karen is rubbing her eyes.

'I hope so.' With Karen's help I manage to manipulate myself out of bed and shuffle painfully with old man steps towards the bathroom, leaning on her shoulder.

'Only a bit further now, Grandpa.'

The sight of my face in the bathroom mirror takes my mind momentarily from the pain in my sides. I am impressed with the purple swelling around my eye and touch it tentatively with my fingertip.

'This is as far as I come, Jamie, you're on your own now. Call me when you need me again.'

I have to support myself against the wall until I have finished. There is no way that I am going to get back into bed, so Karen escorts me to the sofa where she puts a blanket over me and pads into the kitchen to make some coffee, pyjamas over the soles of her feet.

'What have you got to eat?'

'In the freezer compartment there's frozen croissants. Heat them up if you want.'

'Brilliant. Do you want some music on?'

'OK.'

Karen flips through the record collection, pausing occasionally as if about to select one, before picking out an old Roxy Music album. 'I haven't heard this for years. God, they don't make sleeves like that any more,' she says scrutinizing the woman in the ripped red dress on the cover before returning to the kitchen. She brings coffee and croissants into the living-room and sets them on the table before me. 'Here you are, sweetheart. Your milk was yoghurt so it's black coffee I'm afraid.'

'Thanks for staying, Karen.'

'That's OK, I had you pencilled in for last night anyway remember. But I'm not going to give up my Saturday night for you as well. Besides, I expect you're looking forward to the arrival of your favourita.'

'I'm glad it was you who stayed last night.'

'What's this, Jamie? I'm not sure I can handle these sudden compliments.'

'No . . . it's just that . . .'

She smiles at me. 'It's OK.'

'Some people have no problem saying it. Look at Colin.'

'And he really means it.'

'Mad bastard. You know he head-butted somebody at a party a while back who was going to hit me.'

'Somebody was going to hit you! You've suddenly got lots of enemies.'

'Well, it was a bit different. I had just spat in their face.'

'Were you both by any chance somewhat pissed?'

'Colin wasn't too bad but I was wrecked.'

Throwing the House Out of the Window

Karen sighs. 'And the cavalry arrived in the shape of Colin – head-butt first think later – Ferguson. I can just imagine it. He wouldn't let anyone hit you. The very thought of it! Just wait till he finds out about this. You'll have to stop him rounding up a posse of mad Scots.' She blows on her coffee and dunks a croissant in it, lifting the dripping end carefully to her mouth.

'He's already offered that.'

'I'll give him a ring this afternoon and let him know the good news. Eat your croissant, Jamie, it's going cold. Have you got any fags in the house?'

I shake my head.

At lunchtime Ana María arrives. She looks quite pale and ill at ease. Eduardo has sent some kind of herb to boil and drink. He is fond of alternative remedies, which he sees as preferable to the capitalist drugs industry. The fact that they have no noticeable remedial effect does not seem to concern him. He once made me a disgusting concoction of beer, lemon juice, salt and raw egg when I had a cold. It worked in a kind of way, since I forgot about my cold for about half an hour while I concentrated instead on not throwing up.

'Well . . .' Karen picks up her jacket '. . . he's all yours, Ana. I'm off to spend my pay-cheque and prepare myself for a date with a handsome young welfare rights adviser. Bye Jamie, I'll see myself out.'

I suddenly feel awkward alone with Ana María and miss the easy banter and chatter with Karen. It is obvious that the feeling is mutual and I find it difficult to meet her eyes as we are talking. I can hear myself swallowing and feel as if my head is wobbling as I speak. In the end we put the TV on and watch a film about the Norwegian resistance to the Nazis, every now and again attempting half-hearted efforts at conversation. 'Tventy Norvegians,' screams the SS officer, after the death of one of his men, his Nazi eyes bulging with rage. 'Tventy Norvegians vill die for zis.' Ana María wanders off to make a cup of coffee and seems relieved to find that there is no milk. 'I will just go to the shop,' she says woodenly. 'Do you need anything else?'

'I can't think of anything.' I try desperately to think of something I need so that I will have something else to say. Drums roll as the innocent Norwegians are lined up in front of the church. They are all going to die. For a moment Ana María pauses, jacket in hand, to watch their fate. But suddenly the handsome young village priest, who has been urging the villagers not to take up arms, throws off his cassock to produce a machine-gun and begins spraying the German troops with bullets from the window of his church. 'Liberation theology,' I say, and Ana María smiles wanly.

'Are you sure you don't need anything?'

'Yes, I think so. The keys are hanging up by the door.'

'OK.'

The door shuts behind her. I haul myself up with extreme difficulty and make my way to the bathroom again.

When Ana María returns from the shop, the atmosphere is, if anything, more strained. I tell her about O'Leary and she listens attentively but still seems in another world. She responds to things that I say but does not initiate any new topic of conversation. I almost feel like launching into an anti-Castro tirade just to provoke a reaction. It is starting to annoy me – I am the one who is injured, it's up to her to stop being selfish and make a bit more of an effort. But as I watch her sitting with her chin cupped in her hands, her black hair falling around her shoulders, I feel that awful impulse urging me on – tell her you idiot, do something, don't just sit there, you can't go on like this, it can't be more painful than a kick in the ribs. And suddenly the words rise from deep inside, leave my mouth and hover expectantly in the air between us like little humming birds.

'I love you.'

There is an agonizing silence. The words have transformed themselves into malicious imps, dancing mockingly round the room, pulling gargoyle faces and shrieking with laughter at my stupidity. They have been said, there is no undoing it. My bridges burned. Three unretractable words – they echo and glimmer like patterns of light which remain on the retina behind the curtain of closed eyelids. Ana María turns her face towards me.

'Jamie . . .' but she is interrupted by a sudden urgent knocking on the front door. We both look at each other for a moment and then she gets up and walks to the door. I close my eyes.

'*Hola linda! Como estás?*' roars Colin in an excruciatingly bad accent as he bursts into the house and greets Ana María.

'Ah, you have been studying. *Muy bien gracias, y tú?*'

'Sorry, that's all I know. Jamie . . .' he strides into the living-room '. . . how are you? Karen phoned and told me. Fucking animals. I've been thinking of a few guys here we could get together, there's Mikey and Davey, they'd definitely be up for it . . . that's a great black eye you've got Jamie, whaddya think of the Spanish then, eh? Carlita's been teaching me, I'll tell you what . . .' he turns to Ana María '. . . you could teach me a few new phrases and then I could, like, surprise her. These guys, Jamie, have you got any idea where we can find them? Had you seen them before?'

I shake my head, looking at Ana María who is sitting on a chair looking down at her hands. What is she thinking? What was she about to say? Colin, oblivious to the drama around him, produces a bottle of brandy. 'This is what you like, eh, Jamie? I thought if you've got to have grapes when you're ill then they're better out of a bottle than a brown paper bag. Come on then, let's have a drink and I can show you my new dance steps. Jamie, you'll have to sit this one out but I'm sure you won't mind.'

Ana María suddenly laughs out loud, looking up at Colin who grins back at her. 'You can be my partner.'

'OK,' she replied, 'I'll dance with you.'

213

Colin pours us all huge tumblers of brandy. 'Have you got any salsa or anything like that?' he asks me and I shake my head. 'That's OK, I've bought a couple of records today. It's not easy these days. All they want to sell you is those bloody CDs. It calls itself a Megastore and it's got less records than I have at home. Bastards.' And he pulls the records with a flourish from his bag like an excited magician producing a rabbit. 'I was gonna go to salsa classes but I thought they'd be full of wankers, you know, yuppies going for a bit of the exotic Latin so fuck that . . .'

He chatters on with infectious exuberance and Ana María is giggling slightly as he carefully holds the record with his palms, places it on the turntable and blows the dust from the needle. Taking Ana María by the waist, he says, 'Right, off we go then,' and begins to spin her crazily round the room.

'Slower, slower,' she begs, 'you're making me dizzy, listen to the music, move your waist a little more.' They are spinning and laughing as they crash around the living-room until Colin finally manages to collide with the shelf, sending books cascading to the floor and a glass shattering into pieces. 'Oh shit, sorry Jamie, where's the brush?'

'In the kitchen.'

'OK.' He goes to hunt for it. Ana María collapses panting on to the sofa beside me, and brushes her hair out of her face.

'I'm sorry,' I say. 'I didn't mean to . . .' But she shakes her head and puts her finger to my lips. Then she drops her hands to mine and lifts them up to her face.

At this point Colin re-emerges. 'I can't find . . . oh erm sorry . . . I'll just go and . . . maybe it's in one of the other cupboards.' We both laugh at his embarrassment.

'Leave it, it's OK. Don't worry,' I say.

Ana María takes my hand, stroking it gently with her thumb. Colin raises his eyebrows questioningly to me to say, 'What's going on?' and I shrug and shake my head to answer 'I haven't got a clue.' Ana María smiles calmly at Colin, who suddenly says, 'Can I use your phone?'

'Sure, go ahead.'

He crouches down to dial the number. Ana María turns and looks me in the eyes and then rests her forehead against mine.

'Hi, it's Colin. Yeah. Ha ha ha. No. I was thinking of coming down now. Or do you want to come up to mines? Yeah that'd be better, I'll wait for you there then. Then we can go out and get something to eat. OK? Ciao hen.'

He replaces the receiver. 'Right then, you two lovebirds, I'd better get back and clear my place up before Carlita gets there. This is definitely an improvement on arguing about drug traffickers although I have to say, Ana, you could have done better for yourself. Listen right, how do you say 'you've got a fabulous body'?'

Ana María sees him out of the front door, kisses him goodbye and then comes to sit beside me again on the sofa. She puts her arms around my neck and I understand suddenly what the Little Mermaid must have gone through. Ana María notices my discomfort and pulls back laughing. 'I am sorry. I forget your rib.'

'I wish I could,' I reply.

There is a long silence and she rests her head on my chest. I feel slightly awkward. What are we supposed to do now? But it is clear that Ana María is not particularly expecting me to do anything. So we just sit there and I let my hand run through her thick hair like a comb, feeling it close to my nose, touching her shoulder. 'Ay,' she says suddenly as I pull my hand through a slight tangle. We sit silently for a little longer, Ana María playing with each of my fingers, lifting them up one by one as if enthralled by the working of the joints. I can feel my heart beating against her ear. At last, Ana María looks up at me and says softly, 'We could go into the bedroom.'

We get into bed fully clothed, Ana María pausing only to remove her shoes. The air is heavy with our shyness; from outside I can still hear the almost soothing murmur of the afternoon traffic. A small bird flashes across the window. I feel the bed sink slightly under Ana María's extra weight, the duvet pulled up to cover her. I realize that this moment, these seconds of my existence are happening now and that in the future I will always try and recreate them but never succeed. Ana María shifts towards me, I can feel her hair on my cheek, she whispers something unintelligible and then her lips are fluttering against mine.

It is a strange, slow and somewhat painful lovemaking, largely due to the fact that two broken ribs are not the greatest aid to sexual performance. When we are apart again, we lie silently for some time and then Ana María says to me, '*Te quiero mucho*' and we do not say anything else until we fall asleep, not exactly in each other's arms which would be impossible, but arms outstretched, touching each other.

Story Telling

Over the next weeks, the snow stops and the days of clear cold skies and pale sunshine return. The pain in my side grows more bearable, turning into a dull ache; it is not so difficult to get up in the morning and I can actually manage to sleep on my side rather than my back. Roy brings me get well cards from the office. There are cards from the Monitoring Group, Adrian Thompson on behalf of the union, and a few from tenants including a strangely touching card from Mr Peters which says 'So sorry to hear you have not been well.' There is a small article in the local paper about a vicious unprovoked attack on a council worker, with a description of the two men the police are looking for. I ask Roy to bring some work round for me and he arrives with computer printouts so that I can sit and write rent arrears letters and bring my paperwork up to date. He tells me that after the attack things died down for a while but that the car windscreens were smashed with sledge-hammers just a few days ago and that they have taken to urinating through Mrs Khan's letter-box.

Ana María spends most of her time at the flat. We lie on the sofa or in bed telling stories to each other. I tell her about the East End. She listens to tales of the striking match-girls, the victory over Mosley's blackshirts, the siege of Sidney Street, the Poplar rate rebels, the disappearance of old communities and the arrival of new ones, the music halls, synagogues and mosques. Most of all she likes the story of dreamy Sylvia

Pankhurst organizing the working-class suffrage movement while snobbish Christabel retreated to Paris, and of how they delivered her tortured, broken and barely alive body to Parliament to shame the cat and mouse legislators.

In turn she tells me of Chile, of how she travelled the entire length of the country with her boyfriend, from the glaciers in the south to the northern desert, of places where there is only a few hours' daylight in winter and how sometimes in spring the Atacama desert bursts into flower. Gradually, I begin to piece together another Ana María who existed before I met her. There is the teenager in Mexico hanging around with a group of students and would-be artists drinking and idling away the hot afternoons. There is the Ana María who returned to Chile full of lofty ideals, hiding from the water cannon and tear-gas-poisoned air on days of protest. Lurking behind this story, sometimes vaguely alluded to, is a man she loved – I imagine him as a tall and austere figure – who left her for a woman he considered to be of greater social and political importance, a woman from the shanty-towns with whom Ana María could never compete. Sometimes a vague fear grips me that one day I too will be part of a recounted story to some new lover, just another stage in her rootless history. But I banish such thoughts quickly; what's the use in thinking like that?

After a while, I am able to walk without so much difficulty and we wander around together, down to the river, or spend afternoons in the cinema. Ana María shops in the market on the Whitechapel Road, returning with fronds of coriander in brown paper bags, great crescents of orange pumpkin with their pulpy centres, sweet potatoes, and huge bags of onions which cost a pound and last for only a few days. I like the way that Ana María relates unfussily to food. In the early evening, or when people come round, she makes tea which we drink with toast, mashed avocado and tomato salad. She brings tapes of Latin American music and teaches me the words.

We stand on the balcony watching the clouds passing like

convoys of whales and the calm steady progress of planes moving their cargo of people around the world, trying to guess their origin or destination. One day we take the Light Railway through Docklands, gazing at the glittering office pyramids rising above the water. Sitting under the Canary Wharf tower drinking coffee from plastic cups and watching the water rising and falling endlessly from the fountains, I wonder idly whether we will bump into Neil, busily deconstructing our troubled voyage through the perplexing waters of post-modern Britain and gazing at late capitalism's shimmering fraudulent symbols. The thought of him meeting Ana María is rather amusing – his encounter with her meta-narrative would be a somewhat one-sided contest. 'What are you smiling at?' she asks and I shake my head. 'Nothing, I was just thinking of someone I used to know.'

It will soon be time for me to go back to work. Ana María has also to start working, her money has run out and she cannot keep asking me or Eduardo for funds. But she has no work permit. A friend of Eduardo's has said that he can find her a job in the company which has the contract to clean the offices of a large daily newspaper and, although she has decided to try and teach Spanish, she has agreed to start the following week.

One night, as we are lying in bed, the telephone rings. Ana María picks it up. 'It is for you,' she says. 'Somebody called Iona.'

'Hi Iona.'

'Hi Jamie, well I guess I know now why you haven't phoned me for a little while.'

'Things have been a bit complicated.'

'Complicated?' She laughs sharply. 'That's one way of putting it.'

'How's Malcolm?'

'That's not really fair, Jamie.'

'Isn't it?'

'No. You knew about that from the beginning. You could have told me you were seeing someone else.'

'I wasn't.' I twist round to look at Ana María, who is sitting up reading a paper, completely ignoring the conversation.

'What were you going to do? Just not phone me again?'

'Of course I was. There's other reasons I haven't called. I've been ill.' Ana María turns a page crisply and brushes it flat. She sweeps her hair over her shoulder but does not look back at me. 'Look, why don't we meet up for a drink, you know I can't really talk about this now.'

'Yes, I can see it might be a little difficult. Listen Jamie, don't worry about it. I mean I'm just being stupid. It was obvious that something like this would happen. It's just, you know, I liked the times we spent together, and it's finished really, hasn't it?'

I am going to say something bland but suddenly there doesn't seem any point. 'Yes, I suppose it has.'

'OK, Jamie . . .' her voice catches a little '. . . well, I think I'll skip the drink anyway . . .' and the phone clicks down.

Ana María continues to turn the pages of the paper without saying anything. There is a long silence and it is clear that she is not going to say anything. 'That was a girl that I was, you know, seeing before, you know . . .' I trail off, acutely aware of how stupid I sound. She looks up and shrugs.

'Y qué?'

'Well, I'm not seeing her any more if that's what you're thinking.'

'It doesn't matter what I think Jamie. It is your business, not mine.'

'I mean I just told her that I couldn't see her any more.'

'Is that what you wanted?'

'Of course.'

Ana María turns a page. 'I am not sure why it is so obvious. Don't you like her any more?'

'Well, that's not the point, is it?'

Throwing the House Out of the Window

'It would certainly be the point for me. What other reason is there to stop seeing someone?'

'Well, because things are different now. I've started a relationship with someone else.'

Again the stupid clumsy formality of words like relationship. Ana María glances at me slightly condescendingly.

'Ah well, that is up to you. If that is your reason then that is your business. But it's got nothing to do with me.'

'Well, of course it's got something to do with you.'

'No, Jamie . . .' and at last she puts the paper aside '. . . we should get this clear. I will never promise you complete faithfulness because I never promise that to anyone. I could do it easily but that would make me a hypocrite. At the moment I am quite happy and satisfied just being with you but that does not mean it will always be like that.' I start to interrupt but she holds up her hand. 'No wait, I am not an idealist about these things, I know they cause all type of problem. I am a jealous person as well, but I try and fight against my jealousy because I know it is wrong, I know that it is not natural and that it has been created by this society. Now, I don't always win this battle . . .' she laughs '. . . and for that reason I just don't want to know about that side of your life. But don't say you stop seeing this person because of me. I can't stand that. It makes me angry. If I see someone or not, it is because I decide. What happens next is another matter . . .'

'Well, this sounds OK in theory . . .'

'No no, Jamie, don't say that. Please don't say that "it sounds good in theory but it won't work in practice". For me that is completely irrelevant and anyway it is such a boring thing to say. If you have a theory you must try and put it into practice. If you cannot, then either it is not really your theory and you are a hypocrite, or the theory is wrong. Now I have thought about this very hard and I still believe that this idea of finding the right person and being faithful to them for ever is nonsense. I am not denying that jealousy and possessiveness exist, but it is wrong. And, therefore, you have to try and change that. Now, whether it works in practice depends on the people involved. I hope that we will be able to sort it out but if you think that I am going to promise you that I will never look at someone else, or desire someone else, or even make love to someone else then you are wrong.'

'Right, I see.'

She turns to me and laughs. 'Don't sulk, Jamie.'

'Don't talk, don't be boring, don't sulk, any more orders?'

'Yes. Don't be stupid and turn the light off.'

I lie in bed with my eyes open, unable to sleep. There is no point in saying anything to Ana María, as she always falls asleep immediately. Sometimes when I have insomnia I kick her and wake her up because her self-satisfied sleeping is even more frustrating. She just smiles and, with the confidence of one who can slip back into sleep like a seal sliding into water, rolls over on to her other side. I get up and go into the living-room and kneel on the sofa staring out of the window. The headlights of cars stream eastwards on the Whitechapel Road, the spiky TV aerials nesting on the roofs below point eerily southwards, summoning their invisible images, and the dark mass of trees shakes in the night wind. I try and imagine how I would feel if Ana María slept with somebody else but can't. It's not that I particularly disagree with her; everybody has had that drunken conversation about fidelity and monogamy, to tell or not to tell, if you think about doing it then there's no real difference, etc. etc. I know that even now, much as I love Ana María, I wouldn't mind sleeping with Iona again and really why not? Who says you can't? If you know that somebody is thinking like that, and most people are, then why get upset if they actually do it? The problem with Ana María is that she almost certainly will do it if that's what she thinks. I can't rely on it all being abstract philosophizing, as is the case with a large number of people, most of whom don't get the opportunity anyway. And then what would happen?

Total jealousy is what would happen. I slump down on the sofa and lie on my back. Tomorrow I will go to work. Tomorrow I will . . . . I must have fallen asleep because the next thing I know Ana María is kneeling beside me stroking my face. 'Why are you sleeping here, stupid?'

'I didn't mean to fall asleep.'

'Shall I sleep here with you?' She gets on to the sofa beside me and we lie in the dark, listening to the night noises: the crescendo of car engines, the sudden bursting wail of a siren, a shriek of laughter, the yowling of a cat. Her eyes remain open and her hand strokes my back gently. 'I love you,' I say to her.

'Shhh,' she replies, bringing my lips to hers.

Live a Little

An estate manager from Portland office has been covering my patch while I have been ill and my desk is unusually tidy when I arrive at work the next day. It is a shock walking into the office, which is exactly the same as ever. Two or three tenants are sitting sulkily waiting to be seen, a small queue of pink rent-card-clutching pensioners are at the cashier's window, and the receptionist is looking as if an armed robbery would be welcome just to break the tedium. The council policy is that if anybody tells you that they have a gun you should just hand over the money. Like all of the council policies it is well-known and much abused. Most robbers don't bother coming armed but simply push a note announcing that they have a gun through the cashier's window. Nobody yet has tried to call their bluff.

I climb the stairs holding the rail and exaggerating my fragility a little.

'Jamie,' Trevor exclaims, coming out of the kitchen carrying a mug of coffee. 'Nice to see you back, man.'

Bob Townsend grins at me, folding his paper away. 'I've got some good news for you, Collins. Remember your favourite tenant? Anthony O'Leary? Well, he's now the problem of Riverside office, living in a cosy one-bedroom flat on the fifty-eighty floor of the worst tower block in the area. He's no longer around to trouble you any more.'

'What about Mrs Khan?'

'Ah well, Mrs Khan is a bit more tricky. We can't just put her anywhere, you know. But I'm hopeful something will come up in the next few weeks or so.'

'That's really incredible,' Trevor mutters, 'I'm getting the most amazing sense of *déjà vu*.'

'Am I talking to you, Campbell you prat?'

Eileen grins at me. 'I bet you feel like you haven't been away at all, Jamie.'

I pick out a letter from my in-tray. 'Dear Mr Collins, I am writing to complain about my neighbour playing loud reggae music at all hours of the night. I have spoken to Hilda Connolly from the Tenants' Group and she says I must write to you . . .' I throw the letter back into my in-tray. 'Yeah, well, who's gonna make me a cup of coffee then? I think I should be spoiled a little seeing as it's my first day back.'

Trevor and Bob gaze at each other and then bend over their desks. Mike the social worker comes over to my desk. 'How's your pile?' I ask.

'Yeah, not bad, I took the fucker out with a knitting needle . . . no, not really,' he says as he sees me wince. 'Listen, Jamie, Mr Carmichael, remember him?' I nod. 'Well, he's dead I'm afraid. Topped himself.'

'How?'

'Jumped. I suppose he had nothing left to throw out of the window so he kind of threw himself.'

'Not from his flat?'

'No, no. He never went back there. He was back at his mum's in Stratford after he got out. She was on the eleventh floor.'

Karen takes me out to lunch to celebrate my first day back at work. As we walk to the café, a boy with long greasy hair and wide staring eyes asks for money. I give him fifty pence. 'Can I buy a fag off you now?' he asks. Karen reaches in her pocket, removes two cigarettes from her packet and gives them to him, waving away the offer of money.

'London's a cunt,' he observes after lighting the cigarette, cupping the little flame with the palm of his hand.

'It can be sometimes,' Karen agrees.

'But you two are gonna go to heaven,' he continues, and despite my total lack of religious sentiment there is something pleasing about this prophecy.

'How's Ana María?' Karen asks as we settle into a table which looks out on to the street.

I recount our discussion on sexual fidelity and Karen laughs. 'Poor Jamie. Well, I suppose if you wanted somebody safe you could have just stuck with good old Helen. It's no use complaining that Ana María's unorthodox, since you've known that all along anyway.' Karen has always kept her opinion of Helen pretty much to herself and I don't point out that staying with Helen was not an option which was available to me.

'But do you think she's right?'

'Well, yes, on paper, I suppose I do. Whether I could put up with it is another matter. Anyway, it sounds as if you made a bit of an idiot of yourself with, what was her name again? Maybe Ana María was partly reacting to that. Men are so talentless when it comes to those sort of situations.'

I sigh. 'Well, it's not always that easy, you know.'

'You'll just have to wait and see, won't you? See how things turn out. You're lucky that you're with the one you love but you can't expect it just to be a never-ending trip into an eternal sunset. Anyway, it's good the way you argue sometimes. It's more healthy than squabbling about, you know, total trivia like some couples insist on doing. I really hate that. Although the worst was this guy I was seeing once. He was incredibly nice, never raised his voice, never interrupted me. You know he'd read all those books on how men monopolize conversations so he was determined not to do that, but he took it to ridiculous extremes. I used to say totally outrageous things and he would listen politely when I really wanted him to say you're talking crap. Then I realized that he didn't even really care that much. He wouldn't argue 'cause he wasn't really listening.'

She stirs her tea, making a little whirlpool with the spoon.

'Anyway, what's happening about Ana María getting a job?'

'She starts tomorrow. Office cleaning.'

Karen grimaces. 'Welcome to the Third World.'

In the afternoon I decide to go out on the estate. I am nervous as I pull on my jacket and make my way down Jarvis Road, holding a clipboard with details of the visits I have to make. The estate is quiet, the early afternoon sun dazzling the windows of the tower blocks. Two old ladies stand chatting on the pathway, their tartan shopping trolleys extended behind them. In the middle of the estate I meet Karen Reynolds swinging a loaf of bread. 'Oh,' she says as she sees me. 'You're back.'

'Yeah, down but not out I'm afraid.'

She hesitates and then says, 'Can I come and see you in the office?'

'Yeah, of course. What's it about?'

She glances around nervously. 'No, not here, I'll talk to you in the office. Can I come this afternoon?'

'Sure. Come about half three.'

'All right.'

When Karen Reynolds arrives at the office it is very quiet and I can hear the receptionist explaining impatiently that it is not my time to see tenants.

'But he told me to come.'

I lean over the balcony. 'It's OK, Mary, I'm on my way down. She's got an appointment.'

Karen Reynolds sits in the interview room nervously. 'Can I smoke in 'ere?'

'Yes.'

She takes a packet of Marlboro out of her jacket pocket and offers me one. I shake my head.

'You got a kicking, didn't you?' she says suddenly.

'Yes.'

'Everybody was talking about it. It got in the paper as well. I come down the office to talk to you but there was someone else doing your job and I couldn't talk to 'im.'

'Yes, I saw the report. Everyone's famous for fifteen minutes.'

She laughs. 'I don't think I'll even get that. But I'll settle for less. It was to do with that . . . Asian family wasn't it?'

'I think it might have been.'

'I gave you those names, remember? Jason King and Dean Anderton?'

'Yes, that was very helpful.'

Suddenly, she says fiercely, 'They're animals. Scum. You know that now I suppose. But you ain't the only one. My friend Kelly, they done things . . . they really . . . they hurt her bad you know . . . four of 'em. Do you understand now? You know why I told you. She wouldn't go to the police. I tried to make her but she wouldn't. Said there was no point. In the end all I could do was get her one of those telephone numbers for, you know, counselling or whatever. But she ain't gonna get over that. Not ever. She never troubled no one Kelly, she was just looking for Mr Right. Someone to treat her nice.' She laughs bitterly. 'You know the worst thing? One of the boys, he was in her class at junior school. And then they go round saying she's a slag and all that.' She shakes her head. Her face is flushed and angry with the retelling of the story and for a moment she glares at me as if daring me to give an inadequate response. I say nothing and there is silence as she flicks ash from her cigarette.

'Anyway, right, the point is, the reason I come to see you is that I want to do something. You come to see my mum and she told you where to go . . .' she laughs '. . . I can't slag off my mum, she's my mum, right, but everyone knows what she can be like sometimes. I'm moving off the estate, I've got to. No

229

kid of mine's gonna grow up here, you know what I mean, Mr Collins. My boyfriend's got a flat in Manor Park so I'm going to move in with him. Wait till I break that one to me mum! Kelly's coming too, so I might just say I'm gonna live with her. Make everything easier I suppose. Anyway, what I'm trying to say is that if you need someone to get up in court to say who it was giving all that grief to the Pakis . . . sorry, you can't say that in 'ere can you . . . Asian family . . . then I will. I ain't scared of them any more and I want to get them back for what they done to Kelly. Especially that Jason; little animal. So I'm gonna give you my address, where I'm going and everything and the minute you need someone to get up in that court and point the finger at the bastards you just let me know. It will be my pleasure.'

She writes the address down on the pad, holding the pen in a strange grasp in her left hand. As she writes she says suddenly, 'We just wanna live a little. Everyone does, don't they? But it's funny how many people there are tryin' to stop you. Why don't they all just mind their own business? Why do they have to go round troublin' others? You know I ain't being funny but it was when I heard about you that I decided to do something. When's it gonna stop I thought. I remembered you comin' round, trying to do something about all that nonsense and I thought well first it was the Asians, then Kelly and then you and everything. You know my boyfriend he was dead against me comin' down, we had a right row about it, but I can be a real stubborn cow sometimes. He'd better get used to it an' all. Here, this is your pen.'

'Well, thanks very much for coming in,' I say, holding the door open for her.

'That's all right. Don't go wandering down any dark alleys.'

I watch her leave the office. Waiting outside for her smoking is the girl I have seen before, Karen's dark-haired *doppel-gänger*. She must be Kelly. They are wearing almost exactly the same clothing of black leggings and boots and long denim shirts. Karen Reynolds slips her arm into her friend's and they disappear together down Jarvis Road and into the estate.

Roy is back at his desk. 'Witness number two,' I say.

'What time are you thinking of leaving?' Trevor asks me. 'About five all right 'cause I'm going down the gym. I can drop you off at the tube station on the way.'

'What, is your car all right then? I would have thought with a big knock like that in its side you wouldn't be taking it out on the road.'

Trevor grins at me. 'Shit, yeah, I forgot. You'll just have to walk, won't you. Take your chances with the *Waffen* SS on the streets.'

'It's the end of an era,' Bob says, 'Campbell not falling for any more car wind-ups. Don't worry Jamie, we'll find another one. He's so stupid he can only be on his guard for one thing at a time.'

'Why don't you take early retirement, Bob? Even with nobody to replace you the tenants would probably stand a better chance of getting a transfer.'

'I've told you before, clever Trevor, it's no good blaming me . . .'

'. . . It's the system. Yeah, yeah, yeah, change the record my son.'

'Have you two started getting it on or something while I've been away?' I say, ''Cause you're completely obsessed with each other. There's this raw energy between you.'

'It's called hatred,' Trevor replies.

'There's a thin line,' Roy says suddenly, 'between love and hate. Remember that, boys.'

'*I* wouldn't know anything about that,' says Bob.

'Really?' Roy arches an eyebrow campily, 'because I have to tell you that from my experience you have all the hallmarks of a frustrated queer. And I'm rarely wrong about these things.'

'Get out of it, I'm a married man. Family values, me.'

'That,' smiles Roy sweetly, 'is what they all say, Robert.'

Service Economy

In the end I don't take Trevor up on his offer, because I am going to see Ana María at Eduardo's so I travel by bus instead. When I arrive, Ana María and Soledad are sitting at the table drinking tea and eating mashed avocado on toast. Ana María is uncommunicative and clearly uneasy about starting work the next day. I suggest that we go out for a drink.

'I don't know,' she says doubtfully, 'I have to be there very early tomorrow morning.'

'You should go anyway,' says Soledad, setting some toast down before me and pouring another cup of tea, 'otherwise you're gonna get nervous. Just don't go completely mad.'

I paste the bright green avocado on some toast and crunch into it. 'Well, what do you think?'

'No,' she says suddenly, 'I'm going to stay here. Just read for a little maybe and write some letters.'

The dismissal hangs heavily in the air and Soledad looks at me expectantly.

'You're probably right,' I say stiffly. 'I've got a couple of things to be catching up on as well.'

I put the half-eaten toast on the plate. After an uncomfortable half an hour I leave. 'Thanks for the tea, Soledad.'

'I'm going out as well,' she says. 'I'll walk you down.'

I kiss Ana María on the cheek. 'See you.'

'Yes,' she replies vaguely. 'See you.'

As we walk to the stairs Soledad says to me, 'You're vexed, aren't you?'

'Yes,' I answer, although I am more miserable than angry.

'Don't be. That's what she's like. She is the living moody cow, man. If anyone's gonna get it now it's gonna be you. You know that. Anyway, fair enough, she didn't wanna be around anyone. I can understand that.'

'It's not that. She should have just said it properly. After all, it was her that wanted me to come round tonight in the first place. And it was my first day back at work today as well.'

'Yeah? That's a bit out of order. Just leave her for a bit. Make her sweat.'

'That's my problem. I'm not very good at that sort of tactic. What if the other person doesn't get worried and you never hear anything again?'

She turns to me incredulously. 'What! Don't be a wimp, Jamie. Ana María . . . well, I never thought I'd see her like it. Jamie this, Jamie that. She's been driving us crazy. It's *us* that want not to hear anything, we're getting sick of your name, it's worse than her politics. Anyway, you done the right thing. That's why she likes you, 'cause you didn't sit around pleading to stay or whining, "What's the matter?" like some men would have. You just upped and went.'

'Yes, I suppose you're right,' I say, enjoying this version of dignified masculine retreat rather than sulky injured pride.

'They're the worst, you know, Jamie. Whiners. I can't stand 'em. Where you going? Who with? What's the matter? Don't you love me any more? I mean that's no way to make yourself lovable, is it . . . yeah, fuck off!' she interrupts herself to whirl round and give the finger to two boys who have made a comment to her departing back. 'No, you and Ana María man, you're made for each other. Both boring bastards who spend so much time worrying about the world you don't get any time to enjoy it.'

'You cheeky bitch! I forget though, you're only young.

Shouldn't you be running along to your rave and taking some E?'

'Nobody calls them raves any more, Jamie – except the newspapers.'

'Really? Silly old me.'

'There you go,' she grins triumphantly. 'That's what you like best, isn't it? Arguing. That's got rid of your long face.'

We arrive at the bus stop and I say, 'Are you getting the bus?'

'No, I'm walking.'

'Give my regards to Patrick.'

Soledad cackles evilly. 'What gave you the idea it's Patrick I'm meeting?'

'You shameless hussy.'

'No, just young. And you only live once.' She blows me a kiss and strides off down the road.

The next day, I am going to phone Ana María to find out how she got on but when I get home from work I find that she has used the key I gave her in case of emergencies and is curled up asleep on the sofa. I sit down next to her. She wakes up blinking at me, a little dribble of saliva on her chin. 'Jamie.' She puts up her hand to my face. 'I'm so tired.'

'Oh dear, well actually it's a bit inconvenient you being here. I thought I might catch up on some reading tonight or maybe wash my hair.'

She laughs. 'You can't be nasty to me, *querido*, you have to listen to what a terrible day I have had. But first you have to make me something really nice to eat and go out and buy a bottle of wine for us. Expensive wine.'

'Is that right? And what are you going to do?'

'Now? I go back to sleep. Later I will be submissive and tender and obedient. What do they call those Japanese women who are like slaves?' She puts her hands together and bows her head in a mock, and not entirely convincing, show of meekness.

'Geisha girls. I can't see it somehow.'

Walking to the off-licence it suddenly strikes me. Thinking of Ana María sleeping on the sofa I realize that I have never before loved anyone as I love her. What if I lose her? What if she were to die? I imagine a car smashing into her. I imagine somebody deliberately hurting her. I shake my head. But you can't keep people under permanent observation and if you did they would stop loving you anyway, resent you, come to loathe your watchfulness.

The stout middle-aged Sikh who owns the off-licence regards me suspiciously, even though I have been going in there for years. He is an authoritarian who likes to spatter his ship with handwritten signs over and above the usual plea not to bring down offence on yourself by asking for credit. 'Clouse the door slowley' it says on the chiller cabinet and by the till are a battery of instructions. 'Do not offer lose change unless asked for it' and 'Checks not accepted here, even with card'. I scan the wines – fat bottles of screw-top Valpolicella and Lambrusco, cheap French table wine, Pink Lady and Canei – it's a pretty crap off-licence.

'What are you looking for?' barks the owner.

'Champagne,' I say suddenly, 'give me a bottle of champagne please.'

He holds the twenty-pound note which I give him up to the light and examines it ostentatiously from different angles as if expecting to find a watermark which says 'counterfeit' running through it, so I do the same with the five-pound note in the change. Surprisingly, he laughs and slaps the counter hard. 'Funny boy, eh? Can't be too careful these days you know. Here, that bottle's dusty. Let me give it a wipe. Not much call for champagne around here.'

I stand in the kitchen slicing onions and Ana María comes in and puts her arms around my back. Tears stream down my face from the bitter, invisible juices of the onion. 'Look,' says Ana María, taking the top of the onion which I have discarded and putting it on my head like a little cap, 'that is supposed to stop you crying.'

'And how does it do that?'

She shrugs. 'One does not ask such things. You must just believe.'

'Sorry, I've never been one for blind faith. Anyway, what about your job?'

Ana María scowls. 'It is horrible. A tremendous building. I kept getting lost with all the different floors. And the supervisor . . .' she shudders, 'I did not like him at all.'

'What about the other people? What are they like?'

She shrugs. 'Big mixture. Mostly Colombians and Nigerians. There is a Peruvian – he is nice. A couple of Chileans.'

'What are they like? The Chileans?'

'*Rotos*,' she says firmly. 'Lumpen. Eduardo knows some of them. They are always starting fights. Probably they are CIA agents.'

'What, cleaning offices?'

She juts her chin out. I remember the first time I met her and the orange rolling beneath her palm. It looks as if she has woken ready and prepared to do battle. 'Well, what are they supposed to do? Walk around with dark glasses and a gun in their pocket?'

'Yeah, but . . .' I start to laugh, '. . . what are they doing there? I mean you can't just call people you don't like CIA agents. They just sound like wankers to me.'

Ana María hates being laughed at. 'Well . . .' she says huffily, '. . . I wouldn't expect you to understand, having grown up here.'

'Oh, that's original. That's what I like about discussions with you. The delicate way in which you explore the complexities of a situation . . .' She puts her hand over my mouth.

'Shut up, Jamie. Tonight we have a truce. No arguments, yes?'

'Yes, no arguments. I'll drink to that. Anyway you've forgotten about your promise.'

'Oh yes.' She bows her head again. 'Please be gentle with me.'

I take the champagne out of the freezer compartment and hold it to her face. 'Cold enough?'

'*Ay* Jamie, it's freezing.'

I loosen the cork on the bottle and let the champagne hiss into the glasses, watching the foam swell and subside. I am about to sip mine when Ana María says, 'No, we must make a toast first.'

'OK.' We clink our glasses together and I say, 'To secret agents the world over. Even those infiltrating office cleaning companies.'

'*Salud.*' Ana María clinks her glass. 'And to patronizing Western liberals who are going to get a big shock one day when their illusions about democracy are shattered.'

'*Salud.*'

The Mystery of Things

The shifts that Ana María has to work mean that sometimes she does not come round and I mourn the days of convalescence when we were together nearly all the time. One early evening I am waiting for her, as we did not see each other the night before due to her late finish and early morning start. The weather has gone crazy. A huge storm is threatening, with a sky which looks like something from a pathologist's textbook, great purple and blue cloud contusions, and the threatening hiss of the advance rain peppering the window in short bursts. Inside, the room has become almost yellow like an old photograph, although further west, beyond the great mass of cloud, the sky is bright and almost clear apart from a few frantic smoky whisps. I am looking out for Ana María, with the TV on to the local news, when suddenly the announcer says, '. . . and now we can bring you more news of that shooting in East London earlier today. Police have named the dead man as Anthony O'Leary, a well-known local figure with a long police record. Mr O'Leary was shot as he got out of his car with a single shotgun blast to the head and it is believed that he may have been lured to his death. He died instantly. Police believe the killing to be linked to a gangland dispute and are urging anyone with any information to call them in the strictest confidence. And now here's Caroline Kingston with tonight's look at what is happening in the world of show business in the capital . . .'

A fierce wind-blown blast of rain spatters the window. The drops cling to the glass instead of running down, each one swollen with a tiny glimmer of light captured from inside the living-room. 'Oh no,' I say out loud to the empty room, thinking of O'Leary's blue car, the swallow on his neck, his head split open by the force of the pellets. There can't be two well-known Anthony O'Learys. The wind shakes the windows and wails up the old chimney flues like a frantic poltergeist. Lightning flashes. People in the street quicken their pace. How many times have I heard stories like that and paid them no attention? I pace anxiously around the room wondering if anyone will mourn him, whether there will be a funeral. I think of him shaking my hand, patting the baseball bat calmly on his palm, the swallow trembling on his neck when he got angry. I am perplexed by my reaction which is not so much of sorrow but bewilderment. Who was he anyway? Why was he given the name Anthony? What was I doing at precisely the moment that an undispersed fist of lead pellets was blasted into his face? When I had faced my moment of greatest danger he had arrived and saved me. Yet he had not been able to save himself. *And you, O'Leary, let me know what flowers you want for your funeral.*

The doorbell rings and I let Ana María in. She is wet from the rain and her face is a match for the storm which is breaking outside.

'What's up?'

'Wait. I want to make a cup of tea.'

She lights the cooker with trembling hands and places the kettle on the ring.

'Is something wrong at work?'

'Yes. I no longer have job now.'

'What, they sacked you? What reason did they give?'

She laughs bitterly. 'Reason? You remember I tell you about supervisor. The one I don't like. Well, over the last few weeks he has been making comments to me, then he started trying to touch me. I don't say nothing because I think maybe he will stop. But today he make it clear *el muy concha de su madre* that I have two choices: leave the job or . . .' she waves her hand disgustedly. 'So I tell him what I think of him, and where he should stick his job and that is it. *Ciao* job. I can do nothing. I have no rights, no work permit, no nothing.'

Steam genies out of the kettle as it boils. We both watch it without moving and the air begins to fill with the wet clouds until finally I lean over and switch it off. Ana María's fury and frustration bubble up. 'I hate this country, I hate men, I hate everything in this terrible place. I go.'

'Where?'

'How do I know? Chile maybe. Back to Mexico. Anywhere away from this horrible, cold, miserable country.' Her fists are clenched and her lower lip jutting out aggressively. I put my hand on her shoulder but she shrugs it off. 'No. Leave me now.' I am used to this sort of behaviour so I decide not to point out that she can't actually throw me out of my own kitchen. I walk into the living-room and after a little while I hear the bedroom door shut behind her.

After about an hour I quietly open the bedroom door. Ana María is fast asleep, fully dressed and half covered by the duvet. She looks stupid and I can't help laughing. Her face is set in exactly the same frown that she was wearing when she fell asleep. I sit down beside her and lift her hair out of her face. She murmurs something in Spanish and takes my hand. I lie down beside her, pull the cover over us and she curls into my body. Lightning dazzles the sky outside and I wait expectantly for its thunder roll. 'What am I going to do, Jamie?' she asks plaintively.

'I don't know,' I sigh, playing with her fingers. 'Oh yeah, I forgot. You know tonight Karen is having a leaving drink because she's changing jobs? She wants us both to go. Why don't we just get drunk?'

'Yes. I think better when I am drunk.'

I tell her about the shooting of O'Leary and her eyes widen.
'That is terrible. He is the man who help you?'
'Yes.'
We lie silently, listening to the storm receding, the rain diminishing. Did he ever think about me again after moving? Was I as good as gold? What was his last thought? Did his face register terror or surprise? Did it have time to hurt?

'Thank God,' says Colin when he sees us walk into the pub, 'people who can talk about something else apart from bloody housing. This lot have been boring me senseless talking about people in their office. I know all about how unreasonable Patsy can be in the mornings now and how Barry fiddles his flexitime.'
The girl sitting next to him casts him an offended look. Karen, who is already quite pissed and has about three full pints in front of her, grins at him. 'Well, you did invite yourself, you rude bastard.'
'Yeah, big mistake. Right, Jimmy, what are you having? I sold a picture today to some fat American poof so I'm celebrating.'
A boy with a T-shirt with 'Queer love is no crime' on it turns round and glares at Colin.
'Lager please, Mr Politically Correct,' I reply, trying to smile apologetically and receiving a contemptuous stare in response.
'And you, my not so obscure object of desire. Order whatever you wish.'
'Such an English gentleman,' says Ana María, fluttering her eyelashes at him. 'I'll have the same.'
'English!' Colin draws himself up. 'Only someone of your extraordinary beauty and lack of acquaintance with this septic isle can be excused such a crass error.'
'Watch out kids,' says Karen, 'it's the time of the month and this mad weather. His hormones are out of control. Nobody's

safe. Anyway, let me introduce you to Keith. Come here darling and meet my best friends.' Keith is shy and pretty and it is clear that he is one of Karen's temporary flings whose heart and ego will be seriously damaged by the encounter.

'Karen and Keith,' says Colin, returning with a tray of beers and chasers. 'That's beautiful. You can put it on your car windscreen when you move to Ilford.'

'How is Carlita?' asks Ana María, sipping her drink.

'Unfortunately, no longer around. She exhausted me. I had nothing left to give.'

'He means that she finished with him,' says Karen, 'and it was him who exhausted her with his unceasing nonsense.'

'Strange but false. I finished with her. When I found out that she was the daughter of Pablo Escobar.'

'He got scared,' Karen adds, 'that he would end up with his testicles in his mouth or a horse head in his bed.'

'Not true. I got angry 'cause she wouldn't do me any cheap coke.'

'Who's Pablo Escobar?' asks Keith.

'A Colombian drug baron,' I say. 'A dead Colombian drug baron.'

'And she was really his daughter!' Keith is impressed. There is a cruel silence and Colin raises his eyebrows at me. But a sideways glance from Karen is enough to deter any urge he might have to take the piss.

'No,' he says, swallowing his lager, 'she wasnae really his daughter. I'm only joking about it to cover the deep and indelible scars on my heart which could only be healed by . . .'

'. . . A shag,' Karen interrupts.

'Well actually, yes,' Colin says pensively. 'That would be a start. Sex-ual healing. Any offers?' and he stares at the girl he has previously been talking to.

'You couldn't even get a shag off a bus stop mate,' she says coldly.

'So, Colin, you've been busy making friends tonight,' I say, and Ana María giggles. 'You are revolting pig, Colin.'

'I don't think anyone can argue with that,' Karen agrees. 'Come on revolting pig, settle down and ponder on the oft-neglected virtue of subtlety. Or even better, go to the bar.' And she gives him a twenty-pound note.

'I'm just going out to find a bus stop first,' says Colin.

'How is your job, Ana,' Karen asks, and Ana María explains what has happened that day.

Colin, halfway between bar and table, nearly drops the tray of drinks when he hears what has happened. 'Right. Where is this place?' he demands instantly. 'What's the bastard's name?'

'Surely you could put in a complaint of unfair dismissal,' interrupts Keith. 'There's lots of sexual harassment cases in the news nowadays.'

'Get real, pal,' snaps Colin, 'she doesn't – didn't – work for some cushy local authority. No, we'll just have to go and sort the fucker out. Break his fuckin' legs.'

'O'Leary's dead,' I say suddenly. Karen looks at me sharply. 'What?'

'Tony O'Leary. The guys who were looking for him . . . they found him.'

'Shit.'

'Yeah.'

Keith looks confused. 'Is this another joke?' he ventures.

'No,' I finish my pint. 'It isn't.'

'So what are you going to do, Ana?' Karen asks.

Ana María shrugs. 'I agree with Colin. I think he should have his legs broken. But for now I need work permit.'

'Well, you'll have to get married to an Englishman,' Karen says. 'Why don't you get married to Jamie?'

'No, I couldn't marry Jamie. It would be too complicated. Jamie is my *compañero*. I don't want marriage to make everything difficult. I would not be able to separate the reasons. It would have to be just for that motive of getting work permit.

But I could . . .' she suddenly grins wickedly '. . . marry someone who is not English.'

'Wouldn't that defeat the purpose of getting a work permit?' asks Keith.

Karen shrieks with laughter. 'I think she's saying . . .' she chokes on her beer '. . . I think she's saying that she could marry a Scottish person.'

Colin is sitting dumbfounded, staring at Ana María, for once in his life completely lost for words. 'Me?' he finally splutters.

'Why not?' Karen's eyes are gleaming. 'I think that's brilliant. I mean, there could never be any question that there was any other reason behind it. But immigration aren't going to know that, are they?'

Colin is trying to recover his composure. 'Yeah, but wouldn't Jamie . . . I mean it's a bit fuckin' weird, isn't it?'

'I don't know,' I say. 'I can see the logic in it.'

'But what if they come round and start checking the tooth-brushes. I've seen it, you know. On *EastEnders*. Maybe they'll do some big investigation. Come round sheet-sniffing. What's that film with the French radge with the big nose? *Green Card*?'

'Nah,' Karen says. 'And anyway, we can deal with that. Oi . . .' she nudges Keith, '. . . get another round in. We have to drink a toast to Mrs McRefugee.'

We watch Keith struggling at the bar to grab the barman's attention, pogoing forlornly and waving his money in the air like a drowning man. Karen sighs. 'Oh dear. He'll have to go.'

By closing time, we are all hopelessly drunk. Colin has switched from bewilderment to feverish excitement about the prospect of his nuptials. He buys three pairs of cheap socks from an old Scottish man who is hawking them around the pub out of a carrier bag, and presents a pair to the girl who claimed he couldn't get a shag off a bus stop. Then he tries to persuade Ana María that he will be entitled to spend the first night with her. 'We could go on honeymoon to Scotland,' he says. 'It would only be for sex though, no emotional complications. Otherwise of course cash would be acceptable. I believe that it's quite common in these cases for a small premium to be paid to the person involved.'

'I don't want to have sex with you. And I have no money.'

'Well, Jamie can pay. It is, after all, partly so that his beloved can stay with him that we're doing this.'

'You're right,' I reply, 'and I'll tell you what I'm going to do. I'm going to forget that thirty quid you owe me. Can't say fairer than that.'

Back in the flat as we lie in bed drinking water to fend off tomorrow's hangover, I say to Ana María, 'Are you really going to do this?'

'I might,' she says. 'If I stay here I need work permit. But I'm not sure I could marry Colin. Even for that.'

'So you're not still thinking about running off?'

'Ah Jamie, sometimes I just say things. Don't take everything so seriously. I'm sorry.'

'Marry me then,' I say. 'Just for the work permit.' She turns to face me.

'Maybe,' and she pulls me towards her.

Sparks

One morning, after a stream of tenants complaining that their keys to the gate on the arch in Folkestone Road don't fit, Bob Townsend approaches my desk looking very smug.

'Your Mrs Khan,' he says, 'is about to receive an offer of a lovely four-bedroomed street property.'

'Where?'

'Riverside.'

'Riverside!'

'Well yeah, but a good part of Riverside. And you can't have everything.'

'I suppose not. Well, that's good. Does she know?'

'The offer letter went out yesterday.'

'Excellent.'

'So all your troubles are over.'

'Let's hope that Mrs Khan's are. Anyway, they're not, 'cause we're still looking to evict the Kings.'

'Why bother now? I mean, as long as we don't go and put another Asian family in there, things should quieten down considerably.'

I stare at him. 'You stupid ignorant . . . Bob, don't you understand anything?'

His grin fades. 'What? What are you on about, Jamie? There's no need to talk to me like that. I've just done you a favour.'

'Me a favour? You're unreal, you really are.' I am shouting now and Roy turns round.

'All right Jamie, let it go, you've made your point.'

'No, fuck off, Roy,' and I feel a collective flinch from the office at this challenge to his authority. 'I mean, for the last few months, Mrs Khan's had shit smeared on her door, her windows broken, pitbulls outside her house, Maggie nearly gets killed with a brick, I get my face rearranged and nearly have a swastika carved on it, O'Leary's dead . . .'

'. . . What the fuck has O'Leary got to do with it?' roars Bob. 'I got him a transfer as well for God's sake. I suppose it's my fault he went and got himself blown away.'

'. . . And all this stupid bastard can say is that he's done me a favour and we shouldn't put any more Asian families on the estate.'

They can hear the row downstairs now and there is a whisper-punctuated hush over the office.

Roy rises with his hands outstretched trying to calm things down, but Bob is off again. 'Well, this is great. All I ever get is slagged off in this office when it's not my fault and I come and tell someone that their tenant's got a transfer and they start slagging me off again. I'm only human, you know.'

'Really?' mutters Trevor just audibly. He has been sitting pretending to write a letter but has been hanging on every word, and is not going to miss an opportunity to have a go at Bob.

'What? Come on Campbell, out with it. If you've got something to say, say it. You're a bunch of wankers, all of you.'

'For not going down on hands and knees to you for just doing your job? For being a racist?'

'A racist! Me! I'm not a racist.'

'But no Asians on the estate because it might cause problems, right? And don't do anything about people who certainly *are* racists because it might give you a few headaches.'

'You're full of shit, Collins, you don't know what you're on about. I've worked in this authority for thirty years. When you couldn't have turned up for work looking like you do, you

248

scruffy bastard. I was here when you were still in nappies. Thirty years!'

'Thirty years too long,' says Trevor.

'Before people like you were even here, Campbell.'

'What! People like me? What was it like before we were here, eh Bob? Do you want to expand on that one? What exactly do you mean by people like me?'

Trevor is rising from his chair.

'That's enough!' Roy suddenly shouts. 'Shut it, Trevor. Bob, go into the kitchen. I'll come and talk to you in a minute. Jamie, go outside for a walk and calm down. I am not having this in the office. Now, Bob! I mean it, Jamie. You've gone too far.'

'Yeah, well, it's easy for you to say, isn't it, Roy.'

'I'm not even going to bother answering that, Jamie, and don't push me because I could discipline you all for this.'

'So discipline me then, you fucking bureaucrat. I don't give a shit.'

And I storm downstairs and out of the office door followed by the amazed eyes of the social workers and housing benefits staff. Goodbye job. I wander down the main road and contemplate going home, already feeling slightly guilty about what I said to Roy. A bus comes lumbering towards the stop, where a queue of pensioners are grumbling about its late arrival. I consider just getting on it when suddenly Roy appears half-jogging behind me. 'Jamie, slow down.'

'What do you want?'

'Come on, Jamie. Let's go and get a cup of tea.'

'I don't want a cup of tea. Leave me alone.'

'Well, come and watch me drink one. Look, I just want to talk to you. Come on, you know you can't go on like this.'

He takes my arm and leads me towards a café. 'Two teas,' he says to the owner. 'Do you want anything to eat?'

I shake my head, embarrassed because tears are beginning to spill down my face. The owner stares at me uncomfortably.

'What are you staring at?' I demand and he shakes his head and disappears out the back.

Roy laughs. 'Jamie, you can't fight with everybody.'

'Sorry. Sorry.' I am trying to control myself but my face is contorting with the effort and strange involuntary sobs leave my throat. Roy watches me, sipping his tea. He passes me a tissue and I blow my nose. 'God, I'm not even drunk,' I say miserably. 'I'm sorry, you know, that I swore at you. It's just that things have been piling up, you know. Like that O'Leary thing, I can't explain it, I can't say it without it sounding stupid, but some people don't get a chance, they don't ever get happy, like the man who threw everything out of the window and then himself, and sometimes those things can seem so tragic and you can't laugh any more, you can't laugh . . .'

Roy watches me. He is smiling but it is not a horrible smile. 'You know, Jamie, when Danny died I couldn't cry for ages. Even at the horrible funeral with his vile relatives – all loud-mouthed pub owners with loads of money – I couldn't. And then about three weeks later I was in Sainsbury's and I was picking up cans of tuna and trying to decide whether to get it in oil or in brine and which was more dolphin-friendly – I mean you don't give a shit about the way the tuna got squashed into the can – and suddenly everything seemed – well like you've just said . . . and that was it. I was howling, it was so-o-o embarrassing. I just stood there holding this can of tuna and bawling my eyes out and everyone just ignoring me, looking away. Then suddenly this old woman came up to me and took me by the arm and said, "It's all right love, it's all right," over and over again until I stopped. Look, Jamie, I know why you reacted like you did. And I know how sometimes it only takes a little spark. But you've got to be careful with old Bob as well, you know. You and Trevor give him a hard enough time and OK, sometimes he deserves it, but he was right, he is human as well and subject to stress like all of us. When you got hurt in that incident he was really upset, he organized the card and everything. He says things without thinking sometimes and it's good that you pull him up. But you've got to use a bit more suss than just shouting at him and calling him a racist.'

'Yeah, well, normally I would you know, it's just . . .'

'It's all right, I do understand that, but I'm your manager as well. I can't have screaming matches in the office. Especially not when tenants can hear. It's been rough the last couple of months and I really appreciate the work you've put in. You're good at your job, Jamie, even though . . .'

'. . . My paper work is rubbish.'

'You took the words right out of my mouth. Come on, Jamie, come back to work. I'd tell you to take the afternoon off but I think it would be better if you came back in and made your peace with Bob. Also . . .'

'. . . My flexitime won't allow it.'

'If you ever contemplate moving on career-wise, Jamie, you'd make an excellent mind-reader.'

Back in the office, Bob is sitting at his desk eating his liver sausage sandwiches and reading the *Daily Express*. Trevor winks at me and I wonder if my face is red and puffy. Bob looks up sheepishly. 'Listen, Jamie, what I said, I can see now that it was a bit insensitive. I'm sorry.'

'It's OK. I'm sorry I flew off the handle.' Bob holds out his hand to me and even though it feels a bit stupid I shake it.

'Just one thing though,' Bob says. 'When I said that to Trevor, you know, about your sort of people and that. I didn't mean it in a racist way at all.'

'How did you mean it?'

'He frowns. 'I don't know. I suppose I meant . . .' he suddenly brightens '. . . I suppose I meant that he was just a wanker really.'

'And when was this time before there were wankers in this authority?' asks Trevor cunningly. 'After all, you said yourself you've been here thirty years.'

Roy puts his head in his hands but Bob just laughs. 'All right, so I'm a wanker as well. I'm sorry.'

'*Ich bin ein wanker*,' I say. 'Who isn't sometimes?'

'Me,' Roy says, 'I'm the only sane one in this section I think.'

'Well, we'd all be sane,' I reply, 'if we never had to meet any tenants and sat around all day writing reports and sucking up to senior management.'

'Jamie, I think a session on your rent arrears is long overdue. I hope everything is up to date when we go through it at . . .' he looks at his watch '. . . three-thirty this afternoon.'

¡Viva Zapata!

Ana María gets a new job in a Mexican restaurant in Camden Town. At first she thought that it would just be washing-up, but it turns out that her task is to move around from table to table offering the diners shots of tequila, keeping a percentage of every glass that she sells. The downside is that she has to dress up as a Mexican guerrilla, with the tequila glasses replacing the bullets in her gun belt and a special holster for the bottle.

One night we have arranged to go out with Karen and Colin. As Ana María is working that night we agree to meet first at the restaurant with the promise of cheap margaritas. I go to collect Colin from his studio before picking Karen up at Camden Town station. Colin is still working when I arrive. There are several studios in the old white-walled building and Colin's is right at the top, through a maze of corridors and skylights. To describe Colin's workplace as chaotic would not be doing justice to the state of total anarchy which prevails. Apart from the jumble of brushes, oils, canvases and jamjars, there are stacks of empty wine, beer and spirit bottles, piles of newspapers spilling in all directions, and junk of every conceivable type. On the door is a sticker which says 'We don't deal with Cunts' and stencilled on the wall is a giant Elvis from *Jailhouse Rock*.

'Bill, I'm going . . .' shouts Colin to an adjoining studio as he sees me. '. . . Don't forget to lock up.'

We catch the tube, making a list of all the horrible things about Camden Town on the way: the fact that the tube always stops between Euston and Camden Town, the tube station itself, the large proportion of goths and hippies, the crowds on Sundays, the impossibility of getting a cab once the buses have stopped. 'I fucking hate Camden,' announces Colin loudly as we make our way up the escalator. Karen is waiting for us at the entrance and scowls at us as we arrive. 'Thanks for making me wait,' she grumbles.

Ana María's restaurant is not hard to find, it is covered with pictures of large green cacti and men in sombreros riding donkeys. Colin begins to drag his feet. 'Do we have to go in?' he asks. 'Yes,' Karen replies. 'Anyway, I could murder a margarita.'

We are met at the door by a hawk-faced manageress who ushers us to a table. As she hands us some large menus I look around for Ana María.

'We don't really want to eat . . .' starts Karen, and the manageress snatches back the menus.

'You can't sit here then.'

'Why not?' Karen asks.

'Because this part is for people eating. You have to sit at the back.'

Colin looks around him at various empty tables. 'It's not exactly causing you a problem if we sit here though, is it.'

The manageress puts her hands on her hips and stares at him for a second as if she can hardly believe that he is questioning her authority. Colin stares back as if he can hardly believe that she is questioning his right to question her authority.

'Come on,' I say, thinking of Ana María's relationship with her manageress. 'It doesn't matter. We'll move.' I try and smile at the woman but this only seems to increase her contempt for us.

'Look,' says Karen as we take up our new position, 'there's

Ana María. My God.' She covers her mouth with her hand and giggles.

Ana María is dressed in a black shirt and black trousers with two bands of tequila glass bullets crossing her chest. She is wearing a black hat and a black expression, moving from table to table offering the customers their shots of tequila. When she sees us she abandons this task and goes and whispers to the barman. He looks over at us and nods and starts preparing a large jug of margaritas. Ana María brings it over with three salt-frosted glasses. The margaritas are strong. 'I told Giovanni to put some tequila in yours,' Ana María grins, 'they serve them really weak here.'

I notice with some trepidation that the manageress is staring over at us.

'I don't like the look of your manageress,' I say.

Ana María glances over contemptuously. 'Her? She is assistant manageress. She just likes to think she has lots of power. She is Spanish,' she adds as if this is significant. Colin waves at the assistant manageress and she looks away haughtily.

Ana María moves off to serve more tequilas and we attack the jug of margaritas, watching her. It is hard not to laugh, because she does her job with what appears to be a complete lack of interest in whether people buy the tequila or not. Karen is also having difficulty restraining her laughter. 'Do you think she might sell more if she actually . . . you know . . . smiled from time to time?' she whispers to me. But Ana María has clearly decided that the indignity of being dressed up is as much as she is prepared to compromise in this job. Matters are made worse when a second tequila seller emerges who whoops and laughs, insists that the customers really *do* want a tequila when they say no, and consequently appears to sell about twice as much. Tequila seller number two is dressed up like a Mexican bandit even though she has blonde hair, a posh accent and is clearly working her way through drama college.

Colin decides he is hungry so we move back to the eating

area. The assistant manageress is over like a shot.

'I've told you before, you can't sit here. Ana María, come here. You must tell your friends . . .'

'Chill out, Mamacita,' says Colin, 'we're gonna eat now. Bring me one of your giant menus 'cause I just can't decide whether I'm in a burritos or fajitas mood tonight.'

The assistant manageress slaps three menus down in front of us and glares at Ana María.

While we are waiting for our food, three men in suits at the next table to us beckon Ana María over. They have been talking loudly all evening, stopping only to have equally loud conversations on their mobile phones. Ana María comes over, the expression on her face unchanged.

'How much is the tequila, darling?'

'One pound fifty,' replies Ana María, reaching for a glass.

'One pound fifty!' says the loudest of the men. 'I should get more than a tiny tequila for one pound fifty,' and he looks Ana María up and down. Colin puts his glass down but Karen places her hand on his arm. Ana María appears quite unperturbed.

'It is cheap, one pound fifty,' she says, 'but it is up to you.'

'Eet is cheep, one pound fifty,' the man mimics her voice. Ana María stares blankly back at him. 'OK,' she says dully and makes to move away.

'No, no,' he says, 'I'm only joking, love. Give us three tequilas.' As she starts to pour the drinks, he puts a fiver on the table. 'That's four-fifty for the tequilas and fifty pence for the blow-job,' and he roars with laughter. 'Eet is cheep, no?' One of the men he is with looks slightly ashamed and turns away. But this is all just too much for Colin.

'Oi, radge,' he snarls, shaking Karen's arm off his. 'You'd better apologize to her right fucking now.'

The man swings round and focuses blearily on Colin. He has obviously been drinking since he left the office. 'A sweaty!' he exclaims. 'A sweaty sock. Och aye. Hoots mon.' And he roars with laughter.

'Shut up, Gavin,' says the man next to him. 'Just settle down and stop being a prat. I'm sorry love,' he says to Ana María, taking out a tenner. 'Here, give us three more tequilas and keep the change. Ignore him mate, he's just pissed.'

Colin is half out of his seat already but Karen hauls him back. 'Stop it,' she hisses. 'It's all right now.'

Gavin slumps back into his seat but the fragile peace is shattered by the assistant manageress marching over. 'Right,' she says, 'I've had enough of you three. I want you to leave.'

For a moment I think that she is talking to the three men but then she swings round to Ana María. 'Your friends have caused nothing but trouble since they arrived. Especially this one.' She points at Colin. 'Tell them to leave please.'

Ana María stares at her, one hand on the tequila bottle in its holster as if she is about to draw.

'Why should they leave? It was not their fault.'

'Yeah, come on, love,' says Gavin's friend. 'It's OK. Things just got a bit high-spirited, that's all. We're all mates now. Aren't we?'

We all nod except Colin, who is still levitating a few inches off his seat and who has Gavin fixed in a glare that would have probably frightened him had he been sober enough to remember what happened thirty seconds ago.

'I said . . .' spits the manageress through gritted teeth, looking only at Ana María '. . . tell your friends to leave.'

Ana María stares back at her. 'Fuck you,' she says, as I had kind of expected she might.

There is a second of pure silence before the assistant manageress erupts. It is hard to make out what she is saying, as it is a mixture of English and Spanish curses. The gist of it, however, is that Ana María is sacked, that she must leave with us, and that this is the last time the restaurant will ever employ lazy, uncivilized, thieving Latin Americans. Ana María throws off her hat contemptuously and goes to collect her stuff.

'You get out now,' shrieks the assistant manageress to us.

'Not yet,' replies Karen calmly, 'we're waiting for our friend.'

'I call police, I call police now . . .'

'Shut up,' I say, 'we've told you we're waiting for our friend.'

Ana María emerges from the back carrying her jacket and bag. She goes to the bar and says goodbye to the barman, who has been watching the whole proceedings with an appalled fascination. A waitress stands staring with four plates of enchiladas, her mouth open. Only the second tequila seller is moving around quietly urging people to sample her wares. Ana María says coldly to the assistant manageress, 'You think you have hurt me because you sack me. But you cannot hurt me because what are you? You are assistant manageress and you always will be. You are no more than that. And you are so proud to be Spanish, but your ancestors probably carried syphilis to my continent and you are still nothing more than ignorant peasant syphilitic trash.'

'That's you told,' smirks Colin as we make for the door.

As we walk down the street, I notice that Ana María is struggling with her bag, which is making clunking noises. 'What have you got in there?' I ask. She stops and rests her bag on her knee, before opening it to reveal about six bottles of tequila.

'Yeeehaaa,' shouts Colin. 'Back to the studio. I'm in a slamming kind of mood.'

But suddenly Ana María's face just kind of crumples and big tears start falling from her eyes.

'Hey,' says Karen gently, 'it's OK. Don't let it get to you. You couldn't have gone on doing that job anyway.'

But Ana María just shakes her head and sobs hiccup out of her. Karen motions to me and moves away with Colin. I lead her by the arm out of the middle of the pavement and we lean against an advertising hoarding. I take the bag off her. I know she is not crying for losing her job or for the row with the assistant manageress. She puts her arms around me and cries on to my shoulder while Karen and Colin stand facing the other way. Finally she looks up at me, strands of hair plastered to her face. 'I know it sounds stupid, Jamie, but it is just the fact that they dressed me up like a Mexican as well, it made me think . . .'

'I know,' I say.

She smiles awkwardly. 'Come on. Let's go. I'm OK now.'

We rejoin Karen and Colin. 'I'm sorry,' says Ana María.

Colin puts his arm around her. For a moment I think he is going to cry as well.

'Listen, Ana María,' he says, 'you're fucking brilliant. I love you, you know that. And I really think we should just get in a taxi, get out of fucking Camden, go back to my studio and cane a few of those bottles of tequila. Don't go home like this or I'll go home greetin' as well.'

She looks up at him, her face still puffy, and he kisses her forehead. 'How can I say no,' she replies, and wipes at her nose with her hand.

Ammonia

One morning I arrive at work to find two police officers talking to Roy.

'Ah, Jamie,' says Roy. 'Good. Something's happened. We're about to have a meeting.'

Khaled and Paula emerge with a couple of people from the Monitoring Group and there are a clutch of council officers including Tim Broadbent the area manager. Hilda Connolly glances suspiciously at me before turning back to speak to one of the policemen.

'What's happened?'

'Last night there was a big fight outside Mrs Khan's house. Some of her relatives went out to try and sort out some of the boys and one of them got kicked in the head and had ammonia thrown in his eyes. He's still in hospital. Dean Anderton got a kitchen knife in his stomach.'

'Self-defence,' says Khaled, who I notice has got a large bruise on the side of his face.

'I don't know what's happening to this estate,' says Hilda, scowling at Khaled and Paula with distaste, 'and we don't need all these outsiders sticking their noses in. They're responsible for half the trouble if you ask me. Now if we had more gates . . .'

'Nobody did ask you though, did they?' interrupts Paula. 'And if we're gonna start looking for people to blame, then you're well in the frame, love. Maybe it would help if you remembered to invite a few black people to your little meetings.'

'Anyway,' continues Roy, skilfully moving between them, 'the police arrived fairly quickly for a change and there are witnesses who saw Jason King use the ammonia. He's under arrest and is going to be charged with causing GBH.'

'But outrageously enough,' Khaled continues loudly so that the police officers can hear, 'Mrs Khan's nephew is being held as well and may be charged with affray.'

One of the policemen looks over at Khaled. He has a big brutish face, in fact everything about him is big, as if they have taken an American football player – protective clothing and all – and stuffed him into a police uniform. His shoulders are hunched up like a giant Quasimodo about to sprout wings, and his hair seems to emerge from a single point in his scalp. I wonder what it would be like to be so devastatingly ugly that nothing you could do – dieting, spending money on clothes, plastic surgery – would make any difference whatsoever. He smiles awkwardly and nervously as he sees me looking at him and I feel guilty.

'What about the person who stabbed Anderton?' I ask. 'Is anyone going to get charged with that?'

'Doesn't look like it. Nobody saw that. And the knife hasn't been found.'

'Jason King has got quite a record,' Roy adds. 'So if he gets found guilty, which I suspect he will, he's going to be off our hands for a little while.'

'But we still go for the eviction, right?'

'Yes. Definitely. But with Mrs Khan's transfer through and King and Anderton off the scene, hopefully things will settle down a little because that's still going to take some time. Obviously, in a way it's easier because now there's a criminal prosecution as well, although I've sometimes known the courts take a funny attitude in those cases and ask why we're going for eviction when there are criminal proceedings taking care of the matter. We'll have to wait and see. Legal have to sort that one out.'

'What about Anderton?'

'He'll live, although apparently he's in quite a state. He's putting all the blame on King and he's given a statement. He thought somebody had been killed so he was in a terrible panic. He's being charged with affray and something else.'

'And Mrs Khan?'

'She's moving this week. Still wouldn't go into emergency accommodation. Hopefully, it will be Tuesday and I want that flat boarded up straight away and a security door on.'

'Right.'

Roy moves off to speak to the area manager and Khaled takes my arm, his eyes gleaming excitedly as if adrenalin is still coursing through his veins. 'It was brilliant, Jamie. Total ambush. They weren't expecting it at all. There they were and out we came. Akhtar was brilliant. Kickboxed that King bastard after he had sprayed the ammonia and took him out completely.'

'What about the charges against him?'

'He'll be all right. We've got good lawyers. He'll be out this afternoon.'

'Well, I hope it's all over now.'

'It's never over, Jamie.'

In the afternoon I visit Mr Peters. There is a definite edge to the atmosphere on the estate and people watch me carefully as I pass. Everything seems calm outside Mrs Khan's house, with no evidence of the previous night's drama.

'Jamie,' Mr Peters exclaims as he opens the door. 'Nice to see you back, boy. Heard about last night I suppose. Old Bill managed to arrive on time for once and it's a good thing for those boys that they did. The Asian lads were giving them a bloody good hiding. Hold up, I've got the kettle on.'

I sit in the living-room and Sandra, Sarah and Samantha beam down at me through their gap teeth. Mr Peters emerges with the teapot and a plate of Bourbon creams. 'Sarah's just won the talent competition at her school.'

'What did she do?'

'Sang. A Madonna song.'

I don't ask if it was *Like a Virgin*, as I feel that, where his grandchildren are concerned, he might not see the funny side. '*Holiday*,' says Mr Peters, as if reading my thoughts. "Cause they were about to break up for half-term. Good idea, eh?'

'Yes.' I try my best to look sincere. 'Absolutely.'

'She's got talent all right, that one.'

'Well, she mustn't hide it under a bushel.'

'That's what I say. Well, what about you young man? Took a beating yourself I hear. Now if you'd been a boxer you might have had more of a chance.' He snaps a bourbon in two. 'Last night, *that* was a fight all right.'

'Did you call the police?'

'I did. Gave a statement as well. I saw that King boy with the ammonia.'

'What about the boy who got stabbed?'

'What, the Anderton boy? Little fool. Jack Saunders'll be spinning in his grave. This might teach him a lesson.'

'And did you see what happened there?'

He slips his feet into his slippers and taps his pipe out into the ashtray. 'No. Can't say I did. Anyway he got what he deserved. You can't go around troubling people in their homes and then complain if one of them decides to sort you out. Don't matter what colour you are. Pink, blue . . .'

'Maybe you'll get some sleep at night now.'

'Well, some quiet at least. I told you before I don't sleep much. Not since Joyce died.' He gazes at the photograph. 'I miss you, love,' he half-murmurs, as if I am not there, and it is said with such a genuine sense of irreplaceable loss that I feel the ache of his words rather than any embarrassment at the public display of pathos. He wipes at his eye. 'Sorry, mate. I'm just a stupid old man.'

'And why should you not be,' I reply. 'You don't have to apologize.'

'So are we not going to have any more of our little chats now it's going to calm down a bit?'

'Well . . .' I reach out for another biscuit '. . . actually I want to ask you a favour. See if you can keep an eye on the flat because the lady's going to be moving and I'm worried it might get vandalized or something. I could pop round next week and check that everything's OK.'

'Right you are, Jamie. Oh yes, and one more thing. Now that gate. We're very grateful and everything but half the keys don't bleedin' work.'

I cover my ears with my hands. 'I know, I know. It's being sorted.'

'All right,' and as I leave he pats me on the shoulder. 'Don't forget next week, son.'

Better than Lemons

'Lemons are brilliant,' I observe as I impale the yellow dome on the purple plastic squeezer and watch the pips and slushy filaments dribbling out of it.

'Lemons and onions,' agrees Ana María, 'are things you must have in your house at all times.'

She has decided to cook a Chilean meal for us and has also invited the Peruvian from her ill-fated cleaning job. I am squeezing the lemons to make pisco sours, a mounting pile of skins beside me. Ana María is making a dish which seems like a kind of shepherd's pie except with a baked sweetcorn topping instead of potato. She pauses every now and again to feed olives into my mouth. When the lemons are squeezed and the food is baking in the oven, there is still an hour or so before people are due to arrive. 'Come here, Jamie, I want to show you something,' she says and takes me into her bedroom and closes the door.

'What is it?'

'No, come here, you can't see from there.'

I move closer and she grabs me and falls on to the bed. 'Oh no, we're falling,' she says, pulling me after her.

'I've got lemony hands.'

'Let's see.' She takes my finger and sucks it questioningly. 'Yes you're right about lemons. They're brilliant.' Ana María likes the word brilliant and always pronounces it with extra emphasis.

267

We remove each other's clothes quickly. But as our breathing crescendoes we hear the key in the door and freeze, staring at each other. 'Ana María,' Soledad calls, 'are you in?' I put my hand over her mouth to stop her from giggling and move gently inside her. She bites at my finger. We hear Soledad approach the bedroom door, hesitate and then tap gently. 'Ana María?' Then her footsteps disappear down the hallway. After a while Ana María says, 'But some things are better even than lemons.'

We dress quickly and return to the kitchen, as Ana María is worried about the food in the oven. Soledad is sitting in the kitchen drinking tea. 'Oh, you're in,' she says. 'Didn't you hear me?'

Ana María simply smiles at her and Soledad laughs. 'Right, I get it.'

Colin and Karen arrive together with bottles of wine wrapped in green tissue paper. Colin is carrying a guitar case.

'Ah good,' Ana María exclaims, 'you brought the guitar.'

'What's this?' I ask, picking up the instrument in its black plastic case.

'It's a guitar,' Colin replies.

'Yeah, I got that much. But why?'

'"Cause me and Ana María are going to entertain tonight, dumbo. It's no going to be one of your dry English dinner parties. We're gonna sing.'

'Can you play the guitar then?' I ask her.

'Of course,' and she unzips the case revealing the shiny wooden curve of the base of the instrument. She takes out the guitar and begins to strum gently, frowning and stopping briefly to tune it.

'So can I,' Colin says, watching Ana María proudly. 'But I'd better have something to drink first.'

I pour pisco sours for everybody and wrinkle my nose at the combination of bitter citrus juice and strong alcohol.

'More sugar,' Ana María says firmly.

'No, no sweet tooth, this is great,' Colin says, and downs his glass in one, holding it straight out again for a refill.

'I hope Gustavo is not lost,' muses Ana María, glancing at her watch. 'I think maybe we eat anyway.'

Gustavo arrives as we are eating but offers no clue as to the reason for his lateness. He is tall with a gloomy and slightly superior expression and jet-black hair, darker even than Ana María's. 'Can't see his bottle,' Colin mutters to me as Ana María fetches him a plate of food. He does not talk to anybody much except Ana María and occasionally Eduardo, who has also arrived late. He completely ignores Colin, who keeps him under a continuous baleful surveillance. After we have finished eating, we move into the living-room. 'Watch fucking *Sendero Luminoso* over there,' Colin grumbles audibly. 'He's got his eyes on my future wife.'

Karen takes Colin's arm and leads him to the sofa. 'Now Colin, you remember what you promised? You remember you said you'd be a good boy?'

Something about the way they touch each other and the way Karen talks to him makes me start and I remember Karen's leaving drink and the fact that Colin was there when we arrived as well as their joint arrival today. I narrow my eyes at Karen and she blushes and drops Colin's arm. 'Aha,' I murmur, like a detective who has just uncovered a piece of particularly interesting evidence. 'I see.'

Colin picks up the guitar and plays a few chords. Then he begins to sing. He plays well and has a surprisingly good voice and I remember how he used to be in a band when he lived up in Scotland. He sings a strange, gentle version of *Smoke Gets in Your Eyes*, and *Crazy* by Patsy Cline which he dedicates to Ana María. 'You are certainly crazy for trying,' she remarks, as she pours everybody more wine. He passes her the guitar. 'Come on then, your turn now.'

'I do not know what to sing,' she says and Eduardo, who is slightly drunk from the pisco, tells her to sing something by

Victor Jara. I watch her fingers moving swiftly on the strings, her head bowed towards the instrument, singing quietly and hesitatingly at first but then more confidently. I understand only odd phrases but one image sticks in my mind – the other star. Why the other star? Other from what? Ana María finishes the song and then says, 'Now it is my turn to dedicate a song and I dedicate this one to Jamie.' I blush uncontrollably and everybody laughs and claps. 'This is a song by my favourite singer Violetta Parra. She wrote protest songs and songs of love and suffering. But this song is her most famous. It is called *Gracias a la vida*.'

There is total silence as Ana María sings. Once she makes a mistake with the notes but nobody stirs. Again, I understand very little but the subtle melody fills the room, hypnotizing the listeners and leaving a deep silence when the final notes die away. 'That was fucking magic,' Colin finally says. 'What happened to her?'

Ana María laughs drily and puts the guitar carefully down. Eduardo hands her a glass of wine. 'She shot herself.'

'Well,' Eduardo says, 'somebody else's turn. Everybody must perform tonight. Jamie?'

'I can't sing,' I say.

'Well, do something else then. Read a poem, tell a joke.'

'There is a poem,' I say hesitantly, caution slightly abandoned because of the drink, 'that I think I can still remember. Most of it anyway.'

'Well, go on.'

I clear my throat remembering the days of lonely adolescence when I would learn poems by heart. 'Processions that lack high stilts . . .' I begin '. . . have nothing that catches the eye.' The words come back to me as I recite, even though I think I may have missed a line or two, and I gratefully reach the last line. 'Those great sea-horses bare their teeth and laugh at the dawn.'

Everybody claps and Colin glances maliciously at Gustavo.

'Come on then pal, what're you going to do?'

Gustavo takes the guitar without replying and sings a fast, raunchy Peruvian folk song which shuts Colin up. After Eduardo has recited a Pablo Neruda poem and Karen has duetted with Colin on *Love Hurts*, we start to clear up. 'I didn't know you were a poetry man, Jimmy,' Colin says as we carry glasses into the kitchen.

'Well,' I reply, looking him straight in the eye, 'there's one or two little secrets have emerged tonight.'

'It took you long enough to notice.'

'It's not the most likely partnership.'

'Isn't it? Anyway, nobody said anything about a partnership.'

'When did it start?'

'When did it start?' Colin echoes mockingly.

'Well?'

'Technically speaking, that night after we'd been at your flat. When we got a cab together.'

'What?' I am astonished. 'You mean before Carlita? Before . . .' My words die away.

'Don't be so square, Jamie. It's not like that anyway. I thought Ana María might have told you.'

'Ana María! She knew! Fucking hell, how come she knew?'

'She guessed. And asked Karen.'

'And how come she didn't tell me?'

'Maybe Karen asked her not to. Maybe she didn't see how it concerned you.'

'Oh, that's great. Thanks a lot everybody.'

Colin laughs. 'It's not our fault that you're slow on the uptake, Jamie. Anyway, like I said, it's no big deal. Stop being a drama queen. Listen anyway, I'm gonna have a party. I've found a brilliant place. And I want you all to come this time. It will be good. Really.'

Ana María and Karen come into the kitchen giggling. 'What'll be good?'

271

'My party.'

'A party,' says Ana María. 'Good.' She takes my arm. 'Because Jamie and I are going to get married, aren't we Jamie?'

'We are?'

'Yes. I've thought about it and it's the only way.' She turns to Colin apologetically. 'I'm afraid I will have to refuse your offer. It's better that it's Jamie.'

'Well, if you're sure,' Colin says disappointedly.

'I'm sure. And then we have a party and throw the house out of the window.'

'What?'

'It is a Chilean expression. It means you have a big party.'

'It has a slightly different meaning where I work,' I say.

Throwing the House Out of the Window

We stand on the steps of Hackney Town Hall on a cold Saturday morning surrounded by the wind-swirled confetti of other marriages. I am wearing my old suit which has a red ink stain over the breast pocket where I once left a biro in it. Ana María is dressed in a tight white skirt which she has borrowed from Soledad. Beyond us, in Mare Street, the red buses jostle for space and shoppers proceed unaware of the conveyor belt of matrimony which is taking place in the municipal headquarters. Eduardo takes some photos of myself and Ana María standing with Colin and Soledad – who are the witnesses – clutching our arms and grinning broadly. I have told nobody about getting married except my sister Catherine, who has promised to find Ana María a job as a receptionist in the abortion clinic once she has a work permit. Ana María's Spanish will be useful for the overseas visitors to the clinic. Catherine gives us a food processor as a wedding gift even though I have explained the purely practical purposes of the ceremony.

The only hitch in the ceremony is when the registrar reads out Ana María's full name in a terrible accent – Ana María Estela Rojas Zambrano – and Soledad dissolves into giggles. When the time for the exchange of rings comes I slip Ana María's lapis lazuli star, which she gave me the night before, on to her finger and she gives me a simple silver band. Eduardo, ever mindful of future complications, snaps the whole process eagerly with his camera. After it is all over, we go back to Eduardo's flat and get changed back into our normal clothes.

The only other person I tell about getting married is Mr Peters, on one of the afternoons round at his flat. 'Good boy,' he says. 'It's good to settle down, start a family. In my day, people got married much younger. Nowadays, you see all these young girls with prams and no rings on their fingers. Make the most of it, Jamie, they're the best years of your life and they'll never come back.'

I look at the photo of his wife, with her high forehead and half-smile. She is dead now. One day I will die and Ana María and Karen and Colin and Roy and Khaled and Paula and Hilda Connolly and Mrs Khan and Catherine and Robbie and Sarah. A small boy stands at the rails of a ship and drops a plastic boat into the sea because he is curious as to whether it will float. I'm not him any more but I can still remember what he murmured to himself as he trotted down the sandy path in the pine forest and nobody else can remember that. Ben Blewitt had an imaginary dog, a dog so small. And then he tried to push the real dog away, but the puppy stood shivering on the Heath and refused to go. My mum read me that book when I was as young as Ben Blewitt and now I am older and my mum is older and the dog – if it had been a real dog and not just a fictional real dog – would no longer be a trembling puppy.

'Jamie,' says Mr Peters, 'Jamie, you're dreaming, boy. 'Ere, have another biscuit,' and he holds the plate out to me smiling.

Walking back from Mr Peters's house I see Paul King and Gary Knight sprawling on a bench. I pause, but Khaled's words echo in my ears. 'Walk on, we can't turn back.'

Gary Knight nudges Paul King as he sees me coming and two pairs of eyes lock on to me as I approach. Not again, I think, not again. As I pass, Paul King stretches out his legs so that I have to walk round them. 'Don't think it's finished,' he snarls as I pass by. "Cause it ain't. It'll never finish.'

Colin's party is held under some railway arches near the City. 'Jamie,' he murmurs to me as we enter, 'that lassie's here.'

'Who?'

'You know. Iona.'

'With Malcolm?'

'Fuck off. He'll get a kicking if he even puts his face round the door. But I couldn't really stop her from coming.'

'No. Why should you? It's all right.'

I see Iona almost immediately. She is talking to a girl, leaning against a pillar and laughing. I leave Ana María to get some drinks and tap Iona on the shoulder. 'Hi.'

'Hi Jamie. How've you been?'

'Fine, you know . . .'

'Good.'

'Listen, Iona, I'm sorry about the last time we spoke. I was being really stupid. Really, I'm sorry.'

'I've missed seeing you Jamie,' she says quietly.

'Yes. What's happened to Malcolm? Are you still . . .?'

'Well, he's not stupid enough to show up tonight. And we're, you know . . .' She makes a swerving movement with her hand to indicate the crooked path of their relationship and laughs.

Ana María appears with two cans of beer. 'Jamie, once I ask you before to dance and you say no. Tonight you will have to ask me to dance.'

'Well, that's not quite how it's done in these sort of things but will you dance with me?'

'No,' she says. 'Sorry. Orders from Central Committee. Find someone else,' and handing me my beer she walks over to Karen who has just come in.

Iona raises her eyebrows. 'Looks like you've got your hands full there,' she observes.

'Yeah. Listen Iona, I'll phone you, right? Maybe we can get together some time?'

'Take care of yourself, Jamie,' she replies, shaking her head slightly, and turns back to her friend.

I wander around the party watching people dancing. Colin and Karen are on the door and she has her arms around his neck. I finally find Ana María getting chatted up by a man with a pony-tail and leather trousers. 'Chile!' he is saying. 'That's great. I've always wanted to go to South America. Not Chile though. Real Latin America, do you know what I mean? They say Chile's incredibly European. I've always fancied Bolivia. What's your name again?'

'Juanita,' says Ana María. 'So sorry, no speak much Eenglish. Very nice London city. Very lovely Queen Mother.'

'No, your English is excellent, Juanita,' he says with a crocodile smile. 'So what do you do?'

I take her arm. 'Ah, here you are, Juanita. My other star. Excuse me sir, Home Office. Just a few routine inquiries.' And I lead her away by the arm.

'Now will you dance with me?'

She reaches up and takes me by both ears. 'Come on then Jamie,' and leads me away and on to the dance floor.

Later it becomes too hot and we are both sweating so we stand outside in the chill air. From the swaying black pattern of tree branches the birds have already begun to torture the insomniacs. A never-ending goods train clatters along the railway line and high up in the clear sky the red wing light of a plane winks down at the city. 'One day I would like to go away,' I observe as it disappears behind a block of glass-plated offices. 'Maybe we could go to Chile together one day.'

'Yes.' She takes my arm. 'I would like that. One day.'

'Look,' I point to the offices, 'there are people in there.' A dim shadow passes across one of the windows. 'You see?' We watch silently as another silhouette flickers across the glass as if on a TV screen.

'Cleaners,' says Ana María. 'It's the night shift.'

Suddenly, Colin and Karen emerge from under the arch laughing. 'What are you two up to? We thought you'd gone.'

Ana María takes my arm and shivers. 'We're watching the stars,' she says.

Our four faces turn upwards simultaneously to the sky which the pale morning is already starting to nudge aside.

'You know,' says Colin, 'you two are totally mad but I fuckin' love you.' And he grins, opening the door to a burst of light and the turned faces of people on the dance floor. 'Now come inside and let's throw the house right out of the fuckin' window.'